CW00357841

LEAVING THE LIGHT ON

LEAVING THE LIGHT ON

by

Catherine Merriman

LONDON
VICTOR GOLLANCZ LTD
1992

First published in Great Britain 1992
by Victor Gollancz Ltd,
14 Henrietta Street, London WC2E 8QJ

THE RUTH HADDEN MEMORIAL AWARD
The Ruth Hadden Memorial Trust was founded to
commemorate the memory of Ruth Hadden who lost her
life in the *Marchioness* Thames River Boat tragedy in
August 1989.
Ruth, who worked in publishing, was a tireless supporter of
new writing, and the Trust has established an annual award
in her name for the promotion of first books by previously
unpublished authors. *Leaving the Light On* by Catherine
Merriman is the second recipient of this award.

ISBN 0 575 05371 2

Typeset by CentraCet, Cambridge
Printed in Great Britain by
St Edmundsbury Press Ltd, Bury St Edmunds, Suffolk

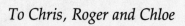

To Chris, Roger and Chloe

1

The South Coast, summer 1985.

'That's Billy,' said Sonia, nudging Barbara as two men entered the pub and shouldered their way through the crowd to the bar. 'The skinny one in front.' She skimmed silver fingernails over her short blonde hair, confirming it was still teased to its best. *The other one*, her eyes added excitedly, *is Len*.

Barbara replaced her glass of cider on the pub table and leant forward to view the men properly. Her gaze rested only briefly on the young man Billy; a slender figure in shapeless khaki t-shirt and paler khaki combat trousers. His streaky brown hair was cut unevenly short at the front but straggled to his shoulders behind, as if he'd attacked it with nail scissors in front of a mirror, ignoring everything he couldn't see. In an earlier conversation Sonia had described him as 'pretty'; but, to Barbara, prettiness denoted at least grace of line, and there was nothing graceful about Billy. If anything crossed her mind before her gaze passed on it was relief she wasn't in for a double date.

Her eyes settled with much more concentration on the substantial figure of Len. He was powerfully attractive in a way that was both stunning and vaguely daunting. Late-twenties, she guessed, wearing cream pleated trousers, and a dazzling purple and green shirt. His neatly cut hair was dark and thick, above features that were heavy and regular, and intensely masculine. She hoped Sonia wasn't going to ask for an instant opinion. All that occurred to her immediately was 'You must be very brave.'

'They'll come over in a minute,' said Sonia confidently, without removing her eyes from Len.

'They're earlier than you expected,' said Barbara.

Sonia replied with an absent 'Mmm.'

Barbara sighed and regarded her friend, irretrievably man-occupied, and then her lap, frowning. The view caused her to wish, reluctantly, that she had dressed up more. Sonia was wearing white silk trousers and a silver backless top, displaying a glossy expanse of tanned shoulder, with glitter round her eyes, and tassels of fine plaited silver at her ears. Walking the ten minutes from the bedsits in the eight o'clock daylight, Barbara had thought her overdressed for a Friday night at the pub. Here, though, where most of the other girls had dressed to kill, she looked no more homicidal than the rest, while Barbara's own cotton blouse and skirt had undergone an unfortunate transformation from pretty and appropriate, to dowdy and out-of-touch. Not that it mattered, she reminded herself grimly, tucking frizzy dark hair behind her ears with resolution, since the only killing she contemplated was literal, and the victim thirty miles away.

Barbara had been in exile now for two months, but thoughts of her ex-boyfriend still made her angry. She felt she had a lot to be angry about. It was he, Peter, who had been unfaithful, but it was she, in the bitter aftermath, who'd suffered. She had lost her home, since the flat had been his, her job – Peter was her boss so she'd had to leave – and, in her retreat, most of her friends. She could hardly believe that she'd once thought of him as her best friend.

The men at the bar showed no signs of rushing over 'in a minute'. Barbara wondered if Sonia knew Len quite as well as earlier conversations had implied. Or if she had a habit of presuming intimacy where she desired it. This seemed possible; Barbara was sometimes astonished by their own friendship, which had been quite simply bestowed on her, fully-formed, the day she'd started work at Fiddick and Watson's. They were to be friends first, it seemed, and find out about each other later. Not that Barbara had objected; she'd been grateful for Sonia's interest and sympathy and vigorous endorsement of her every bitter complaint, even if Sonia never seemed to get as angry as she should. 'Men are so horrible,' Barbara would insist, savagely dismissive. 'Aren't they,' Sonia would agree, but almost happily, as if their capacity to be horrible was, in truth, part of their appeal.

And then, a week ago, Sonia had presented her with the bedsit. 'Got you a place,' she had announced, just like that, only days after Barbara had been complaining about being treated like a twelve-year-old convalescent at her parents' house. It was the bedsit below her own, an airy, uncluttered cooker-and-sink bedsit, the sort that was never advertised because word of mouth was enough, and Sonia, whose mother was friendly with Mrs Barnstable, the landlady, had used her clout to snap it up.

'What would you have done if I hadn't wanted it?' Barbara had asked, deeply touched. It seemed extraordinary that Sonia should have thought of her, away from the office.

'No problem,' Sonia had replied breezily. 'There's queues for places like that. And I wouldn't have got it at all if I hadn't been definite.'

So now she and Sonia worked together and lived a flight of stairs apart. Barbara told herself she had better like Sonia, under the circumstances.

Sonia had also taken it upon herself to rehabilitate Barbara, hence this evening. 'Ah, go on,' she had urged. 'You've done the little woman bit. Four years, Christ, shacked up with some dreary guy. Take a break. Live your life backwards for a while.'

Barbara admired Sonia for that sort of remark: she liked to think she underestimated her. She had agreed, recklessly. 'Just tell me when I hit fourteen,' she joked, 'I was awful at fourteen.' She envisaged, with Sonia's help, a summer of irresponsible and adolescent selfishness. The rest of her life, Peter-less and effort-laden, could wait.

She wondered if the whole evening was to be spent like this, she and Sonia at their table, the men they were supposed to be meeting lounging at the bar. In fact at present Len was doing all the lounging; Billy was engaged in some sort of foraging expedition, moving from one group of drinkers to the next, receiving brief words and nods or headshakes in reply to some enquiry. At intervals he returned to Len's side, as if reporting back. Barbara puzzled over it a while, until she saw him approach a noisy group, buying flagons across the bar. Partygoers. Of course; she remembered the ritual. He was action-seeking.

She realised she was content to sit and watch. She and Peter had rarely gone out to town pubs, and in any case the pubs in Hastings weren't as exciting as these; this was a real city-by-the-sea bar, fast and bright and shark-infested, probably, under the steamy glamour. (It was cigarette smoke really, but Barbara saw it as steam, wisping from all those tanned and barely clothed bodies.) The place and the people reeked of sea. You could taste it in the atmosphere, see it in the whites and primary colours, hear it in the languages. She wondered, staring around, how many here tonight were English. Not those girls in the corner, she decided: wild-haired blondes swaying in a close circle, arms strewn across each other. Too tall, too blonde, and too free with their hands to be English. And English girls wouldn't be wearing shorts, or not so confidently. Language school students, she guessed, not tourists. Seasoned adventurers, their loose limbs said, well shark-nibbled already.

'You want a drink?' asked the young man Billy, appearing from nowhere and addressing the general space around them.

'A gin and tonic, please,' smiled Sonia, although she had been drinking cider. She put a hand on Barbara's arm. 'This is my friend Barbara. She's just moved in below me.'

'Hi, Barbara.' Billy smiled briefly at her and waited for her order.

Barbara asked for half of cider.

Billy smiled again. 'It's OK,' he said, flapping the five pound note in his hand. 'It's Len's dough.'

Barbara glanced toward Len, who had broken off his conversation with a tall man by the bar to stare across at them.

'Just a cider,' she said firmly. Billy shrugged and departed. She saw Len turn back to his companion, a brown-haired man of similar age with intelligent eyes and two-inch side-

boards. His mouth was curved down at the corners, convey-
ing amusement at something Len was saying.

'That's Dave Len's talking to,' Sonia whispered. 'They
work together. And Jane, Dave's wife.'

Barbara hadn't noticed the young woman at the bar, mostly
because she liked restrained male faces, and, despite the
sideboards, had been watching Dave. Also the woman was
small and from a distance, unspectacular. Closer inspection,
however, suggested that this was probably deliberate. The
sleek chin-length dark hair and poised stance suggested an
intentional discretion, confident of greater things elsewhere.
The man Dave said something to her and she smiled back at
him faintly. She looked well dug in by the bar and unlikely
to gravitate to female company.

Billy returned with the drinks and drifted back to hover
round the others. Sonia lifted her glass to Len, who failed to
notice, and sipped it.

Barbara guessed her friend was annoyed with Dave and
Jane, detaining Len at the bar. With an inner smile of malice
– directed not at Sonia, but at the non-cooperation of her
quarry – she propped her elbows on the table to scrutinise
the group, and for a delightful moment saw them as actors,
screen-testing for her appraisal, their every moment deliberate and significant. Len would be angling for the starring
role: macho, and sex-and-action packed. She conceded it,
ungrudgingly. (This was a male-interest film, not one she'd
personally care to see.) Dave would make a perfect lawman,
sideboards perhaps a trifle longer, strong and incorruptible
and with right, possibly pigheadedly, on his side. Billy, on
the other hand, couldn't honestly expect to land more than
'foolish young man', the type viewers wouldn't bother about
much, as he was obviously expendable and could well get
killed off in the first half. None of them looked anything like
Peter, whom she had once seen on a similar mental screen as
handsome-and-responsible doctor type, but now saw as a
ruthless and womanising go-getter. There was nothing of the
cowboy in him anyway, a thought that made her smile. Of

11

course: the cast in front of her were cowboys – maverick, sheriff, and greenhorn.

Beside her, Sonia gave a breathy squeak. She had managed to catch Len's eye and was beckoning to him, smiling brightly. Len said something out of the corner of his mouth to Dave, who turned and glanced in their direction. The group moved slowly towards the table.

'This is Barbara,' Sonia announced, when they were close enough, and before conversation could restart. 'She's taken the bedsit below me.'

Len surveyed Barbara briefly. Barbara made an effort with her forehead ('Don't frown so much,' Sonia kept exhorting her, 'you'll get lines,') and said, 'Thanks for the drink.' She added a polite smile. Len nodded. She was made to feel her smile overdone and, offended, reminded herself how much she disliked people – it was invariably men – who couldn't be bothered to return smiles. She lowered her eyes but found, disconcertingly, that she was still seeing him, raising his glass slowly to his mouth, even when she wasn't looking at him.

'Hello, Barbara,' said Dave, with ostentatious courtesy, possibly to make up for Len. He added a grin hinting at commiseration, which he then spoilt by turning to Jane, as if it were a joke she could enjoy too. Jane said nothing, but included her in the return smile to Dave. Barbara thought Dave looked harder, close to. Coarser-skinned and definitely more Len-like. She downgraded his attractiveness, and put him at over thirty.

Sonia reached out and tugged Billy on to the seat next to her. An anchoring tactic, Barbara guessed; he was probably the only one she dared manhandle. She removed her jacket from the stool beside her so someone else could sit down, but no one chose to. The standing trio resumed where they had broken off at the bar, and Sonia chatted to Billy, who nodded and smiled and appeared to let it all wash over him.

Barbara could hear only snatches of Len and Dave's conversation, because it was happening so far above her, and

12

the little she did pick up rather shocked her. It appeared to concern some workmate.

'Lets his wife screw around too,' she heard Len say scornfully. 'Common knowledge.'

'Wanted kids, didn't he,' Dave snorted back. 'Probably grateful for the help.'

Christ, Barbara thought, hurriedly shutting it out. Sonia's conversation with Billy was sheer nonsense. She began to feel deserted. And then suddenly unnerved, as a familiar sensation pricked the back of her eyes. Oh, no, not here, she prayed: the tendency for her eyes to fill, without warning and at the obscurest triggers, was a distressing feature of recent weeks. She'd told Sonia it was hayfever. She tried insisting it to Peter too, whose image always surfaced at these times, looking unbearably attractive and remorseful. Just after blinking the image away, her gaze was caught firmly by Jane and directed sideways towards Sonia, who was remonstrating with Billy about something in an exaggerated manner, holding one of his hands and tapping it with an imaginary ruler.

'Naughty boy,' she was giggling, pushing her face into his. 'You naughty, naughty boy.'

Barbara was almost grateful to feel cross: with Jane for trying to make her laugh at a friend, and with Sonia for deserving it.

The low spot of the evening came a few minutes later, as Billy was sent off to buy another round – his main purpose in the group, as far as Barbara could see, was to make himself useful – and Sonia took advantage of his absence to squeeze out and lodge herself next to Len, who shifted ground fractionally, still talking to Dave, allowing her to slip an arm round his waist. Barbara couldn't bring herself to stand up too and felt completely – and publicly – abandoned. She was grateful to Billy when, after distributing the drinks, he sank down on the stool next to her, even if she couldn't think of a thing to say to him.

After a while she tried, 'Do you usually come here?' which she immediately realised was excruciatingly close to the hackneyed, 'Do you come here often?' She hoped she wasn't going to get an equally excruciating reply back.

Billy was sitting with his feet up on the crossbar of the table, tapping his knees sticking up in front of him. Their boniness was accentuated, rather than disguised, by the baggy folds of his combat trousers. He turned his face to hers and smiled disarmingly. Something in her expression told him he was being addressed. He stopped tapping and said, 'What?'

Barbara gave an inward sigh. She had spoken perfectly distinctly. He had khaki eyes, she noticed, to match his t-shirt, heavily flecked with yellow.

'Do you usually come here?' she repeated. It sounded even more fatuous a second time. She looked at his arms; he was very brown, browner even than Sonia, whose tan was artificially assisted. He had some job on the seafront, she recollected, which doubtless explained it.

Billy was nodding slowly, as if giving her question serious thought.

'Yes,' he said finally. 'Nearly always.' He smiled again, revealing very small teeth, like baby teeth, and resumed the tapping.

She didn't bother with him again. The evening dragged on, hot, smoky and tedious.

At closing time she was informed that they were all going back to Len and Billy's place.

'It's really nice,' Sonia whispered as they left the pub. 'He's got some great stuff.'

Barbara, relieved to be in the fresh air – the others drank much too fast – smiled and nodded. She was aware that, to Sonia, these things were important. And that it was very much part of Len's appeal that as well as being good-looking and having 'presence' (though Sonia's definition of this was imprecise) he also owned a car – a brand new Montego, no less – and a whole house. Billy, she knew, was merely the tenant.

The Montego, however, was not in evidence tonight. They travelled in Dave's Rover, making a detour into the centre of town so he could pick up a takeaway Indian meal. Dave, she gathered, was permanently hungry.

Sonia was perched on Billy's knee beside her on the backseat. She had wrapped his arms round her waist and spent the entire trip accusing him playfully of molesting her. 'Ooh!' she squealed, every time the car swung round a corner – Dave drove with some panache – 'Billy! Ooh!'

Barbara doubted Billy had enough gumption to molest the most willing of victims. By the journey's end she was almost ready to molest Sonia herself, if it would have shut her up. She was also, due to the convoluted route, completely lost.

The house was small and bayfronted, in a yellow-brick terrace. Barbara was aware of Sonia's eyes on her, dancing with anticipation, as they followed the others inside.

'Brilliant, isn't it?' she hissed when they reached the sitting room, under cover of Dave's clattering for plate and cutlery in the kitchen.

Barbara stared around. She'd been mistrustful of Sonia's judgement and found herself agreeably surprised. The door between sitting room and kitchen behind had been removed, and the doorway widened and converted to an arch, giving, for such a small house, an impressive illusion of space. The furniture looked chosen too, rather than simply acquired, and with a discretion curiously at odds with the personal flamboyance of its owner. The colours were muted, mostly shades of white and grey. White walls and a slate-coloured carpet. Plain darkwood dining table in the front bay, a smaller, lower, coffee-table version in the centre of the room. In the alcove to the right of a Victorian tiled fireplace, an expensive-looking hi-fi system. The three-piece suite, with a studio sofa of the type that folded back into a bed, was in a restrained navy corduroy, and much more Habitat than Hollywood.

Dave and Len settled themselves beside Jane on the sofa. Sonia patted Barbara into one of the armchairs before curling up on the carpet at Len's feet. Billy was already crosslegged on the floor in front of the fireplace, an LP cover, cigarette papers and tobacco in his lap. As she sat down Barbara saw him unwrap a small screw of foil and realised, with a flicker of alarm, that he was rolling a joint. She hadn't been in a room where drugs were taken since her last year at school, six years ago. It's only cannabis, she reassured herself.

Billy also turned out to be responsible for dealing with the tapes in the hi-fi, a duty he performed with enthusiasm and much concentrated twiddling of knobs and dials, as if the tapes, rather than being pre-recorded blends of sounds, were the raw instruments themselves, in need of regular monitoring and supervision.

'Give it a rest,' Len said testily after ten minutes or so, when Billy had got to his knees to make yet another adjustment.

'Yeah,' said Billy, though he carried on twiddling.

Len slumped back with a sigh, and raised an exasperated eyebrow at Dave. Dave pushed his empty plate away and looked at Billy with contempt.

'Lay off it, Billy,' he snapped.

Billy removed his hands instantly, without glancing behind him, and returned his attention to the half-rolled joint on the floor.

Barbara thought Len's request reasonable, assuming it was his equipment, but didn't see why Dave had to be so unpleasant about it.

While she was thinking this, Len pushed a small tumbler and a whisky bottle towards her. Belligerently she filled the glass. But then changed her mind, remembering the cider, and sat back.

Half an hour passed. She got up to use the bathroom, in a ground-floor extension at the back of the house. Re-entering the kitchen she had to skirt round Jane, making herself a coffee.

'Do you want one?' Jane asked.

'No, thanks,' Barbara smiled, but hesitated, since she could see Jane was about to say something else. This had the appeal of novelty, as no one had been saying much to her in the other room. Len and Dave had been discussing cars.

Talking shop, in fact; Len, she remembered, was a car salesman. Which meant Dave must be one too.

'What do you do, then?' Jane asked, with the air of someone who liked to get people sorted out as quickly as possible.

'I work at the same place as Sonia,' Barbara said. 'Fiddick and Watson's, the solicitors. I'm Mr Fiddick's secretary.'

'Oh,' said Jane.

'What do *you* do?' Barbara received the impression that more had been expected of her. She assumed Jane did do something; she looked an unlikely mother or housewife.

'I run a travel agency,' confirmed Jane, and heaped coffee into a mug.

'Goodness, that must be interesting,' Barbara said. Jane had beautiful hands, she noticed: creamy and slender, with perfectly oval nails. She never normally noticed hands; it was the way Jane used them – or rather, didn't use them – holding the teaspoon and coffee jar with the tips of her fingers, as if conscious of their loveliness and afraid excessive wear might disfigure them.

'Mmm,' Jane glanced up and smiled. 'It is. We specialise in the Far East. It's an expanding area. People who don't fancy Majorca or Corfu any more, you know. And it means I can do a fair bit of travelling. Dave and I went to Bali last year. Fantastic.'

Barbara wasn't sure if Jane was being deliberately superior, or if drink-induced paranoia was making her interpret it like that.

'I've been to Japan,' she said, more aggressively than she intended.

'Have you?' Jane looked impressed, or maybe surprised; again Barbara couldn't tell.

'Yes. I went on a business trip eighteen months ago. With my boss. I used to work for a software firm. Computers, you know.'

'That must have been wonderful.' With a delicate fingertip Jane released the silky hank of hair she had tucked behind her ear to make the coffee, and sounded more genuinely

17

friendly. She leant against the work surface and lifted her mug. 'What did you think of it?'

Barbara plumbed her memory for intelligent things to say about Japan. The images that sprang to mind, like the way Japanese women covered their mouths with their hands when they laughed and the profusion of pornographic magazines everywhere, seemed inadequate.

'It was more beautiful than I'd expected,' she said finally. 'I'd thought of it as one vast city, like Hong Kong or somewhere, I don't know why. We didn't really get to know many Japanese, though. I don't think they're very like us. Peter – my boss – didn't think so either. He's got this flip sense of humour . . .' – she began to smile and suppressed it – 'and he said he felt he had to watch himself at meetings. They were very earnest and serious. He reckoned it was a different way of approaching things. I mean they definitely had a sense of humour too, but they didn't mix it with business. We didn't spend very long there,' she admitted, realising her first thoughts would have sounded much more interesting. 'Only five days.'

'Still,' Jane said, 'It must have been an experience.'

'Oh, yes.'

'We must have a chat about it some time.' Jane pushed herself away from the worksurface. 'I'd like to hear more.'

'Yes.' Barbara recognised that the exchange was at an end. She wondered how she'd scored. She didn't think she liked Jane very much, and hoped it wasn't envy.

She returned to her armchair. Len and Dave were still talking shop. Sonia, who in her opinion should have been either attempting to change the subject or striking up a rival conversation with herself or Jane, seemed content to gaze kittenishly up at Len and murmur at intervals, 'Oh, that sounds fun' or 'Well, I never knew that'; all of which went quite unacknowledged in the discussion above. The atmosphere in the room was now heavy with scented smoke. Barbara felt a shroud of boredom settle around her. She picked up her brimming glass of whisky.

*

Towards one o'clock it entered her mind, hazily, that Sonia might be intending to stay the night – in fact undoubtedly was – and that she had no idea how to get home. While she was still pondering this, Dave and Jane got up to go. She knew this was the moment to ask for a lift, but couldn't find a space large enough in the farewell conversation and missed her chance. They should have offered, she told herself crossly, also suddenly worried by how incapable she felt. Thankfully not as incapable as Billy, however, who was now unconscious, lying on his back in front of the fireplace with his mouth open. She had watched his collapse earlier with concern – his head had almost hit the grate, on its sagging way down – but nobody else had paid him any attention, as if it were all part of the normal evening ritual.

Len, evidently, had failed to notice altogether. 'Put another tape on, Billy,' he ordered from the door, returning from seeing the others out.

'You'll be lucky,' giggled Sonia. She was still sitting on the floor, looking blearily beyond her best, Barbara thought. In case she looked as rough she opened and closed her eyes several times.

'Shit,' muttered Len, and stepped across Billy to do it himself. Watching him between blinks, Barbara decided he was rather improved by late-night jadedness: less overbearingly glossy, almost rakish. She had always thought Peter irresistible when he was tired.

Len replaced the tape and turned to look down at Billy. He tilted his head, studying him. Then he stepped back. His raised foot, crossing Billy obliquely, trod directly on his outflung hand.

'Len!' squealed Sonia, snatching him on, and then reached forward to stroke Billy's stomach protectively. 'Poor Billy,' she cooed.

Billy remained motionless. Barbara stared at his hand, the fingers returning slowly to a relaxed position, curled over his palm.

She saw Len's action again in her head. He'd trodden, quite deliberately, on someone who was unconscious. She watched

Sonia's caressing hand, rumpling the khaki cotton over Billy's midriff, and had to suppress a fierce desire to shake him awake and tell him to go to bed at once, this minute.

Len returned to his seat on the sofa and placed a hand idly on Sonia's head. His fingers played through her hair, tugging and rubbing; then stretched wide, encasing the blonde tufts from nape to forehead. His gaze lifted and swung to Barbara.

Barbara looked away, towards the fireplace, but found, as she had in the pub, that it was difficult to blot his image out completely. His expression, she thought, was speculative. Drunkenly, she decided not to speculate on what he was speculating on. After a minute or two his head tipped away, and the fingers in Sonia's hair resumed their movement.

At the end of the tape he leant across Billy to switch off the stereo, grunted, 'Bed,' and left the room. Sonia rose and followed, casting an apologetic smile behind her, but no clue as to how to get home.

Barbara thought this extraordinary and frowned over it a while, wondering if something obvious had escaped her. No answer was forthcoming.

She stood up. There was a phone on the windowsill; a taxi, she thought, but then realised she didn't know the address, and couldn't face searching the house for letters, nor the road for street names. The navy expanse of the sofa opposite yawned at her invitingly.

She went through to the bathroom. On the way she bumped her shoulder twice, first on the archway and then on the bathroom doorjamb. Christ, you've drunk too much, she thought, take it steady. Swilling her mouth out with tepid water from the cold tap, she wished she carried a spare toothbrush in her handbag, like Sonia. She returned to the sitting room and squatted down beside Billy.

'Wake up,' she whispered, and shook him lightly. Apart from a faint stirring, and a brief crease of his forehead, there was no response. She watched the rise and fall of his chest, and reminded herself that no one else had seemed worried about him. Then she recalled who everyone else had been. She lowered herself to her knees. He should at least be on his side, in case he was sick. She put one hand on his shoulder, the other on his hip. 'Turn over, Billy,' she said, and pushed. Slowly, with a groaning sigh, he rolled over. His face came to rest on the decorative tiles of the fireplace surround, so she wedged a scatter cushion from the armchair under his cheek.

There, she thought, getting to her feet, and mentally dusted her hands off.

She circled the room, switching off lights. Under the table in the bay window she spotted a cardboard box; stuffed into the top were the quilted folds of what was unmistakably a sleeping bag. She pulled it out. It was green, faded the colour of stew-bleached peas. She held it to her face and sniffed: seawater, at a guess, not actually unpleasant. She carried it back with her to the sofa and kicked off her shoes. It occurred to her to convert the sofa, but then it seemed too much effort. She unzipped the sleeping bag till it was no longer a bag, lay down on the corduroy and spread it loosely around her.

Look, she told Peter, as she reached behind her to turn the table lamp off, I'm spending the night with an unconscious man, sod you.

She lay back. Light from the kitchen strip still flooded through the archway, but she wasn't going to turn that off. She didn't want to be in complete darkness with a strange man, however insensible.

Some time in the night the sofa seemed to collapse around her, someone pushed her sideways, and a body settled itself with a groan against her back. Startled fully awake she lay rigid, trying to work out the configuration of the man behind her, without turning to look at him. She was now lying on the flattened back of the sofa, and the wall of the sitting room was less than twelve inches from her nose. After a minute or two she cautiously twisted her head, to see a khaki back, with no apparent designs on her. She shifted position slightly and pulled the metal zip of the opened-out sleeping bag off her jaw. This is lunatic, she thought, sighing. I feel an idiot. I shall send someone a postcard about it.

21

2

In the morning Barbara's bladder woke her. Also there was a knobbly obstruction digging into her hip, which turned out to be Billy's spine, pressed hard against her. Billy, she thought. And Len. She lay staring at the ceiling, trying to summon the energy to make the day start, knowing that even if she did get up, which would mean climbing over Billy, she certainly wasn't climbing back again. Finally she had to go. She mumbled, 'Sorry, sorry,' as she scrambled out.

The house looked shabbier in the daylight, like a place someone had taken an interest in a few years ago and filled with quality stuff, but then got distracted from and left to look after itself. The ornate hardwood frame of the bathroom mirror was encrusted with toothpaste spray, and the louvred slats of an adjacent pine wall-cupboard were grey with dust. One of the panes in the frosted-glass window had been broken, and replaced with tacked-in cardboard. In the kitchen there was a girly wall calendar courtesy of A & M Motors, two years out of date. Or perhaps 1983 had been a particularly well-endowed year, as garage calendars went. The address at the top was local; bet it's where Len works, she thought. She pulled a sour face at the bare breasts and set about finding the coffee.

'That's Len's,' a voice said warningly behind her, as she opened the door of a cupboard above the kettle.

'Oh, sorry,' she said automatically, turning to see Billy leaning against the wall in the archway, scratching an armpit. *So what*, she silently replaced it with, a second later.

Billy pointed to a unit beside the cooker. 'In there,' he said. 'Help yourself.' He yawned inelegantly and withdrew.

From what she could see, peering into his cupboard, Billy's larder consisted of white bread, instant coffee, white sugar, baked beans and Cocopops. She removed the coffee and sugar and switched on the kettle. Then poked her head round the archway, meaning to ask if he wanted one too. Billy was standing in the middle of the room. He appeared to be getting undressed. His feet were bare and he was pulling his t-shirt off over his head. She retreated hurriedly, and debating her reaction to – what? – propositions? assaults? – fiddled with kettle and mug.

'Shit,' said his voice wearily, close behind her. She swung round to catch him disappearing into the bathroom, in white t-shirt now over the khaki trousers, and flipflops. She looked into the sitting room and saw the large cardboard box that had been under the table now in the centre of the room. It appeared to contain clothes. She stood staring into the room until he emerged.

'Is this your room?' she asked, mildly appalled.

'Yeah,' nodded Billy. Water droplets glistened in his unbrushed hair. The white t-shirt was streaked with damp splash marks.

That's why they let him go to sleep on the floor, she thought. Aloud, she said, 'Sorry, I didn't realise. I shouldn't have stayed.'

'S'OK.' Billy jerked his head at the door. 'Len's gone, has he?'

'Where?' said Barbara distractedly. She wished Sonia would come down.

'Work, 'course.' He glanced at his watch, frowned, and squinted past her to see the clock on the cooker. 'I gotta go soon too.'

Barbara placed her coffee mug on the formica surface of the kitchen table and sat down. Len's absence seemed to take the pressure off. Of course, cars were sold on Saturdays. She wondered if he had seen her and Billy asleep in the sitting room – which he could have hardly avoided if he'd used the bathroom – and what he'd made of it.

Billy was flexing his hand and staring at it with a frown. A memory surfaced from last night. She thought of saying,

'It's stiff because Len trod on it,' but didn't. It was true, though; Christ, Len had *trodden* on it.

Billy took a bowl and spoon from the washing-up rack and sat down beside her. Despite his claim about having to go soon there seemed no urgency about it.

'What d'you do, then?' she asked, making the effort to be conversational. 'Something on the front, isn't it?'

'Yep.' Billy mounded Cocopops into the bowl and tipped a vast quantity of sugar straight from the packet on to them. 'The playground. The slides and swings and things, next to the funfair. They have someone there in the summer. For the tourists. Want some?' He pushed the cereal packet towards her.

'No, thanks.' Barbara regarded his bowl. She watched him eat, and wondered how he stayed so thin. 'What time d'you have to be there?' she asked. It was already nearly ten o'clock.

'Half-ten.' He shrugged. 'Eleven's OK.'

'So what d'you do in the winter?'

'Dunno.' He took a large mouthful of Cocopops. Barbara realised he was taking this as meaning next winter. 'Depends,' he said. 'Go on the dole, maybe. Long time till then.'

'Billy?' asked Barbara suddenly, hearing sounds from upstairs that had to be Sonia, and realising she must have known where Billy slept. 'Where are we?'

'You are an idiot,' giggled Sonia, as they walked home. 'I told you they only lived round the corner. That's how I met them, remember?'

'I forgot,' groaned Barbara. 'And going for that Indian meal confused me. I didn't recognise the street.' She did now; in the five days she had been at the bedsit she had passed within a hundred yards of the house, twice daily, on her way to and from work.

Sonia grinned. 'Why on earth didn't you say something?'

'I'm not sure. I think I was too drunk. I was waiting for you to say something.'

Sonia giggled again, and leant on Barbara's arm.

'I feel a fool,' Barbara sighed. 'Aren't there two bedrooms upstairs?'

Sonia shook her head. 'Len's knocked it all into one. It's great. Don't worry,' she said reassuringly, 'Billy won't have minded. He doesn't care about anything.' She nudged Barbara's ribs, grinning. 'You didn't . . . you know . . . ?'

'No,' said Barbara, firmly. 'I didn't.'

'Oh, he's sweet,' Sonia murmured, in the tones one might use for praising a favourite pet.

Barbara decided to sound like the person she was trying to be.

'He eats Cocopops,' she said loftily. 'I couldn't possibly have sex with someone who eats Cocopops.' It sounded good; she smiled to herself.

'You enjoyed yourself though, didn't you? You did, didn't you?'

Barbara hesitated, and then nodded to please her. And then wondered, having allowed the idea, if it might not be true. Len was awful, preposterously so; Jane and Dave unpromising, and Billy hopeless. She'd been bored, or uncomfortable, or disapproving, most of the time. But . . . lots of things had happened that had never happened to her before . . . she had been surprised several times – even shocked. What she'd been looking for, in a sense, she'd found. And God knows, cowboys were as adolescent as you could possibly hope for. So maybe, looked at like that, she had.

Billy stood in the archway between sitting room and kitchen, so he could see both rooms.

'Calm-wet,' he said under his breath. Then he spelt it out aloud. C – he looked behind him; all the cooker switches were off. A – in front, ashtrays clean. L – he shook his head, no washing today. M – he turned round, grabbed the milk bottle from the table and put it in the fridge. W – his eyes swept the windows; all closed. E – no empties to return today. T – both coffee table and kitchen table shone back at him damply, just wiped.

He nodded, satisfied. A deeper, self-congratulatory pleasure coursed through him too, as it did every time he performed the ritual: so much achieved, by the simple invention of a word. A word Len had given him, the evening he'd made him write the letters on his arm. All he'd had to do was change one of the Ws to L (for Launderette, because two Ws were confusing) and reorder them into something he could remember.

He left the archway and swung open the bathroom door. Everything looked OK. Then he spotted a yellow comb, tucked behind one of the taps on the washbasin. It wasn't Len's, so it had to be Sonia's, or Barbara's. Billy tugged at his ear. He wondered if Len would say anything about her staying, and if it might somehow end up being his fault. He thought it more likely he'd say something if he saw reminders so, in case the comb was hers, he picked it up and disposed of it in the kitchen bin.

He let himself out the back door, locked it, and carefully pocketed the key. Then turned the handle again, checking. A day like today was straightforward; it was more complicated when Len and he left together, out the front. Guiltily, his eyes shifted to the piece of cardboard in the bathroom window. He hoped Len wouldn't fix it too quickly: card was easier to punch in than glass, and easier to replace too.

Out on the pavement he peered at his wrist, to see how late he was going to be for work. The digital numerals of the watch were dying, after its immersion in the sea yesterday. Len supplied him with as many watches as he wanted because he could get them free from work, where they featured as special offers. They claimed they were waterproof, but Billy had discovered they lied.

The watchface said, very dimly, 10.25. Billy set off towards the seafront at a strolling pace, pleased that without really trying, he was only going to be a quarter of an hour late.

3

Sonia and Barbara had known each other six weeks, the length of time Barbara had worked at the firm of Fiddick and Watson, Solicitors and Commissioners for Oaths. Barbara was Mr Fiddick's secretary, Sonia the receptionist and switchboard operator, and also, since the dramatic reduction in her workload following modernisation of the telephone system, filing clerk for the two junior partners, Mr Watson Jnr and Miss Delaney. Old Mrs Renson, their secretary, had the office directly behind the reception desk and, until Sonia's reassignment, had been severely overworked, legal output bearing scant relationship to seniority.

The firm occupied the ground and first floors of a Regency townhouse in the city centre, Mr Fiddick and the juniors downstairs, Mr Watson Snr, two clerks and associated secretarial staff upstairs, and tended to operate as two socially distinct units, linked via the telephone and Sonia. Barbara had only twice been upstairs, although she was on chatting terms with Mr Ramsey, one of the clerks, because he lived out near her parents and, until her move into town, had given her lifts to and from work.

The two secretaries upstairs, both women in their late forties who had been with the firm upwards of ten years, kept themselves and their Earl Grey tea to themselves. Sonia, who regarded with pitying condescension any female the same generation as her mother, referred to them as the Queen Mum and Miss Piggy, based on their telephone manners. To Mrs Renson on the other hand – a generation older still – she adopted a co-operative and protective attitude. Old Ma Renson (as Sonia called her, out of earshot) had only recently come to grips with electronic typewriters and lived in terror of wordprocessors. It was to Sonia, who had no fear of technology, high or otherwise, she turned when the photocopier refused to copy, or the new telephone memories failed to remember. 'You're an angel,' she would gush admiringly, as Sonia pressed the appropriate call button on the console, or refilled the toner for the copier. 'You could do so much better for yourself, you know, a clever girl like you.' To which Sonia would joke variations on, 'Mmm, brain surgery exams next week,' setting Mrs Renson off into chortles of motherly pleasure. But despite their affection for each other, they weren't confidants in the way Sonia and Barbara's predecessor, Sandra, had been. Mrs Renson wouldn't have wanted to know who Sonia was sleeping with, or which contraceptive pill she was on. So when Sandra had resigned, to get married and move with her new husband to Haywards Heath, Sonia had been left ready for a new intimacy; and Barbara had been flattered to be taken up so eagerly.

Most of these intimacies took place in their lunch hour, which they spent together on the front, weather permitting, on one of the municipal seats overlooking the lower promenade and the sea. Barbara had, by now, told Sonia everything about her relationship with Peter and the break-up – everything, that is, except those aspects guaranteed to induce a rush of liquid to the eyes, or in other ways suggest a legacy of grief.

These days, with the corpse dissected and spread out before them, they were at the bone-picking stage. A bitter morsel here, another there. 'And when we were in Japan,' Barbara might say, leaping several years from a similar illustrative crime, 'he told me that he couldn't imagine sleeping with anyone else, ever again. And a month later he's in bed with this tart. My God. Men are such liars.'

Sonia, as always, would agree. 'Aren't they,' she'd sigh. And with an indulgent chuckle, 'Why do we bother with them?'

Barbara found Sonia's contributions – and the attitude to men revealed by them – alternately admirable and infuriating. She allowed men, for example, in almost every sphere of behaviour, a licence she didn't extend to women, but it

28

wasn't clear if this was for the approvable reason that men were inherently inferior, and therefore less could be expected of them, or was sexist double standards, with women the losers. She winced at the way Sonia took men's possessions into account in her estimation of them, yet at the same time rejoiced in it, seeing it as a counter-exploitation, a mercenary revenge for the superficial way men regarded women. She approved Sonia's predatory attitude to men, for much the same reason, but again knew that because it was couched so heavily in the silly-female tradition, the males she preyed upon were unlikely to see it in that light, which confounded the issue completely. Len and Dave, for instance, scarcely appeared to hear a word she said, let alone feel threatened by the presence of a manipulatively superior force.

Recently however, with the conversation moving increasingly from specifics to generalisations, Sonia had started to provide her with genuine anti-male ammunition, gleaned from the battered wife affidavits she filed for Mr Watson Jnr. He dealt with most of the legal aid cases, and because he had acquired a reputation for being sympathetic and efficient, had a sad procession of ill-used women requiring his services. Sonia reckoned she could spot a Watson Jnr case walking through the door: all those haggard and trembling women, and adolescent-looking criminal men. The women were even easier to recognise if they were accompanied by a Refuge worker. 'All lesbians, you know,' she told Barbara disapprovingly, an assertion based purely on rumour and non-use of make-up. Sonia herself seemed largely inured to the catalogue of humiliation and violence attested to in the affidavits; so much of it, she complained, was monotonously similar. And why did they put up with the abuse for so long? They might now be bringing an end to it, but for most it seemed ridiculously late in the day. He'd be out on his ear after the first punch, she told Barbara, if it were her husband.

To Barbara, however, even the most commonplace accounts were new, and quite appalling. And there were some shockers that outraged even Sonia. 'And then when he caught up with her – it was in the middle of the high street, but he said she was hysterical, which she was of course, and seeing the doctor, so everyone took his side even the policeman – he dragged her home and that night he tied her leg to the bed post to stop her escaping again. She had to lie awake all night while he snored beside her and in the morning she was desperate to go to the loo and her ankle was all swollen up, and he said he was sorry and tried to have sex with her, and when she said she didn't feel like it he told her she was a frigid old cow and knocked her front teeth out. Imagine!' There was one as dreadful as that about once a fortnight.

What Barbara couldn't tell Sonia, though – indeed she could scarcely tell herself – was that this information, so enthusiastically provided, was in fact the kind she least wanted to hear. Intellectually she welcomed it, but at heart it was painful. Shamefully a resentment towards these unfortunate women festered. Despite all their sufferings – and she could see they were real sufferings, even if, like Sonia, they occasionally exasperated her – they had at least been wanted, or needed, by the men who treated them so cruelly. And to be wanted or needed, however brutally or pathologically, seemed at certain, self-pitying times a definite improvement on being as she had been, unwanted, and unneeded. Her rational self said stoutly, 'Well, at least Peter wasn't like that!' but deep inside, a pathetic Barbara disagreed. Peter had never been obsessively jealous, never disciplined her for failure in her feminine duties, never tied her leg metaphorically, let alone literally, to a bedpost. Of course if he had, he would have been a different person, and she wouldn't have wanted him; but it didn't stop the little voice wailing, on the occasions she too passed the drawn, end-of-tether faces in the corridor, 'Why should any man want that? Why didn't Peter want me?'

Walking to work with Sonia on Monday morning, however, Barbara was in excellent spirits for once, and had been ever since Saturday night, when events, in a matter of hours, had transformed her. Gone was the conventional, shockable, sidelining Barbara of Friday night: in her place, still aglow with newness, was a defiant, outrageous, devil-may-care Barbara. She was in the process of composing a news item for the local paper in her head about it, and had already settled on the headline, which had to be 'Scorned Girlfriend Turns to Crime'. The authentic sound of the article itself was being spoilt by not knowing Len or Billy's surnames.

'What's Len's surname?' she asked.

'Barstow.'

'And Billy's?'

'Dunno.'

Barbara pursed her lips, decided that would have to do, and incorporated them. The article now read: 'Desperado Len Barstow, Svengali of the South Coast, struck again last night, accompanied by trainee desperado Billy Dunno, shapely blonde Sonia Butterworth (22) and attractive brunette Barbara Henson (24) at the flat of self-styled feminist Ms A. Mascura. Raven-haired Miss Henson, of previous unblemished character, placed the blame for this lapse into crime entirely on one Peter Sampson, her erstwhile lover and employer, who, on being confronted with his faithlessness, had cruelly rejected her, calling her a millstone and parasite, and forced her into exile . . .'

'What are you grinning about?' inquired Sonia.

'Saturday night.'

Sonia laughed.

It hadn't, of course, been intentionally criminal. (Would it have mattered if it had been? Well, yes, even the new, disreputable Barbara could see it would.) Walking back to Len's house after an unremarkable evening drinking at the same pub (although no Dave or Jane this time, so there had been more general conversation) Len had suggested they pay a surprise visit on someone called Mal. They'd cut down a sidestreet and ended up outside a converted townhouse in which Mal apparently had the first floor flat. There were no lights visible, however, and no one answered the bell. 'Still boozing, the sod,' was Len's deduction. Sonia urgently needed to use a lavatory and suggested they go back to the house, but the idea had got a hold on Len and he was reluctant to admit defeat. He and Billy had roamed about, mulling it over, and then Len noticed that the front sash window of the flat was slightly open, and decided it would be even more of a surprise for Mal when he returned to find visitors actually in residence. Billy seemed willing to try, so while Sonia hopped up and down, telling them to get a move on – Barbara couldn't recall what she'd been doing, probably just watching, openmouthed – Billy clambered up on to Len's shoulders in front of the ground floor window and started to feel his way up to the sill above. She'd been astonished by Len's composure when just after Billy had eased the upper window open, a ground floor light came on, and the curtains of the downstairs window were pulled back to reveal the startled face of a middle-aged woman, not eighteen inches from his own. Despite still having Billy's trainer-clad feet on his shoulders he lifted a hand in neighbourly salute, threw back a reassuring, 'No sweat', to Sonia's panic-stricken shriek, and as the curtains were hurriedly redrawn, calmly pushed the feet up with his hands. They heard a clatter, as Billy slid headfirst into the flat, followed by a silence, and then the front door opened and there was Billy, grinning at them triumphantly.

'Mal'll explain, if it comes to it,' Len said confidently, leading them inside.

Looking back, it seemed extraordinary how long it had taken them to realise that this Mal, whoever he was, didn't live there any more, or possibly never had, since it turned out that Len and Billy had only been round there once before, and that a while ago, and could have mistaken the house, as they all looked much the same. Len and Billy wandered around, commenting on the incredible changes since last time: 'Hey, he's got a new stereo,' and 'Jammy sod, where'd he get the loot for this lot?' Sonia, emerging refreshed from the bathroom, wanted to know who his girlfriend was, and swirled around narcissistically in a Chinese silk dressing gown she'd found hanging behind the door. Barbara had thought the reading matter on the extensive bookshelves revealed a man ill-at-ease with his gender, comprising as it did little except feminist tracts and novels by women. But the obvious conclusion didn't become inescapable until discovery of letters on the desk in the sitting room, all, without exception, addressed to a Ms A. Mascura; and even then, no one openly admitted the mistake. Len helped himself and everyone else to wine from a bottle he'd found in the kitchen, announced he'd give Mal five minutes and if he didn't turn up they'd go, in case the old bag downstairs had called the police. He even insisted on scrawling *Sorry mate, see you around*, on a piece of paper to leave by the empty glasses, which at the time Barbara had thought a ludicrous humbug, though afterwards could see wasn't such a stupid idea. They waited for the seconds to tick by and, when the time was up, galloped down the fire escape at the back, Sonia breathlessly squeaky and Len frowning, though still firmly in command. Billy alone appeared relaxed and unconcerned, as if absolved from all responsibility by Len's leadership and prepared to trust entirely to his judgement, however unsound. They'd had to leave the back door unlocked – even now, this caused Barbara more than a twinge of guilt, though at the time she'd comforted herself with the argument that they'd probably reduced the risk of a real burglary, since the chances of two invasions in one night must be negligible.

It was on their way back to Len's place that euphoria hit. It was relief, partly. But also a sense of self-discovery. A sense of rebirth, almost. They had careered into the house and talked and laughed about it all for an hour or more, tanking themselves up with whisky to counteract the sobriety that had descended in the last few minutes in the flat. And then Billy had collapsed in a stupor against the sofa, and she had left Sonia with Len – whom she didn't actually like any more than on Friday, but who had, more than anyone, contrived the excitement, and thus the rebirth – and walked home alone, at two in the morning. She had slept until twelve and spent the rest of Sunday nursing a mind-crushing headache and an unquenchable thirst, entirely compensated by a glorious sense of having behaved quite disgracefully, and got away with it. Peter would have been appalled.

Barbara was humming to herself as she strolled down the office corridor to her cubby-hole next to Mr Fiddick's room, and even broke briefly into song – Mr Fiddick wasn't in yet – as she switched on the kettle and began sorting the post. Mr Fiddick would receive a cup of coffee when he arrived and would greet it with a smile of grateful surprise and 'Splendid, just the thing!' as he did unfailingly, every morning.

Mr Fiddick specialised in probate, which Barbara had assumed would be yawningly dull. It had turned out not to be, partly because she found she was actually learning something and partly because Mr Fiddick's evangelical approach was catching, adding a sense of excitement and urgency to the most mundane codicil. At the interview he had startled her by inquiring if she had made her will, and responded with a pained frown when she confessed she hadn't. The omission was soon rectified, without charge; it was a service to all employees, she discovered, as Mr Fiddick couldn't countenance the idea of anyone in his sphere of influence dying intestate.

Barbara's will now resided alongside Sonia's in the documents cabinet. She had left everything to her parents. This morning she didn't feel like someone who had written her will. The old Barbara had done it quite seriously, even morbidly; the new Barbara, if she did it at all, would prefer something along the lines of Sonia's, which was reputedly an epic, with dozens of individual bequests mostly spurred by her desire to present mementoes to all her ex-boyfriends, who would then feel obliged to attend the funeral en masse. Barbara hadn't seen it, but was going to take a peek one day, if only to see who Sonia had left her collection of knickers to. She couldn't believe they wouldn't rate a mention. Sonia's knickers filled a whole drawer in a not insubstantial chest of drawers – Sonia had shown her – and ranged from exquisite silk French shorts, through dainty cotton lace-trimmed briefs, to G-strings and saucy bikinis with rude messages on them.

34

Sonia was a fervent believer in personal hygiene, and changed her knickers at least twice a day, as well as carrying a spare pair in her handbag, along with the toothbrush. She took scrupulous care with her clothes too: the space beneath her dressing table was occupied by a gleaming army of tree-filled boots, and the bedsit bathrooms were permanently festooned with her handwashing because there was so little she would risk at a launderette. She also, carrying fastidious-ness to excess, Barbara thought, disliked the idea of handling library books, because of where they might have been.

'What d'you think people do with them?' Barbara had asked, her imagination reeling, 'besides reading them?'

It wasn't what they did with them, Sonia explained, but who might have been doing it, and she wrinkled her nose with distaste.

As she made the coffee Barbara wondered, grinning to herself, what Mr Fiddick's reaction would have been if she had been arrested last night and called him out. Technically, she supposed, he was now her solicitor. He'd probably have been superb, she decided, splendidly matter-of-fact and nonjudgemental. She was briefly enthused by the idea of becoming a solicitor herself: contrary to repute, it seemed quite an exciting life, if you chose your area carefully. Mr Watson Jnr was always dashing off in his Audi to police stations and other places of high drama, and met all sorts of bizarre people. It would mean going to university, she imagined, which she'd spurned in a fit of pique when Bristol and Sussex turned her down. She'd refused East Anglia's last-minute offer. And by the time disdain wore off she was already employed at Sampsons and undetachably in love. *Ruined my career too, the toad*, she muttered inwardly, though half-heartedly, since life this morning didn't honestly seem so bad.

'D'you know,' said Barbara, ripping the foil top off her lunchtime yoghurt carton, 'that you can rewrite anyone's will after they're dead? You've got two years to do it. It's called a

Deed of Variation. I'm just typing one up now. I bet not many soap-opera writers know that.'

Sonia looked alarmed. 'I hope no one rewrites mine. I took a lot of trouble with it.' She tugged her skirt up to let the sun on her thighs. Sonia was a natural blonde, and had never shaved her legs: stretched in front of her they sparkled with fine down, slender and flawless. A middle-aged man eating his sandwiches further down the bench refolded his newspaper to obscure less of the view.

Barbara laughed. 'All the beneficiaries have to agree. I should think you're quite safe.' She dipped her teaspoon into the yoghurt, smiling. She was reluctant, today, to pursue topics that might dent her good mood. While she ate she stared out over the mottled blueness of the sea, and then along the length of the lower promenade beneath them, beyond the glinting jumble of the funfair, to where she knew the playground lay.

'Funny to think of Billy and Len existing in the daytime, isn't it?' She leant forward to toss the empty carton into a litter bin attached to the cast-iron railings in front of them. 'I mean, being normal sensible people.'

'Len goes to work in a suit,' replied Sonia, closing her eyes and tilting her face to the sun. Her tone suggested that while she couldn't absolutely vouch for Len's being sensible or normal, his mode of dress implied it.

Barbara watched her wriggle her nose and flick absently at her closed lids to ward off a fly. She wished, generously, that Sonia's boyfriends could sometimes see her as she did, when she was unconscious of being watched. Stripped of artifice, her face possessed a genuine, thrilling beauty, rather than mere prettiness, and gained at least twenty IQ points. The sight of her once on the telephone to Miss Piggy, pencil clamped between bared teeth, eyes rolled heavenward in exasperation, had made Barbara want to clap. It occurred to her that Sonia, who would only have seen herself self-consciously in mirrors, or statically in photographs, could herself have no conception of the true quality of her beauty.

'When are we going to see them again?' she asked, surprising herself with the enthusiasm in her voice.

Sonia dipped the corners of her mouth. 'Friday, I expect.'

Barbara nodded; she'd more or less known the answer. Sonia rarely saw boyfriends midweek. Two evenings were reserved for visiting her mother and married sister – despite her professed indifference to both – and Wednesday she attended a Keep Fit class, not so much for the exercise, Barbara suspected, as for the girls' night in the leisure centre bar afterwards. Her previous boyfriend, Harvey – whom Barbara had heard much about but never met – she had seen more frequently, but only because he had the bedsit on the ground floor of their house, directly beneath Barbara. He was an American, and back in the States for three months. Mrs Barnstaple had been persuaded to let him keep the room on at three-quarters rent, which said something about her softheartedness, but even more, Barbara thought, about Harvey's resources. Sonia claimed that neither expected the other to remain faithful, under the circumstances, but Barbara guessed that she expected to pick up with him again, if things didn't work out with Len.

'How old d'you think Billy is?' she mused, her eyes still on the lower prom. She shook her head and grinned. 'He's peculiar, isn't he?'

'He's twenty,' Sonia said. 'His birthday was in May. I remember.'

'Is that all? Oh, well . . .' That explained a lot, Barbara thought. 'And Len?'

Sonia shrugged. 'Dunno. Twenty-seven, eight. I asked him once, but all he said was "old enough to know better".'

Barbara smiled. 'If he won't tell you, that probably means he's older than he looks. Anyway, you can't tell with his type. They look the same for years.' She sat up abruptly, feeling a sudden desire to do something different this lunch time, something active. 'Let's go for a walk along the front,' she said, turning to Sonia energetically. 'We could surprise Billy. Go on.'

'I can't,' said Sonia. 'I've got to go to the dry cleaners.'

'Ah.' This meant Sonia would be occupied for at least half an hour, catching up with the latest moves and countermoves in the shop assistant's feud with her landlord.

'You go,' Sonia urged. 'Honestly. I'm off now, anyway. Give him my love.'

'Right,' said Barbara, struck on the idea now. 'I will.'

She clacked down the purple-railed steps to the lower prom, skirted coaches abandoned while their passengers enjoyed a day out, and strode eastwards towards the playground. On her left steam and tinny music issued from the bars and cafés built into the foundations of the coast road above, their cream walls salt-blasted and peeling. On the seaward side untidy structures littered the upper beach: clapboard huts, winches, bottom-up boats, mountainous heaps of red-and-white deckchairs. At intervals dark slot-machine enclosures backed on to the pebbles, their cavernous design shielding punters from distractions which might tempt them into cheaper, more independent amusement.

Ahead, where the pavement widened and the beach receded, the funfair was laid out on its permanent site. Groups of young men, on the look-out for customers, hung around the machinery. What is it about fairgrounds, Barbara wondered, that makes their minders so swarthy and villainous-looking? In her former incarnation she would have felt self-conscious as she passed; today she felt confident enough not only to be unconcerned about the deployment of her arms, but to stare across at the young men. The two nearest met her gaze and grinned. She smiled back, but removing her eyes, so she was smiling at the contact, not at them, and was exhilarated by her courage.

The children's playground, beside the tawdry glamour of the funfair, looked dated and dreary. Nothing but the old traditional structures, set on concrete; just to ensure, Barbara thought sourly, that mothers foolish enough to allow their children on the equipment would be suitably punished by the injuries inflicted when they tumbled off. As a child she had once caught her knee under a playground roundabout, and the momentum of the thing had prevented her terrified mother from stopping it until it had made two more circuits, skinning her flesh to the bone.

Billy did exist in the daytime, she discovered, though not conspicuously normally or sensibly. She could see him from the perimeter rail, slumped in a deckchair in front of a beach hut, expressionless behind dark glasses. He was wearing a green corporation jacket, sleeves rolled to the elbows, over a bare chest, and, below, jeans and flipflops. She thought he was asleep, until she spotted an outsize cigarette in his hand. My God, she thought, a flicker of shockable, responsible Barbara surfacing, and glanced around at the dozen or so children scattered about the equipment; none appeared in imminent peril.

She waved a hand at him and ducked under the rail. He must have seen her because his head lifted minutely; after a long hesitation he raised a hand in reply. Perhaps he doubts my existence in the daytime too, she thought.

'Hi,' she said, as she stood over him.

Billy sat up properly. 'Hi,' he echoed, sounding bemused. He stared at her, as if checking she wasn't a temporary apparition. 'Want a deckchair?' He jerked his head at the hut behind them.

She fetched a deckchair, unfolded it, and sat down. Billy inspected the end of his half-smoked joint; it appeared to have gone out.

'Taxing work,' she observed, gazing round. A gaggle of young teenage girls, French-looking, was collected just inside the rail the far side of the playground, thirty yards away. Strictly speaking, no one over the age of twelve was supposed to enter, unaccompanied by a child. 'See you've got an audience,' she added.

Billy nodded, called 'Oi!' and flicked a get-out thumb at them. The girls giggled and took no notice.

'I tried voolay voo piss off, but that didn't work either,' he complained. 'Maybe I said it wrong.'

Barbara laughed, since she assumed this was a joke. She looked at the children high on top of the slide, and wondered what would happen if one of them hurtled to the ground, whether that would galvanise Billy into action. Sitting there, she was conscious that he must, physically, be capable of action. He seemed larger here, without Len's bulk to diminish him. Sprawled beside hers, his legs stretched an ankle and foot's length further across the concrete, and his chest beneath the open jacket, though hairless and not noticeably muscled, gave an impression of fitness, because of the tan. It was a leathery tan; as he twisted to retrieve matches from the ground, the dark creases across his stomach looked almost like thongs, cutting into his flesh.

Billy relit the joint. They sat for a few minutes not speaking. Barbara found the silence not uncomfortable, but dull.

'Don't you get bored?' she asked eventually. 'What're you meant to do, anyway?'

Billy exhaled a stream of sweet-scented smoke. 'Just sit here. Keep the drunks and perverts out.'

'Really?' With raised awareness she viewed suspiciously a car pulling on to the yellow lines adjacent to the playground. The driver leant out of the window and shouted to two boys, who hared across the concrete and pushed and shoved to be the first in the back. She turned back to Billy. 'D'you get many drunks and perverts, then?'

'Na,' he said. 'A few drunks. And big kids wanting to lark around. If they won't go when I tell them, the mums usually sort 'em out. They get fed up pretty quick, anyway. It's a nice job. Easy.'

'Mmm,' Barbara smiled. 'I can see that.'

He offered her the joint. She shook her head. She was thinking about his age, and his accent, which sounded local.

'So how long have you been at Len's place?' she asked.

Billy considered. 'Bit over a year.' He nodded. 'Yeah.'

'Where do your parents live, then?' It seemed odd for a boy of nineteen to move in with someone like Len.

Billy said his parents were dead. He sounded so unconcerned that Barbara nearly asked if he was sure.

'I'm sorry,' she substituted, very taken aback.

'S'OK,' said Billy. He took a last drag on the joint and stubbed it out.

40

Barbara couldn't think of anything else to say. Despite his tone, the subject of dead parents seemed unfollowable. Discreetly she twisted her wrist.

'Christ,' she said, making the movement obvious and hiding her relief. 'It's quarter to. I'll have to go.'

'Oh, right,' said Billy.

Rising, she said, 'Sonia sends her love.' She made her voice kind. 'We'll see you at the weekend, I expect.'

''Spect so,' he nodded, and smiled at her briefly.

After she'd gone Billy slumped back in the deckchair and closed his eyes. Muzziness from the joint washed over him, tumbling the sounds in his ears: children's cries, distant adult voices, the thrum of traffic, thudding funfair music. His mind drifted over them, identifying and peeling away, until it found what it was looking for: the white noise rush behind everything, the omnipresent sound of the sea. As his senses locked on to it it seemed to find him too, and swelled to a roar in his head. He folded his arms across his chest and sank deeper into the chair.

In truth the main attraction of the job for Billy was not that it was easy, but that it was by the sea, which he'd lived within a mile of all his life. He swam almost every day in the summer, before or after work, for at least an hour. He would swim out until he felt the first ache of tiredness – a long way, as he was a strong swimmer, far beyond most other bathers – then turn on his back and relax completely, closing his eyes and letting his ears fill with water. The world was then blotted out, leaving nothing except the rocking, swaying motion of the waves, the warmth of the sun above (if he was lucky) and, beneath, a cold awareness of enormous depth. The sea never let him down. If he asserted himself, lifted his head, say, or his arms, he began to sink; but that was his fault, not the sea's. As long as he trusted and did nothing, it held him. When he had tested this to his satisfaction and found it still true, he would open his eyes and tread water while he located land, which could be anywhere now, after such relinquishment. Swimming back, he would experience

41

the giddiness and disorientation that comes from floating far too long, and if he was already stoned before he set off, the sensation was intoxicating. He could scarcely keep his footing as he lurched up the beach, and when he sat down and closed his eyes he could get the whole world to cavort around him. Billy liked anything that transported him to otherworld-liness, because he wasn't too keen on the real one.

'Billy says his parents are dead,' Barbara told Sonia that evening, on their way home from work.

'Mmm,' nodded Sonia. 'I know.'

Barbara frowned. She wondered when, and how. And wouldn't dead parents have left possessions behind them? All Billy seemed to possess was a box of clothes.

'Has he been in care or something?' she asked. 'When did it happen?'

'No idea,' shrugged Sonia.

'How awful. Something must have happened. Most people's parents aren't dead by the time they're twenty. Not both of them.'

'Well ask him,' suggested Sonia, 'if you're interested.'

'I can't interrogate him about something like that.'

'Why on earth not? He wouldn't mind. I told you, he doesn't care about anything.'

This was possibly the dozenth time that Sonia had told her – approvingly – how little Billy cared about anything. Barbara thought people ought to care about some things. Themselves, at least.

'Well,' she said stubbornly. 'I think it's very odd.'

4

On Thursday evening Barbara got the chance to show off her bedsit to Billy.

They met at the checkout of the local supermarket. Barbara had managed to join a queue behind a woman who had forgotten to get her vegetables priced at the back, which meant one delay, and where the till roll had just run out, meaning another. She was waiting for the woman to produce her cheque book, which would mean a third, as the supervisor would have to be called. She told herself that people didn't really faint from frustration, whatever it felt like, and that dizziness in queues was probably a common and well-documented stress reaction; however it didn't make the dizziness go away, nor reduce her fury at experiencing it.

Grateful for any distraction, she responded to Billy's 'Hi, Barb,' with more enthusiasm than it deserved, considering the hideous abbreviation.

'Your shopping night too?' she inquired brightly. She looked at his basket. He was stocking up on Cocopops and baked beans. There was also a packet of hamburgers, and some crisps and polos. Dear me, she thought.

Billy hesitated, as if her question had been more than a pleasantry, and then said yes. He put the basket down on the floor between them. Other till queues were moving faster, but he appeared not to notice.

Looking at him, Barbara thought he could do with a good tidying up. His hair was salt-encrusted and standing in matted clumps from his head, and the faded Sussex University sweatshirt he was wearing was not only a con, but a disgrace. The seams at shoulder and wrist were coming apart, and the general shapelessness and rotted-away appearance suggested something washed up out of the sea. As the queue slowly advanced he pushed his basket forward with a flipflop-soled foot; his toenails were long and winc-ingly ragged, though remarkably clean.

Barbara's shopping filled four carrierbags when her turn eventually came, because as well as groceries she was buying basics for the bedsit, now she'd had a week and a half to list them. She considered asking the girl to look after two of the bags while she dashed back with the others, but when she mentioned the problem to Billy – whose shopping barely filled one bag – he obligingly offered the solution.

'It's really nice of you,' she said, as they made their way back to the bedsit. She had to wait a second for him to catch up. Due to a physical misunderstanding in the shop Billy had ended up carrying four of the five bags, and they were banging awkwardly against his knees. She held out her empty hand. 'Are you sure you wouldn't like me to take one?'

'S'OK,' murmured Billy, adjusting his grip with a frown.

At the house she led the way up the steep uncarpeted stairs and flung open her bedsit door.

Billy stepped in past her. He stopped in the middle of the room and looked from bed to table, from sink to cooker. 'Hey, it's great,' he said.

'It is, isn't it?' she agreed, pleased. She waved down at the golden timbers that edged the green and brown patterned carpet. 'Got a stripped floor and everything. Almost as good as a flat really, even got its own bell. The bathroom's on the landing, but there's another upstairs, so it's almost like having your own.'

'Can you see the sea?' He walked over to the sash window and peered out.

'Too low. Sonia can. She's got the room above. Just put them on the floor.' She indicated the bags he was still holding.

'Oh, yeah.' He put them down, then tested the bed, which was a large single, before crossing the room to inspect the sink and Baby Belling cooker.

'How much d'you pay, then?' He looked impressed.

'A hundred and fifty . . . A month,' she added, grinning, because of his expression.

'Oh.' Billy's forehead cleared. 'What's that a week?'

Barbara realised he was waiting for her to work it out for him.

'About thirty-five.' Was he really as stupid as he made out, she wondered; or did he just not bother to use his brain for some reason? 'It's pretty cheap, actually,' she went on. 'For a place like this. Mrs Barnstaple's about a year out of date. I mean she could rent it as a double, almost, and probably get sixty.'

'Jeez.' Billy stared around.

'It'll be even nicer when I've got the stuff from home,' Barbara continued. 'I'm going to get it tomorrow evening. I've got a dressing table, which I thought would go there – ' she pointed to a long space under the window, ' – and the portable telly, and a load of books and things. One of the clerks from work's going to give me a lift out and I'm borrowing my parents' car.'

Billy nodded.

'You want to give me a hand tomorrow as well?' she asked, half joking.

'Sure.' He was still gazing around, not attending.

'Really?' It would solve the problem of how to get the dressing table up the stairs, if she couldn't persuade Sonia to stay in long enough to help. 'What time d'you get off work?'

Billy blinked at her, as if suddenly realising he'd let himself in for something.

'Half-five, six,' he said uncertainly.

'We could pick you up on the seafront. Say six o'clock? It's only twenty minutes or so. We've just got to load up and drive back. Should be done by eight, easily. It'd be a great help.' She caught his frown; he was looking hustled. She backtracked slightly. 'Only if it's really OK with you, that is.'

'Sure,' said Billy slowly. He thought a moment, and then nodded. 'Sure,' he repeated. 'No sweat.'

'Well, that's great. Thanks.' Barbara smiled at him and

picked up the kettle. 'You want a coffee now? I'm going to have one.'

Billy shook his head. 'I gotta go.' He moved towards the door.

'Don't forget your bag,' Barbara said quickly, seeing he was about to leave without it.

'Oh, no, right.' He picked up the bag. 'Seeya,' he muttered, and left.

Billy had lied three times to Barbara during the last half hour. All were spur-of-the-moment, convenience lies, and as he walked slowly away from the house, all bar one was forgotten.

The first had been his agreement that Thursday was his shopping day. In fact he had no regular shopping routine. The only special feature of Thursday was that it was his day off; today had been spent on the beach, as usual. Basically he shopped when, like tonight, he discovered that there was nothing left to eat and, having forgotten all the cookery he'd been taught at school, his choice was limited to packets that came with simple instructions, or needed no cooking at all.

Then he had lied about it being OK that he was carrying four of the shopping bags. The fingers of one hand had become completely numb from the weight. However it had seemed simpler to continue carrying them than stop on the pavement and sort things out more comfortably. Anyway, Barbara had seemed in a hurry and it might have irritated her. On their own he found her rather alarming, and definitely someone to keep on the right side of.

The third lie was that he would like to help Barbara out tomorrow night, and it was this lie that was now occupying his mind.

As he stood at the corner of the street, waiting for a gap in the traffic, he suddenly remembered she'd said they'd be back by eight, at the latest. His anxiety eased, as it had when she'd said it. Len didn't expect him home till after seven, anyway.

He jogged across the road, slowing to his usual amble the

other side. In his mind's eye he saw again the interior of Barbara's bedsit. It was nice, he thought, nearly as nice as Len's place. All it was missing was a sound system. The rent, though . . . he guessed Barbara must earn a lot more than he did.

He turned the corner into his own street. As the house came into view, anxiety about tomorrow night surfaced again. Then his mind made an inspired leap backwards, and he realised it needn't happen at all. He could just forget about it, which was what he wanted to do anyway, and it wouldn't happen.

Relieved, he swung the shopping bag from his right hand to his left, and dug in his jeans pocket for the back door key.

'Billy's coming back to my parents' with me this evening to give a hand with the stuff,' Barbara announced to Sonia as they clattered downstairs first thing on Friday morning. 'I bumped into him last night.'

'Brilliant,' said Sonia. 'Then you won't need me.'

'He carried my shopping back from the supermarket,' grinned Barbara. 'Four enormous bags.'

'Clever you,' Sonia said, and flashed her an approving smile.

However, when Barbara arrived with Billy at her parents' house on Friday evening, she found no car on the hard-standing outside because it was in the garage quarter of a mile down the road, irretrievable till the morning.

'I tried to ring you, dear,' said Mrs Hanson apologetically, laying the table for three in the kitchen. 'But they said you weren't in.'

Mrs Hanson resembled a softer, more tentative version of Barbara. The creases round her eyes hinted at anxiety, not determination. It was one of nature's self-corrections, she and her gentle husband could only assume, that they had produced such an irascible daughter.

'I haven't been back to the bedsit,' said Barbara. The onset of a familiar, despairing rage made her voice wobble. She hadn't given her parents Fiddick and Watson's phone number, in the interests of peace and quiet, but her mother could easily have looked it up in the book.

'Oh, Christ,' she moaned. 'What am I going to do?'

'Well, you can stay the night, dear.' Mrs Hanson gave her a hopeful smile. 'It's only the exhaust. It's lucky it happened when I was almost home. You can get it first thing in the morning. They open at half-eight.'

Barbara inferred from this that the work was already done and that there would have been nothing to stop her mother collecting the car *before* the garage closed for the night.

'But I've brought a friend back to help,' she said bitterly. Why was her mother so stupid?

Mrs Hanson stopped what she was doing and said, 'Oh, dear me.' Then helpfully, 'Well, perhaps she wouldn't mind staying too. Or there's always the bus. I think there's one more.'

'It's a he,' said Barbara aggressively. 'Billy.'

'Oh,' said Mrs Hanson, in a rather different tone.

Barbara rolled her eyes. Billy, who had been hanging back out of earshot in the hall, came to the doorway.

'This is my mother, Billy,' Barbara announced, adding, in her expression, *who has just ballsed everything up*. 'Guess what? The car's in the garage. We can't get it till tomorrow morning.'

Billy nodded at Mrs Hanson and then stared at Barbara as if waiting for the solution. Barbara felt like hitting both of them. She should have abandoned the whole idea the moment she found Billy not ready at six o'clock. He'd obviously completely forgotten about the arrangement. It was only by luck she'd spotted him on the beach. Mr Ramsey had had to wait around on double yellow lines for him to get changed out of his swimming things, and she hated apologising.

'How d'you fancy staying the night?' she suggested with vicious cheerfulness, knowing it would dismay her mother. 'We could be off by nine, soon after. You don't have to be at work till eleven, do you?'

Billy looked at her as if she were mad. Barbara's determination hardened. He was only going to be out drinking himself silly with Len, after all.

'It'd be OK, wouldn't it?' she said. Her mother was regarding Billy with consternation. She'd been fond of Peter and hadn't, Barbara knew, given up all hope. Since the break-up he'd rung roughly once a week, and although Barbara had refused to talk to him, she knew her mother had. Billy looked confused, as if aware that more than a logistical argument was going on, but at a loss as to how to respond to it.

'Billy'll stay, he'd like to, wouldn't you, Billy?' she said, making it impossible for her mother to mention the bus.

Her mother glanced at Billy, but knew better than to argue.

'Your bed's already made up, dear,' she murmured, without a trace of a blush.

Barbara wanted to scream 'You're obsessed with beds,' because she linked the remark with the glance at Billy, but instead said smoothly, 'I'll deal with Billy's,' and flashed her mother a dangerous look.

She parked Billy in the sitting room and ran upstairs. While she was making the bed she heard the front door slam – her father was back. She waited for the click of the bathroom door and ran back down to the kitchen. Her mother was draining peas at the sink.

'Billy's just a neighbour,' she hissed. 'I've only known him a week. Don't you dare interrogate him.'

'Of course not, dear.' Mrs Hanson tipped the peas into a bowl and gave her a brave smile. 'Call your father, will you. Supper's ready.'

It was fish pie. Billy sat beside Barbara and ate what he was given.

'Have some more,' Mrs Hanson urged him, poking the serving spoon encouragingly into the crusty remains of the pie.

Billy shook his head at her and moved his lips, though no sound emanated. God he's pathetic, Barbara thought: how could anyone be nervous of her parents? Irritably she pushed her own plate away.

Her father, the other side of the table, put his knife and fork together with an appreciative grunt. As usual he'd returned from work looking as if he had spent the day hauling his desk round the office, rather than pushing paper across it. His thinning hair jutted out in horizontal wings over his ears and several inches of polka-dot tie hung down untidily from the breast pocket of his corduroy jacket.

'What d'you do then, Billy?' he asked politely, nodding at his wife and holding his own plate out.

'He works at the playground on the front,' Barbara chipped in, before Billy got round to it. It wasn't the first time she'd leapt in to answer for him. This is a mistake, she thought heavily. Billy's hating this. I should have put him on the bus.

After supper Barbara and her mother washed up. Billy didn't offer to help, but didn't follow Mr Hanson through to the sitting room either. Mrs Hanson kept having to say, 'Excuse me,' as she manoeuvred around him to put things away.

When the washing-up was finished Billy sidled up to Barbara.

'I gotta ring Len,' he whispered.

'Oh?' Barbara said, drying her hands, and detecting criticism. 'Why?'

'He doesn't know,' said Billy. 'I gotta ring him.'

'Christ, Billy,' she said impatiently. 'He's not your bloody father.' She shrugged and pointed towards the hall. 'Oh, go on, then. It's out there.'

Len had already gone out. Billy finally put the phone down, frowning unhappily. Barbara was exasperated with him.

'Sonia'll tell him where you are. God, it's not a big deal. Why're you bothering? She'll be seeing him.'

'Yes,' said Billy, looking as if the thought gave him no comfort.

Barbara sighed, and wondered bleakly how they were going to spend the evening. It would have to be the village

50

pub. She told her parents and borrowed one of her father's sweaters for Billy.

Walking down the village street she felt she was escorting a complete stranger. She had regressed to last week's will-writing self – contact with home, even without other irritants, invariably had this effect – and he seemed lost, cut off from his own territory and Len. They passed the garage on the way and caught a tantalising glimpse of her parents' Cavalier estate through the padlocked slats. Yesterday's Barbara would have toyed with some daring rescue plan; today's sighed and plodded law-abidingly on.

As they approached the pub a female voice bellowed 'Barbara!' at her from a yellow car pulling into the forecourt. A young woman with curly hennaed hair leapt out and rushed towards them.

'Barbara!' The young woman clapped a hand to her chest in delight. 'How wonderful to see you! It's been years. God, you haven't changed at all!'

'Sammy,' laughed Barbara, after an orientating second. Sammy had had straight hair at school, nondescript brown. They hadn't been close, but not enemies either. Just different league – Sammy and her friends had had big houses and ponies, and fathers who were Something in the City. A fair-haired young man tugged briefly at the passenger door of the car before strolling towards them. 'Goodness!' she exclaimed, recognising him. 'Paul as well!'

'We're married now,' Sammy announced. 'Last year.' She had a loud resonating voice and used to be called Bugle at school, Barbara recalled, a fitting variation on Bogle, her surname. Billy had taken several steps backwards, as if retreating from the blast.

'Look!' trumpeted Sammy, reaching for her husband's arm. 'It's Barbara! Terrific! You are going in, aren't you, not leaving?'

'Just arrived,' nodded Barbara. She had to turn round to retrieve Billy. 'Sam, Paul, this is Billy. He's a neighbour,' she explained, making her voice offhand, so Sammy shouldn't get the wrong idea. 'He's come to help me move some things from my parents' place.'

'Oh, right,' smiled Sammy.

They found seats in the snug, in a red-plush alcove. At first everybody made an effort with Billy, but he wasn't co-operative.

'Don't mind him,' Barbara said dismissively an hour later, when Billy had wandered off for the second time. By now the conversation had drifted to where it had wanted to go all along, into reminiscences of shared pasts, and mutual acquaintances, and what lots of people Billy had never heard of were doing. His own fault, she told herself crabbily: he had his chance. She shrugged. 'He's hopeless, honestly.'

'I expect he's shy,' Sammy said understandingly. She leant forward and gave a noisy snort. 'You probably frighten him. Barbara the Barbarian, remember?'

Barbara grinned and got up to use the Ladies. On her way through the main bar she caught sight of Billy at the swing doors, obviously just returned from using the payphone in the lobby. You stupid boy, she groaned to herself, cross with him for making her feel guilty.

But by closing time she had mellowed, and, walking home, allowed herself to pity him.

'Try Len again,' she whispered, as they let themselves in the back door. She locked it behind them. The pub hadn't emptied until eleven-thirty, and her parents would have been in bed an hour. 'Go on,' she urged. 'He might be home by now.'

Billy glared at her, as if he didn't trust her not to be needling him. 'It's OK,' he said, with an edge of hostility. 'It doesn't matter.'

During the night Barbara got up to use the bathroom. Afterwards, padding back to her room, she noticed slivers of light round the door of her brother's old bedroom, where she'd put Billy. Three in the morning suddenly seemed not a bad time for apologies, if he was awake too; so with a cautious glance in the direction of her parents' room –

although she wasn't sixteen, she reminded herself, and could visit as many men as she liked in the middle of the night – she eased the door open.

Billy was lying on his stomach on top of the single bed, fully clothed, his face turned towards the wall, arms wedged beneath his chest. In the stark glare from the central light the room looked bare and impersonal. Smooth mahogany surfaces, empty shelves, limp undrawn curtains. She saw the room suddenly as a spare room, not her brother's, and felt a small shock of loss.

'Billy?' she whispered, shielding her eyes against the light.

He didn't stir. The room felt chilly and unaired. He must be cold, she thought with a shiver, but there didn't seem to be anything she could do about it, without waking him.

I'm not responsible for him, she told herself as she quietly withdrew, though she couldn't escape the sense that she was, a little. She left the light on, in case he remembered.

Climbing back between her own sheets she realised she was hurt, too, that he couldn't even accept the hospitality of a bed. Punishment for her, it seemed, for abducting him.

The following morning the car was loaded by nine o'clock, the dressing table in the estate back, the portable television, cardboard boxes and potted plants on the rear seat. Her father had offered to come as well, to save her having to bring the car back, but there wasn't room. It was obvious to everyone how much simpler the operation would have been if Billy hadn't been there.

As a peace offering Barbara asked him if he'd like to drive; he said he couldn't.

'You ought to get Len to teach you,' she said kindly, belting herself into the driving seat. Billy didn't reply.

'Why don't you come back for lunch?' her mother asked, leaning down to the car window. 'You could get the two-thirty bus back in to town.'

'Maybe,' said Barbara, and then more graciously. 'Yes, OK.'

Mrs Hanson smiled weakly at Billy, and, as she turned

away, gave a small sigh. Barbara knew she'd just been to Billy's room to strip the bed, and seen it hadn't been slept in.

As they pulled out on to the main road Barbara waved at the glove compartment. 'D'you want to put a tape on?' she asked. 'There are some of mine in there.' She wouldn't have bothered herself, for such a short journey, but Billy didn't seem in the mood for talking.

He removed three cassettes, inspected them, and pushed one into the player. Thready jazz strains filled the car.

'What's this?' frowned Barbara.

'Miles Davis,' said Billy. He nodded grudgingly. 'He's good.'

The name meant nothing to Barbara. It had to be one of her father's. She watched Billy's hand make an adjustment to the balance control, and, returning her eyes to the windscreen, felt she'd been handed a small unexpected present.

'Well, thanks,' she said sincerely, after they had lugged the stuff upstairs. It was stacked in front of them, on the green and brown carpet. She decided to take the car back straight away and leave reorganisation of the room until the afternoon. She wished she could think of some way of repaying Billy, since she knew he hadn't enjoyed himself and she hadn't been at her best, but didn't think she could offer money.

'Maybe see you tonight,' she said, smiling. 'I'll buy you a drink.'

'Maybe,' muttered Billy.

'You won't be late for work, will you?'

Billy shook his head, making for the door.

'Explain to Len, it's all my fault,' she called after him, and instantly regretted it.

Len should have been at work, but his car was still outside, so Billy rang the front door bell rather than letting himself in the back.

'Oh, it's you,' said Len, throwing the door open.

'Yeah,' agreed Billy, pushing past and making for the kitchen. Len followed.

'You see Sonia last night?' Billy asked, and, wanting to make himself useful, decided to make Len a cup of coffee.

'She told me.'

'The car was in dock. We had to stay the night.' He filled the kettle and turned his back on Len. He was very aware of how large and close he was, and how angry.

'Have a good time?' Len inquired, after a few seconds.

'OK,' said Billy indifferently, his back still turned. He lost his grip on a mug he was removing from the cupboard. It fell and smashed on the floor.

'Prat,' said Len. 'Pick it up.'

Billy squatted to retrieve the bits.

'Good lay, was she?' Len asked, standing over him.

'Tried to ring you,' murmured Billy.

'You've missed a bit.' Len kneed Billy's back in the general direction. 'I don't give a shit what you do. It's nothing to me.'

Billy put the bits in the bin and said, 'You want a coffee?' Len didn't reply, but he removed a second cup anyway.

'Taken a fancy to her, then, have you?' said Len.

'No,' said Billy. 'It was just a favour. I didn't want to stay.'

'Toffee-nosed bitch,' commented Len. 'You want to watch out she doesn't get her claws into you.'

Billy said nothing.

'Seeing her again this evening, are we?'

Billy still didn't reply. Len reached for the mug Billy was about to spoon coffee into, and inspected it.

'Wash it out,' he ordered.

Billy took the mug and rinsed it under the cold tap.

'Properly,' commanded Len. 'I don't want to catch your fucking germs.'

Billy made the coffee and gulped his down, although it was much too hot.

'Gotta go,' he said, throwing the mug into the sink. 'See you later.'

'Drop these off on your way,' ordered Len, indicating a collection of empty beer bottles on the floor below the sink.

'It's the wrong direction,' objected Billy. 'I'll be late.'

'Then fucking be late,' snarled Len.

Billy piled the bottles into a carrier bag, with every intention of dumping them behind the first wall he came to.

'I'll walk up with you,' added Len, as if suspecting him of planning just that.

Billy sighed, but knew there was no point in suggesting Len took them, then. He thought he had probably got off lightly, in any case.

5

The bedsit looked so different, so cosy and familiar now, that Barbara nearly went up to Sonia's room after her six o'clock pizza and told her she wasn't going out. The dressing table in particular delighted her: it provided a new quality focus to the room, and matched the yard of stripped pine between carpet and walls exactly. Even the hideous veneer-topped table had become acceptable now that it was covered in a checked tablecloth, and the other eyesore, the chipped painted locker by the bed, had disappeared under the folds and fringes of an unwearable paisley shawl. Her orange-shaded pottery lamp, with the failsafe power to warm the bleakest surroundings to an intimate snugness, stood above. As for the rest, well, it was remarkable what thirty paperbacks and half a dozen potted plants could do.

She had admired the room from every aspect: from the door, as if entering – necessitating the immediate transfer of her lacquered Japanese trinket boxes from the window sill to the dressing table, which otherwise looked bare; from the bed, as if awakening – the tablecloth came into its own here, its hanging sides blotting out the mess of bottles and packets beneath the sink; and sitting in the armchair – an odd experience, she'd thought, gazing around her, almost embarrassing to do alone.

Now she wanted to see the room with the curtains drawn against the dark outside, and the bedside lamp exerting its magic. She imagined taking a luxurious bath once the house had emptied, and settling down with the portable television. But then a glance at the newspaper confirmed that, like most Saturdays, there was nothing worth watching till nearly midnight. Curiosity began to creep in too, about Len and Billy, and she didn't want to be thought to be avoiding them.

Moreover she had promised to buy Billy a drink, which he deserved.

So, reluctance overcome, she dressed up – in black and gold – and was rather pleased with the result. Sonia said, 'Wow, Barbara, brilliant!' when she came down, which was gratifying too.

When she and Sonia arrived at the pub, Len and Billy were already there with Dave and Jane. Dave was propped next to Len, back against the beaten-copper bar, long legs crossed at the ankles, expression amused. Jane, at his other side, looked much as she had last weekend, elegant and understated. Billy was hovering in front of Len.

There appeared to be a holiday discussion going on. Len was boisterously mulling over the idea of going to Morocco in the autumn, or maybe Tunis, '. . . or Algiers, you've been there, haven't you?' – an exaggerated nudge to Dave's ribs, eliciting a wincing grin – 'Whaddya think?'

'Try Saladin Tours,' said Jane, leaning forward to see him past Dave. 'Tell them we sent you. They'll give you a discount.'

'Or maybe Libya,' Len grinned at Dave, as if Jane hadn't spoken. 'You think they do holidays to Libya?'

'Taking Billy with you?' asked Dave, and they both eyed him speculatively. 'Better look after him if you do,' he sniggered. 'Real freaks, the Arabs.'

'I dunno,' mused Len, scratching his neck. 'Better than travellers' cheques, eh, Billy? What d'you think? All in a good cause.'

Billy smiled, and plucked at his ear.

'Be overheads, of course,' sighed Len. 'Have to keep him up to scratch.'

Dave laughed, shaking his head. 'Just alive,' he said. 'They're not fussy.'

Barbara suddenly grasped what they were talking about. She was first outraged – this wasn't a holiday conversation at all, but something much nastier – and then acutely distressed for Billy. She turned abruptly away into a crowd of drinkers behind Sonia. Over her friend's shoulder she caught a glimpse of Jane's face. It had averted itself from the discussion, and wore an irritated frown.

She pinched Sonia's upper arm, making her say, 'Ow', and turn round.

'How can you listen to this?' she hissed. 'They're being so horrible.'

Sonia glanced back and said, 'Aren't they,' with a light laugh, as if it were a fact of life that men were horrible to each other. 'Billy doesn't mind,' she added, with a hint of impatience. 'Look, he thinks it's funny too.'

Barbara had been looking, but didn't think Billy's smile indicated anything of the sort.

A few minutes later Len sent Billy off on a scouting expedition, and Barbara found herself cornered by Dave.

'You're looking exceptionally attractive this evening,' he observed. He grinned, showing his teeth. Barbara assumed that, despite wolfish appearances, this wasn't a pass, since Jane was standing less than two yards away. His full attention was disconcerting all the same.

'You're being exceptionally horrid to Billy this evening,' she retorted.

'Am I?' He raised his eyebrows. 'Maybe Billy brings out the worst in me. I've got an aversion to creepy-crawlies.' He looked entertained, rather than reproved. Barbara received the frustrating impression that her remark had been taken as a gratifying forwardness, not a criticism, a difficulty she'd encountered before when attempting to reprimand over-confident males.

He flicked his eyes at Sonia, then back to her, and lowered his voice.

'You must come out and see us some time. We'd like that, wouldn't we, Jane?' He reached for Jane's arm and drew her close. 'I was just saying, Barbara must come out and see us.'

Jane smiled and nodded, as if this was something they'd discussed earlier.

'Thank you.' Barbara thought the prospect daunting. She felt like someone specially selected for something, and was relieved when the conversation moved on.

59

Billy returned to report a party, a good one, over in the maisonettes half a mile away. Barbara watched the eager, confidential way he imparted this to Len, as if everything earlier was forgotten, and withdrew her sympathy for him in disgust.

'Might call in,' conceded Len, and sent him off to buy a flagon. He told him to get it wrapped, in newspaper if necessary.

Jane and Dave had a brief conference and backed out.

'We'll get some food,' said Dave, catching the keys Len tossed at him. 'See you back at the house.'

Barbara gathered from this that the partygoers weren't likely to do more than call in, and was disappointed. The thought of a party – new faces, different, maybe even civilised, conversation – had seemed positively appealing.

'Do we know the people giving it?' she asked Sonia, as they tramped up the street towards the flats. Billy and Len were some way in front, playing conspirators now, huddled into each other and crashing shoulders as they walked.

'Dunno,' shrugged Sonia. 'Don't expect so. Probably get booted out. Half the fun, really.'

'God,' said Barbara, and mentally braced herself for a new kind of fun.

At the maisonettes the front door was opened by a young woman wearing orange tigerstripes of blusher on her cheeks and an excess of gold jewellery. Len planted a kiss on one of the tigerstripes and waved the flagon at her.

'Sorry, are we late?' he shouted, over the din of voices and loud music. 'Just stopped for a quick one.'

The young woman looked half taken in, and then, as Len and Billy invaded the hallway, out of her depth. She retreated, possibly to find someone with more clout.

Billy sidled into a darkened room off the hall, where the music was coming from, while Len led Barbara and Sonia towards the bright lights of the kitchen. They stopped at the drinks table. Barbara, who had envisaged a student party, with wine in plastic cups, regarded the rows of spirit bottles and raised her eyebrows at Sonia in silent appreciation. Two

Barbie-doll blondes squeezed unsteadily by, their heavy make-up mask-like under the strip lighting. None of the male guests looked like students; more like successful bank robbers, or off-duty policemen.

'Don't bother to pour yourself anything,' murmured Len, scanning the crowd. 'They're going to throw us out. I'm not going to argue.' He reached across to pick up an unopened bottle of gin from the back of the table, placed it next to him, and transferred the wrapper from the flagon to it. Affronted voices approached from behind.

'There were two blokes,' a female voice said and, with a squeal of recognition, 'That's one of them!'

'D'you mind,' said a large beefy young man with a tight smile. 'This is a private party. Where's your friend?'

'Hey,' said Len, raising a hand and smiling easily. 'No offence. I brought something to help.' He indicated the wrapped gin. Sonia moved close to his side and contributed an innocent smile.

'Sorry,' said the young man, scarcely looking. 'Try somewhere else.'

'Right,' said Len, tucking the gin into his jacket pocket. 'I will.' He put his arms round Sonia and Barbara's shoulders as if to say, and I'm taking these treats away with me too. Barbara was intensely conscious of the weight and warmth of his arm and, glancing up at the unpleasantly belligerent face in front of them, momentarily proud of it.

They were shepherded back into the hall, where several other young men were gathered now, clearly on standby. Barbara thought Len extremely wise not to look for trouble. The young woman was at the doorway of the darkened room, anxiously trying to point Billy out.

'In the black bomber jacket,' she said, pointing. 'There!'

Billy was removed, less politely.

'Hey, lay off him,' Len frowned, looking every bit the injured party.

'It's OK,' grinned Billy. His jacket was zipped to the neck, as if he'd expected to be outside again almost immediately.

'Well, that was a waste of time,' gasped Barbara, as they

galloped down the stairs. Her heart was pounding in her chest. Billy and Len were further down, laughing and jostling like a couple of schoolboys.

'Got the gin, didn't they,' giggled Sonia. 'Reckon that's all they went for. No wonder Dave didn't bother.'

The mood of triumph persisted back to the house. Dave and Jane had only just arrived themselves, and were unpacking dripping cartons of glutinous Chinese food on to the kitchen table.

Len waved the gin trophy at them. Jane said, 'Christ, Len,' with weary amusement and Dave snorted, 'They don't see you coming, do they?'

'Hey,' said Billy, standing over the sofa. He unzipped his jacket with a flourish, releasing a cascade of cassettes on to the corduroy.

Sonia gave a squeal of delighted outrage. Len stared at the cassettes, and then grasped him by the shoulders and shook him, laughing proudly.

Billy started calling out the titles, tossing the cassettes across the sofa. Dave inspected a couple flung in his direction, caught Jane's eye and smiled. After calling out the last title, Billy collected up the cassettes and began to stack them on a shelf above the stereo, with an air of exultant satisfaction.

Barbara watched the scene, speechless. They're bloody thieves, she raged inwardly, much more scandalised by the tapes than the gin. She made a clear distinction between drink and goods. She looked at Billy, his face shining with pride and pleasure. He's done it for Len, she thought in sudden despair. How incredibly putrid.

'Barbara disapproves,' sneered Len, nudging Billy.

Billy laughed, and eyed her excitedly. The vengeance in his expression shocked her; he looked evil. A violent pricking attacked the back of her eyes. She attempted a disdainful shrug and turned away.

Sonia was behind her. 'Here,' she giggled, holding out a glass of whisky. 'Aren't they naughty?'

Barbara took the whisky. 'Yes,' she said, keeping her voice

steady. 'They are.' She blinked rapidly, and sat down in one of the armchairs. And they're like kids, she thought, like horrible little boys. Always have to have a best mate and someone to get at.

She stuck it out for half an hour, till Dave and Jane left. Nobody except Sonia said goodbye to her. On the walk home the streetlights looked huge and blurred, and her throat ached.

Her room, when she switched the light on, looked anything but cosy and home-like. It looked makeshift, and lonely, and pathetic. She drew the curtains, and pressed the switch on the orange-shaded lamp. Nothing happened; the bulb hadn't survived the journey from home.

She sat down on the bed, and began to weep. Streams of unstoppable tears. In seconds her face and hands were soaked, slippery wet. Droplets fell from her chin, to the black and gold of her dress.

She struggled into her nightdress. Climbing into bed she saw in her mind's eye, glisteningly superimposed on the faces she had just left, a square uncomplicated face with honest eyes and an artless mouth. Oh, Peter, she implored silently and lay back, swamped by longings his name invoked; but couldn't bring herself to express them in words, even in her head.

6

'I give up with them,' grumbled Barbara on Sunday afternoon, sprawled beside Sonia on the bed, watching a fifty-year-old film on the portable.

She rolled on to her side and regarded the rain-spattered window morosely. Everything was grey today: the view outside, the film on the television, her mood. She felt drained and fragile after so much night-time crying, though no longer pathetic. They weren't worth getting upset about, she kept telling herself.

Her elbows came to rest on the novel Sonia had returned to her earlier, abandoned after four chapters.

'Nothing happens,' Sonia had complained, riffling through the pages disparagingly, as if to demonstrate their inertia. 'They just think a lot.'

'Well, that's like most people's lives, isn't it?' Barbara had argued, crushed by this verdict on one of her favourite books. 'I mean, it feels true, doesn't it?'

But Sonia evidently wanted action, not truth, and said she thought the heroine a boring wimp who didn't know when she was well off and made an awful fuss about everything instead of pulling her finger out and getting on with it.

Barbara dislodged the book and thumped it on to the bedside locker. There was a slightly precious, middle-class feel to it, she had to admit. It hadn't occurred to her before. The impressionist nude on the cover was staring – rather wetly, it now seemed to her – at a hazy reflection of herself in a gilt-edged mirror. Her navel was clearly visible. How apt, she thought sourly, and sighed.

'I can't be bothered with them,' she insisted, more forcefully this time, since Sonia hadn't responded.

'Oh, come on,' encouraged Sonia, detaching her eyes from the screen. She patted Barbara on the arm. 'It's fun.'

'No, it isn't,' said Barbara. 'I'm fed up with them. They're enough to put you off men for life.'

'I thought you already were,' Sonia reminded her.

'Oh, you know,' Barbara muttered. 'They're so horrible.' She searched around for examples that didn't involve her, to appear unbiased. 'Look at the way they were getting at Billy last night. All that stuff about Morocco. Disgusting.'

Sonia sighed wearily. 'For God's sake. It was only a bit of ribbing. They're always doing it. Billy doesn't mind, I keep telling you.'

'Well, he bloody well ought to,' Barbara snapped. 'That's exactly what's so peculiar about him. In fact the whole set-up's peculiar. He does anything Len says. It's really pathetic.'

'He does anything anyone says,' Sonia said mildly. 'Perhaps that's the way he likes it. No one's forcing him. Perhaps he needs someone like Len.'

Barbara could see that there might be some truth in this, now it was pointed out to her. She was tempted to argue that personally she'd need someone like Len like a hole in the head but refrained, since she wasn't sure how much loyalty Sonia attached to men she was prepared to sleep with. In fact she disapproved of Sonia, too, today. Everybody, it seemed, was leading lives incomprehensible to her. Len and Billy were involved in some complicated and undoubtedly pathological servant and master game, Dave and Jane appeared to inhabit a private and superior world that over-lapped only marginally with the rest of humanity, and Sonia was performing what should be intimate acts in a non-intimate relationship with a man most women would think twice about approaching with a cattle prod. And yet it was she who felt the outsider.

'They shouldn't steal,' she muttered, feeling frumpily old-fashioned.

Sonia giggled. 'No, they shouldn't. But it was funny, wasn't it?' She screwed up her nose. 'They were only tapes. And, I mean, d'you really mind stealing from gooks like that? Christ, you saw them. Billy was drunk, it was just a stunt.

You thought it was funny last weekend, when we got into that flat.'

'That was different.' It was; it had been a mistake. Nobody had set out to hurt anyone . . . What was really rankling had to come out. 'And they don't like me,' she added bitterly. 'I know they don't.' Even Billy, she thought, upsetting herself again. She hadn't deserved that look. It still hurt.

'Oh, rubbish,' said Sonia airily. 'Anyway, I don't see why that should bother you, if you don't like them. People can still be fun, whatever you think about them. Christ, I know loads of people like that. I thought you were just out to have a good time and to hell with it.' She jiggled Barbara's arm. 'Hey,' she wheedled, 'Don't go all straitlaced on me. I like you coming out with us. Who else am I going to talk to? Think of me.'

You should be talking to Len, Barbara thought, but said, 'You've got Jane.' She turned to Sonia suddenly. 'D'you know her? Properly, I mean? I can't make her out at all. Apart from that first night she's hardly said a word to me, but she doesn't seem shy. Anything but, in fact.'

'She's a cow.' Sonia swung her legs off the bed abruptly, and reached out to switch channels on the television. The stilted tones of thirties actors were replaced by the high-pitched scream of Formula One racing cars. She winced and switched back again. 'I think she only comes out to keep tabs on Dave,' she said, flopping back on to the bed. 'Make sure he sticks to the straight and narrow. I've heard he and Len used to be right tearaways in the old days. Fights and all sorts. You ask the landlord.'

'Really?' said Barbara. This information was slightly alarming. She wondered what 'the old days' meant.

Sonia nodded. 'I reckon she's got him under her thumb.'

Barbara found this hard to imagine. On the other hand, if Dave was going to be under anyone's thumb, it could well be Jane's. And it was Len and Billy who stole things, and broke into people's flats. Briefly she saw a picture of them: Len slapping Billy proudly across the shoulders, Billy grinning back at him, triumphantly elated.

'You know,' she reflected, 'I think you're probably right. About Billy and Len, I mean. Perhaps Billy does need Len. I've just been seeing it as Len bossing him around. You're quite clever sometimes, you know.'

'Meaning I'm not usually,' jeered Sonia. 'Thanks a bundle.'

Barbara shrugged, but couldn't suppress a smile.

Sonia giggled. 'Well, I think you're funny, you know that? Half really clever, and half incredibly stupid.' She assumed an expression of supplication. 'But you will come out again, come on, you will, won't you? After all . . .' She smiled reasonably, '. . . you've nothing else to do.'

Barbara snorted. She was beginning, reluctantly, to approve of Sonia again. Nobody else could employ such a tactless argument and render it inoffensive, simply by stating it.

But she shook her head. 'Sorry. I really don't want to. I'm not enjoying myself. If it was just you . . .'

'But it is, really. That's what I'm saying.' Sonia lifted her hand. 'Don't decide now. You'll feel different in the week.'

'I don't think so.'

'Bet you will,' said Sonia. 'Leave it open, OK?'

'OK,' sighed Barbara.

'Had another awful one this morning,' Sonia said breathlessly, as they were hurrying along the pavement towards their seafront bench on Wednesday at lunchtime. 'Old Ma Renson told me. She was spitting. This woman had divorced the bloke months ago, but he'd broken into her house and wrecked everything. Cut up all the sheets and curtains, even the baby's nappies and cot sheets, and smashed up the furniture. He left a note saying she wouldn't be able to live without him and he was coming back, so she'd better look out. He was really clever too, because it was a council house and he didn't touch anything that wasn't hers, none of the windows or kitchen units or anything, so she couldn't get the council on to him. He sits outside the house in his car and follows her everywhere. They're going to try and get an injunction to keep him out of town. Mrs Renson told Mr

Watson that if the judge had any sense he'd take his car away from him, and Mr Watson said that was a jolly good idea, but that judges didn't have much sense and they might not even get the injunction, because lots of the things he wrecked were half his and he hadn't hurt her.' She shook her head in disbelief. 'Amazing, isn't it?'

Barbara absorbed this depressing story over twenty yards or so. 'What I don't understand,' she said finally, 'is why, if he hates her enough to do all those things, he wants her back. I just can't understand it.'

'Careful.' Sonia grabbed her arm as she was about to step off the kerb into a sidestreet. A speeding car screeched past. 'Well,' she said, as they jogged across the road, 'it's a bit like you and Peter really, isn't it?'

'What?' Barbara stopped on the pavement the other side and looked at her with astonishment. 'What on earth d'you mean?'

'Well, you had that row and he said all those dreadful things to you, and chucked you out . . . all right – ' she acknowledged Barbara's squeak of objection, 'made you have to leave. But then he still kept ringing you, didn't he? You said he did. When you were at home. I mean that's like hating you and wanting you back too.'

'He doesn't want me back,' said Barbara scornfully, walking on. 'He just doesn't want it to be all his fault. I know him. He wants to have a good grovel so he can feel better about it. I don't know how Mum can be so gullible.' She felt her jaw harden. 'He still rings her now, you know, even though I'm not there. God.'

Conversation was briefly suspended while they negotiated the coast road. 'Over there,' Barbara said, pointing to a four foot space on a bench to their left. They hurried over to it and unwrapped their lunches.

Sonia bit into a cottage cheese sandwich. ''Course it's not just men,' she said, chewing thoughtfully. 'One of the girls at Keep Fit was so angry with her boyfriend once that she put all his sweaters into the machine on boil.'

'Oh, no. Really?' Barbara thought this rather funny. It

didn't seem nearly as aggressive or reprehensible as cutting things up; though the result, she reluctantly supposed, must have been much the same. 'What happened?' she asked.

'Dunno. They're a weird couple. One week she says she's going to leave him because he's such a B, and the next they're all loveydovey and she's buying him expensive presents and things.'

Barbara sniffed. 'Sounds very tiring.'

'Takes all sorts, I suppose,' Sonia said. 'I mean it's quite hard, isn't it, deciding what you want?'

Barbara had already said, 'Suppose so,' before it occurred to her that Sonia had made a rather perceptive remark. 'Actually that's very true,' she said, nodding. 'Very true.'

Sonia looked amused at her earnestness. 'So about Friday – have you decided?'

'What about Friday?' The change of tack – or was it? – left Barbara confused.

'Whether you're coming out or not.'

'Oh . . .' Sonia was always doing this, leaping away from subjects the moment they became interesting. Before she could say 'No, I don't think so,' Sonia said, 'You've got to. Please.'

'Why?' Barbara laughed shortly. 'Why have I got to?'

'Because we're going to that new place.'

'Which new place? And so what?'

'The place near the clock tower. It's got live music. I don't know anyone there. You've got to come.'

Barbara said, 'You'll have Len and Billy,' aware that she was deliberately missing the point. Sonia was referring to having to arrive at the pub alone, and then, probably, having to wait for the men to turn up.

'Oh, come on,' said Sonia. 'You wouldn't like having to sit in a strange pub on your own, would you?'

'Well, no,' admitted Barbara. 'But . . .'

'And there'll be music. Dave and Jane are coming. It was Dave's idea. Please.'

Barbara debated. There'd be a crowd, always was for live groups. Maybe even dancing. She didn't absolutely have to stay with the others. What else would she be doing? Watching television?

Weakening, she said, 'Couldn't you ask someone from Keep Fit? You'll see them tonight.'

'No,' said Sonia. 'Either they've got boyfriends or they're, you know . . .' She pulled a face.

Barbara sighed.

Sonia took this as assent. 'You will come, won't you? I knew you would.' She squeezed Barbara's arm gratefully. 'We'll have a great time,' she promised. 'We will, honestly.'

7

Barbara had to brace herself for the Friday night date – just really on the walk there – but in the event found it quite unnecessary. Len greeted her almost indulgently (like a magnanimous victor, it occurred to her) and Billy had already called her Barb several times, which made her sound like a sharp spiky object, but appeared to be intended affectionately. Also, although the live music hadn't materialised – much to Dave's disgust; he was querying it now with Len and the landlord at the bar – the new surroundings made it feel like a fresh start.

'Hey, guess what!' Sonia hissed, returning from the Ladies. She sat down and grabbed Barbara's arm excitedly.

'Over there,' she whispered, pointing with a tiny gesture. 'See? That's Len's wife!'

'That's what?' Barbara assumed she had misheard her.

'Len's wife!'

Barbara pulled away from Sonia and stared at her. 'But Len isn't married, is he?'

'Well, he must be,' Sonia insisted, wide-eyed. 'Because that's her, in the purple shirt and beads.'

'But . . .' Barbara searched for a purple shirt and beads, '. . . how d'you know?' Sonia was being infuriating. This was a bombshell, surely?

Sonia visibly took a grip on herself. 'I just met her in the lav. She came up to me and said, honestly she did, "And how's that – "' Sonia dropped her voice, '" – shit of a husband of mine?" Her exact words. She must have seen we were with him. Hey, look . . !' her voice rose to a squeak, '. . . she's coming over!'

'I can't imagine Len being married,' whispered Barbara, before the woman was in earshot.

Len's wife had shoulder-length frizzy hair and a lived-in

face, verging on hard. But then you'd have to be fairly hard, she thought charitably, to be married to Len. She looked well into her thirties too; Len's presumed age took an experimental leap forwards.

'Hi,' said Len's wife, scraping one of the bentwood chairs back from the table. She put her glass of wine down and glanced over her shoulder to the bar. Dave and Jane appeared to be leaving. Dave was standing with his hand on the open bar door, shouting something over the crowd to Len, who was making 'right-on' gestures with his thumb.

Len's wife sat down. 'So tell me more.'

Sonia caught Barbara's eye and giggled nervously. Len's wife frowned, snapped open her tapestry handbag and removed a cigarette packet. Barbara felt the need to compensate for Sonia's manner.

'I'm Barbara,' she said politely. 'I don't know Len very well, I'm afraid.'

'Lucky you,' said Len's wife drily, lighting a cigarette. 'I'm Maggie. What's Len doing here? I thought I'd made a good job of avoiding his stamping grounds.'

Barbara felt a twinge of guilt, for being associated with the invader. 'We don't usually come here,' she said. 'It was Dave's idea. He saw an advert for live music.'

Maggie made a tutting noise, as if Dave, above all, might have been expected to know better. 'You've got the wrong day. That's Sunday. And I know it says folk-rock, but it's mostly folk. Not up his street, you tell him.'

'He's just left, actually,' Barbara said, looking over to the door. 'He's probably gone to get something to eat.'

Maggie smiled, played with the stem of her wine glass. 'I expect so,' she agreed. She looked behind her again at Len, who was now talking to Billy in typical stance, grasping him firmly by the upper arm, face pushed close to his ear. Sonia was sending indiscreet messages with her eyes that Barbara chose to ignore.

'Who's the lad you came in with?' asked Maggie, turning back. 'The one he's talking to now?'

'Oh, that's Billy.' Barbara covered a frown to Sonia. 'He lives with Len.'

'Does he now?' Maggie looked astonished. 'Wow. How long has that been going on?'

'I'm not sure exactly.' Barbara looked at Sonia, wondering if she'd like to take over, but she was sulking. 'A year or more, I think.'

'Well,' Maggie snorted. 'That explains a lot.'

'Oh, it's nothing like that,' Barbara protested, and then felt silly; she guessed Maggie was joking. Sonia giggled rudely in the background. 'He lodges there, I mean,' she said lamely. 'He's got the sitting room.'

'Fancy,' said Maggie, grinning at her. 'I didn't know that.'

Barbara couldn't think of any reason why she should know, if she had been avoiding Len as diligently as she implied. Or perhaps she was just a bit drunk and giving off exaggerated signals.

'I didn't know Len had been married,' she ventured.

'No, well, it was a few years ago.' Maggie swivelled to stare across at Len again, and this time caught his eye. She raised her glass to him and he did likewise, with his pint. If he was surprised, Barbara thought, he hid it well.

'Ah,' Maggie sighed, turning back and shaking her head in mock-admiration. 'Good-looking bastard, isn't he?' She grinned at Barbara, who grinned back. I like her, she thought. She's a bit drunk, but she looks as if she can take care of herself, and she's not scared of Len. Thinking this made her realise that she might be, just a little.

Maggie was still grinning. 'Ah, well,' she declared, slapping her hand on the table and preparing to rise. 'Nice to meet you. You look after yourselves now. Better go and say hello to the old sod, I suppose. Might not see him for another couple of years, with any luck.'

As she strode away Sonia dissolved in giggles.

'Cor, what a slag,' she hissed.

Barbara looked at her in surprise, and then at Maggie's back.

'What d'you mean?' she said indignantly.

73

'Well,' shrugged Sonia, making a face. 'Looks like she's been around.'

'Honestly, Sonia,' Barbara said stiffly. 'Listen to you. I thought she seemed very nice.'

'She was pissed.' Sonia picked up her own glass.

'And why shouldn't she be?' Barbara was outraged. 'It's Friday night. Christ, you're legless most weekends.' She regarded Sonia priggishly. 'You ought to watch yourself. You know what they say about women's livers.'

'Oh, shut up.' Sonia looked away.

She's jealous, Barbara thought. She doesn't like the idea of anyone knowing Len better than she does. Although perhaps Maggie had been a bit tactless. Very tactless, really. It just hadn't seemed like that at the time because of her own opinion of Len. It must have come across rather differently to Sonia.

Billy was walking over to them, glancing behind him. Sonia patted the seat next to her but he appeared not to notice, and squeezed into the bar-facing seat beside Barbara.

'Dave didn't stay long, then,' said Sonia, pointedly directing the remark at Billy, not Barbara. 'Thought it was his idea to come here?'

'Said he was hungry.' Billy's tone was mechanical. He stared across the room. Len and Maggie were at the far corner of the bar, turned away from the crowd, talking with a kind of aggressive intimacy.

'That really Len's wife?' he said.

'Looks like it.' Barbara grinned at him. She was suddenly, despite Sonia's sulkiness – or maybe because of it – positively enjoying herself. She leaned closer to Billy. 'So you didn't know he'd been married either?'

'No.' He frowned. 'She asked me who'd been sleeping in her bed.'

'What?'

'That's what she said. "Who's been sleeping in my bed?"'

Barbara patted him on the hand. 'She was joking. Goldilocks and the Three Bears. We told her you had the sitting room.'

Billy said, 'Oh,' sounding relieved. Barbara grinned at Sonia but got no response. So she crossed her eyes and stuck her tongue out.

Sonia said, 'God, you do look stupid,' but then poked the pink tip of her own tongue out, and grudgingly smiled back.

Billy continued to watch Len and Maggie intently. His expression when Len eventually returned was spaniel-like. Barbara couldn't decide whether she despised Len for encouraging such dependence, or admired him for putting up with it.

Len made no reference to Maggie except in the general remark 'This place is a dead loss, isn't it?' He suggested they try the beer keller on the seafront tomorrow, which had been option two on Dave's list.

'It's miles away,' objected Sonia. 'We'll have to get the bus.'

We? What's this *we*? thought Barbara, but goodnaturedly let it pass. Maybe they'd discover another wife.

'Give you a lift,' conceded Len. He sat down and put an arm around Sonia's shoulders. Barbara noticed Maggie, seated with another woman three tables away, and suspected that this display of affection was for her benefit, not Sonia's.

'Dave'll drive,' pronounced Len. 'I'll tell him to pick us up at my place, half-eight.'

Billy knocked off work at three o'clock on Saturday afternoon, since the rain that had started to fall at noon hadn't abated and showed no signs of doing so. His only charge for the last hour had been a small boy droning in the sandpit with a toy JCB, whom he recognised as the son of the woman who ran the candy floss stall.

He locked the hut, tucked his damp swimming things under his arm – he'd swum first thing, but forgotten to hang the towel and trunks out in the morning sunshine – and set off for the town centre. The rain was so heavy that up on the coast road he draped the towel over his head and shoulders and broke into a jog; even so, by the time he reached the main shopping streets, his jeans and sweatshirt were soaked through.

He ducked through the automatic glass doors of the town's largest department store, and followed a familiar route past women's gloves and hosiery, down the basement escalator to household and crockery, and through this to the hi-fi department. They had old-fashioned listening booths here; two of the three, he noted as he passed, were presently unoccupied. Ahead was the record counter. And behind it, the dapper male assistant, leafing through a glossy catalogue.

Before Billy reached the counter he stopped to gaze at a display of personal cassette players, their earphones extended over white polystyrene dummy heads. Several had special offer signs on them. He'd been promising himself one of these for weeks; the notion of being able to encapsulate yourself in all-round portable music seemed to him tremendously exciting. It would be like the swamping effect of the booths, only better.

The cheapest appeared to be just under twenty pounds. It didn't sound much, he thought, when you took home nearly seventy a week. He wondered if he could risk buying one, the day he got paid, and let the rest of the week look after itself. He reached out to finger the controls of one of the players. It was at times like this he wished Len had fixed him one of the other jobs on the front. Twenty pounds would be nothing then. The deckchair attendants fiddled at least that on top of their seventy, and the arcade maintenance lads on the pier were always flush with cash. Len said thousands went astray there, over a whole summer.

'Hello there,' said the assistant into Billy's right ear. He swung round.

'My,' the young man smiled, 'you're wet.'

'Yeah.' Billy looked down. A corner of the sodden towel under his arm was hanging to his knees, dripping rainwater on to the floor.

'I'll get you a bag for that,' said the assistant. 'Don't flap it around.' He walked over to the counter and returned with an LP carrier bag. 'Stuff it in there.'

'Thanks,' said Billy. 'Sorry.'

'Don't mention it.' The young man looked amused. When he wore this expression Billy knew he was gay, though he didn't count the fact either for or against him.

'You interested in those?' The assistant indicated the cassette players.

'Yeah.' Billy nodded. 'I'm going to get one soon.'

'That's the best.' The young man tapped a Sony make, priced at nearly thirty pounds. 'It's worth paying the extra. Specially if you've got a good ear.'

Billy doubted he would be spending thirty pounds but inspected it out of good will. He knew he was being flattered. He'd told the assistant once that he'd got perfect pitch; he wasn't sure what it meant, beyond being able to hear in his head what middle C sounded like (which was all that stuck in his mind from the test he'd taken at eleven), but the assistant had seemed impressed.

'It's really nice.' He stepped back from the display. 'Next week, maybe.'

The assistant grinned, and started walking back towards the counter. 'You want to hear something now?' he asked over his shoulder. 'Got a couple just in you'd like. Aswad and a live Bob Marley.'

'Yeah?' Billy followed him. 'Can I see the covers?'

'Take them in with you.' The young man flicked through a stack of covers in a pigeonhole behind the counter and removed two. 'Booth three,' he said, handing them over and moving to the counter turntables. 'One side of each, OK?'

'Great,' said Billy.

An hour later, his head throbbing with the rocking, melodic tones of Bob Marley, Billy emerged from the store. It was still raining, but the sky had lightened to a yellow mistiness and the rain was gentler. His clothes remained clammily damp from their drenching an hour ago; he barely noticed any additional wetness on the short walk home.

He let himself in the back door and turned into the

bathroom to strip off. As he did so a voice from the sitting room – Len's – called, 'Oi!'

'Yeah?' He pulled off his sweatshirt and tossed it into the bath.

'C'm here, Billy.' Len's voice was soft, almost inviting. 'There's someone here wants to meet you.'

Billy froze, his hands on the button of his jeans. 'Who?'

There was a short silence. Then Len appeared at the bathroom door. He was smiling.

'You got a visitor, Billy,' he said. 'Eager sort of fellow. Came round an hour ago. He's been down to the playground and back again. He's waiting for you in the sitting room.'

'Who is it?' asked Billy, frightened.

Len moved into the room, scratching his jaw. 'Someone who makes me think you've been doing some fibbing, kiddo.'

'I gotta go,' gasped Billy, and snatched up the sweatshirt.

'Hey yey,' said Len, and caught him by the arm. He pulled the sweatshirt out of his hand and tossed it back into the bath. 'Calm down. He's not going to eat you. Just wants a chat. I'd like to hear it, too.'

8

Sonia insisted on going round to Len's house earlier than eight-thirty, convinced the others would leave for the beer keller without her, given any excuse. Barbara hadn't finished drying her hair, which became an undisciplined frizz if the process was rushed, so – rather bravely, she thought – said she'd catch her up.

Strolling along the road at eight-thirty-five she wondered – provoked by Sonia's anxiety – if Len would take the opportunity to hustle everyone away before she arrived. And would Sonia object, if he tried to? A picture arose in her mind, of Sonia protesting, 'Oh, no, we must wait for Barbara,' while at the same time tripping obediently out to the car. The vision was so persuasive she had consciously to ungrit her teeth as she turned the corner and saw Dave's Rover still parked outside the house.

The front door was ajar. She entered the hallway and hearing voices within, pushed open the sitting room door.

Len and Dave were on the sofa, Sonia curled up small in one of the armchairs. There was no sign of Jane. Nobody looked up as she walked in. Everybody's attention was on Billy, who was sitting rigidly on a hard chair near the fireplace, opposite Len and Dave.

'Little fraudster,' Dave said accusingly, as she perched herself on the arm of Sonia's chair. 'Poor little orphan Billy, eh, and all the time he's got doting parents down the road.' He turned a disgusted face to Len. 'Ever get the feeling you've been had?'

Barbara shot a startled frown at Sonia, who put her finger to her lips in a silencing, I'll-explain-later gesture. Len had his arms folded across his chest and was regarding Billy judiciously. Billy's mouth was open. Barbara could see – almost hear – his breathing.

'My dad is dead,' he said faintly.

'OK then,' Dave conceded, flexing his arms in the manner of prosecuting counsel. 'Mum, then, doting mum. Same difference.'

Barbara nudged Sonia. She wanted to know what was going on, now. Dave caught the movement. 'The Sally Army were round today,' he said, glancing from Billy to her. 'Turns out Mum is looking for the little jerk.'

Barbara stared back at him blankly.

Sonia whispered, 'The Salvation Army. Missing persons, you know. They trace them.'

Barbara hadn't known, but nodded. So Billy was a missing person. And his mother wasn't dead. But it didn't explain Dave's hostility.

'You going to go and see your Mum, then?' she asked. She made her voice as conversational as possible, because she was suddenly afraid Billy was going to cry. Insensitive clods, she thought angrily, can't they see he's in a state?

Billy stared back at her, then shook his head.

'Well, they'll tell her you're OK, won't they?' She heard herself and winced. It sounded grotesque, looking at him.

'They're moving house,' explained Len loudly. 'His mum and stepdad. They wanted Billy to know, in case he ever decides to visit.' He picked up a piece of paper with something written on it – torn, Barbara noticed, as if it had been argued over – and flapped it around. Billy followed its movement hopelessly with his eyes.

'Only take twenty minutes in the car,' Len said cajolingly. 'Wouldn't you like to go see them?'

Billy shook his head again.

Sonia unfolded her legs from the chair.

'Honestly,' she said. 'I think you're both being beastly. Billy's mum is his own business, isn't it, Billy?' She smiled at him kindly, and then added sternly to the others. 'I don't know how you can be so mean.'

Barbara gazed at her in admiration, wishing she'd said it. Len and Dave ignored the interruption. Across the room Billy shifted on his chair. Barbara was suddenly conscious that they were all sitting in his bedroom, that he had nowhere else to go. Poor Billy, she thought heavily, he has to live his life in front of everyone.

Len got to his feet, smiled first at Dave then, widely, at Billy. He put a hand on his shoulder and shook him lightly.

'C'mon,' he said, as if nothing had happened. 'Let's go out.'

The beer keller was hot, damp and crowded. They had to stand for more than half an hour before they could unstick their feet from the floor and appropriate a table. Barbara thought Billy was going to fall over. Len did all the fetching and carrying for once, barging through the crowd with armfuls of litre mugs, issuing 'mind your backs' and 'watch it's to obstacles in his path. The beer was extremely strong and gassy; Barbara had difficulty finishing the first litre Len bought her and only managed a few sips of the second. Sonia, who disliked beer of any description, insisted on being bought unfamiliar German liqueurs, since they didn't stock ordinary spirits. Dave spent the first hour eyeing Billy with irritation and Len with exasperation, and the rest of the evening at a different table entertaining an American redhead with rolling eyes and free-hanging breasts. She'd introduced herself with, 'Sorry, handsome,' as she fell over him trying to squeeze past, and appeared captivated by the texture of his sideboards. Len scarcely seemed to notice the desertion; his attention was on Billy, who swallowed everything pushed in front of him and became increasingly pale and drunk. He also became increasingly pathetic and grateful, and said he was sorry several times, loudly and embarrassingly, to which Len replied, 'That's OK, kiddo,' as if he did, indeed, have something to apologise for.

Barbara spent a lot of time, when Sonia wasn't chatting to her, watching Billy, and thinking. She found she had actually to hold him in her field of vision, in the chaotic, mindbattering atmosphere, to recall the scene in the house. As the evening progressed a deep gloom settled over her. It's the alcohol, she told herself muzzily; this awful game isn't my business, it's Len and Billy's, why should I care?

But she couldn't shake off a sense of foreboding. Just before closing time she found herself studying Billy's face minutely, and, pulling away, realised she had been memorising it, in case she never saw it again. It wasn't until they left the pub, and hit the brain-cleansing seafront air, that the darkness of the mood lifted.

'I'm going to ask Dave to drop me off,' she whispered to Sonia, as they weaved their way across the coast road back to the car. Dave was saying goodnight to the redhead against the wall of the pub, mostly, it appeared, with his knee. Billy was so unsteady on his feet that Len was having to steer him across the road.

She nodded at them. 'Billy looks like he needs to crash.' A stab of anger made her add, 'I can't stand much more of Len's smarminess, anyway.'

Sonia yawned without inhibition, unoffended.

'OK.' She blinked rapidly. 'God, those liqueurs. They're stronger than they taste.'

Keep an eye on Billy, Barbara suddenly wanted to say; but knew it was pointless.

'So what you got against your mum, then?' Len said, slumped on the sitting room sofa late on Sunday morning. He was in a black tracksuit, his bare feet up on the coffee table. A pair of scissors and a small heap of nail-clippings were pushed into the corner of the table.

In the kitchen Billy heard the question, just, over the gush of tap water into the washing-up bowl. He frowned and turned the cold tap on harder.

'Oi,' said Len, raising his voice. 'You heard me. You sulking or something?'

Billy turned off both taps. 'No.'

Len got up, swept the nail-clippings into his hand, and came through to the kitchen. He tipped the clippings into the wastebin. 'So what you got against her, then?'

'Nothing.' Billy squeezed washing-up liquid into the water. Len peered over his shoulder.

'You should do that first, moron. Swish it up with your hand.'

Billy obediently swished his hand in the water. A few bubbles formed on the surface. Len sighed, and stepped back.

'So why don't you see her? Eh? You gotta have a reason.'

Billy shrugged. 'Just don't.' With a clatter he pulled a stack of plates and cutlery from the draining board into the water. He wiped the top plate with a cloth and put it in the rack to his right.

'She throw you out?' Len asked.

'Nope.'

'You must have had a bust-up. Something. You get into trouble?'

'Nope.' Billy wiped the second plate and, lifting it clear of the water, caught it against the overhanging spout of the cold tap.

'Watch it,' Len said. 'You break one of those, you pay for it.'

Billy lowered the plate back into the water. He couldn't do this with Len standing over him.

'I know,' said Len, with a note of triumph. 'You been in hospital. Screwball, aren't you?'

'What d'you mean?' Billy swung round in confusion.

Len twisted a finger into his temple. 'Loony bin. Mental hospital.'

'No.' Billy shook his head, turning back to the washing up. ''Course not.' He picked up the cloth again and carefully wiped the edge of the plastic washing-up bowl. There was a period of silence.

Finally Len said, 'You're not going to tell me, then?' His voice was flat.

Billy murmured, 'Nothing to tell,' and rested his hands on the sides of the bowl. The surface of the washing-up water was spotting with gobs of grease, drifting up amoeba-like from the submerged cutlery.

'Mystery boy, aren't we?' Len said unpleasantly.

Billy stared at the blobs of grease. Should he be answering yes or no? But then it didn't matter: Len was striding towards the door.

'Just get the fuck on with that,' he said, and disappeared upstairs.

'You know,' said Barbara, after finishing her Monday lunchtime roll, 'I think there's something wrong with Billy.' They were in her office cubby hole this morning, as it was raining.

'I think you're soft on him,' replied Sonia, brushing croissant crumbs off her lap.

'Shut up,' said Barbara. 'I'm serious. I spent most of yesterday thinking about it. I don't know why I never saw it before. Or maybe it just didn't register. You kind of accept people as they are, don't you, when you first meet them? As if that's how they should be normally. It's only changes you notice. And somehow . . . well . . . you almost expect people to behave oddly at night-time, with all the boozing and smoking. But if you think about it . . . the way he lives . . . and that stuff about his parents . . . and how much he drinks, and smokes. I know it's only dope, but still . . .'

'Len does the same.' Sonia's expression had become uncooperative. Much, indeed, as it had on the walk to work, when she'd dismissed a casual speculation on the break-up of Len's marriage with, 'Can't blame him, can you, imagine coming home to that.'

'I know he does.' Barbara made her tone conciliatory. Sonia, she was beginning to realise, considered Len and Billy her property, and resented other people claiming insights into them. 'But he can handle it. He never looks out of control. That's exactly what I'm getting at. Billy does look out of control. On Saturday night I imagined him dying.'

'Barbara!' Sonia looked shocked.

Barbara thought back to Saturday night. The overall memory was hazy, but specific recollections were not. She nodded. 'I did. And it does happen. You hear about it all the time. Specially young men. You know, they end up doing something stupid, and dying. And everybody says they're surprised, as if it's the last thing they expected, but when you actually look at their lives, from the outside that is, it's obvious something was wrong. It just isn't to the people who know them because they've got used to it, or perhaps because they don't care that much. It happened to a friend of Peter's. He was a really manic sort of guy, life and soul of the party type, and he used to go on about being skint all the time, and flirt outrageously, and get impossibly drunk, and everybody used to think what a laugh he was and never took him seriously. And then he wrapped his car round a lamp post one night and died, and it all came out, about his business going bust, and the affairs he had, and how miserable his wife was. It was an accident, the crash, but it wasn't really, it was all part of the same pattern, everything being hopelessly out of control. None of us saw it, till afterwards.'

'Billy isn't anything like that,' Sonia objected.

Barbara made an exasperated noise. 'It was only an example. I'm just trying to explain what I mean. The principle's the same. Billy seems out of control. I was watching him on Saturday night and at the back of my mind I was thinking, I'm watching someone who could be dead soon. I was. I'm sure there's something wrong with him.'

'I think there's something wrong with you,' Sonia said. 'What a thing to say. Billy's all right. He's always been like that.'

'But he is odd.' Frustration made Barbara's voice rise. She was being made to feel she was criticising him, not expressing concern for him. 'You must see that.'

'Lots of people are odd. Specially kids. It doesn't mean they're going to die. It's not something sudden.' Sonia leant forward, stressing her words. 'Really, Barbara, I do know.'

Barbara sighed. Sonia had known Billy less than a year and was making it sound like a lifetime. On the other hand, voicing her fears did make them sound overdramatic.

'I don't care,' she said, though less certainly. 'I think we're all missing something. He looked really ill on Saturday. Christ, Dave was so cruel. And Len's meant to be Billy's friend. Some friend. He didn't have to tell everyone, did he? Honestly, Sonia . . . I don't know why you bother with him. What on earth d'you see in him?'

Sonia gave a dipping smile and looked down at the teaspoon in her hand. She twiddled it one way, then the other. 'You don't think he's attractive at all, then?'

'Well, of course he's attractive,' Barbara said impatiently. 'Physically, that is. Any fool can see that.'

'He is though, isn't he?' Sonia raised dreamy eyes. 'He really is. He's got the most amazing body. He can do incredible things with his stomach muscles.'

Barbara gave a snorting laugh. 'Like what?'

'He's got all these exercise machines,' Sonia confided. 'Up in his room. Lots of them. There's one, you pull the straps in and out – ' she demonstrated, as if drawing an imaginary bow, 'or squeeze the ends in – ' the invisible object became on accordian, 'They must really work.'

Barbara couldn't help a giggle. She experienced a flicker of admiration for Len. She had always imagined ownership of such appliances to be guilty secrets, the things themselves hidden away at the back of wardrobes and only smuggled out when coasts were clear.

'I had a go once,' confessed Sonia. 'It was quite fun.'

'Oh, Jesus.' A mental picture was conjured up, of Sonia wrestling with some machinery while Len supervised, and then of him demonstrating how it should be done, while she gazed on, enthralled.

'Well,' she said weakly, 'I'm sure it must make him very . . . um . . . athletic.'

Sonia smiled but didn't reply. She twiddled the teaspoon again. Her smile became diffident.

'Actually . . .' she glanced at Barbara and away again, 'he says I'm a prude.'

Barbara's own smile fixed. 'What d'you mean?'

'Well . . . you know . . . about things . . .' Sonia frowned down at her lap. 'He's said it lots of times. He always sounds surprised.'

Barbara made a noise between a gulp and 'Dear me.' Sonia

appeared to be telling her something rather private – and possibly rather appalling too – without being properly aware that she was doing so.

'I wish Harvey would come back.' Sonia looked wistful. 'It's been over three months.'

Hopefully Barbara asked, 'Are you going to ditch Len when he does?' She felt a rush of affection for her friend. How dare Len call her a prude.

Sonia sighed. 'Maybe. I'm not sure. It's not so much fun with Harvey when we're out, but he is kinder. I mean, I know Len isn't a very nice person. But I do like going out with him. I like the excitement. All sorts of things happen with Len. Nothing much happens with Harvey. It's more personal, between the two of us. I do like it, and I like him, but it's fun to go round with a group too.' She shook her head. 'I don't know.'

Barbara gave a bleak laugh and started to clear the lunchtime debris from her desk. 'You're hopeless,' she said. 'Why not just admit that you know Len's a bastard, but you fancy him like hell. I suppose even I can see he's got something. You can't not notice him.'

'You're right.' Sonia sighed again. 'And I feel so good beside him. I really do. There's nothing wrong with that, is there? There can't be, can there?'

Barbara thought there almost certainly was, but couldn't put any non-moralistic name to it.

'I suppose not,' she said grudgingly.

9

At eleven o'clock on Thursday morning Barbara was waiting in hazy sunshine at a bus stop to the north of town, more than a mile from her work. She had been to the dentist and was concentrating more on exploring the frozen parts of her mouth with her semi-frozen tongue than on her human surroundings. She didn't notice a woman approaching with a pushchair until she spoke.

'Hi,' the woman said. 'It's Barbara, isn't it?'

'Hello,' said Barbara vaguely, seeing an untidy figure in denim skirt and pink t-shirt, and then realised who it was. 'Hello,' she said again, with more enthusiasm. 'Maggie.'

Her voice sounded peculiar to herself because of the frozen parts. 'Sorry.' She put a hand to her face. 'I've just been to the dentist. I'm all numb.' She stared at the child in the pushchair, who looked female, though it was difficult to tell.

'Poor you.' Maggie glanced up and down the road. 'You're going to have a bit of a wait, I'm afraid. You've just missed one.'

'Oh, hell,' groaned Barbara, and wondered if it would be quicker to walk.

Maggie smiled at her. 'I live just round the corner. You fancy coming back for a coffee while you thaw out? Or are you dashing off somewhere important?'

'Only back to work,' grinned Barbara, in so far as she could grin. She considered a moment. The invitation, which should have been surprising, for some reason wasn't.

'Yes,' she said, suddenly feeling adventurous. 'Thanks. If you don't mind me dribbling.' She looked at the child again.

'This is Jacey,' said Maggie. 'Here,' she added to the child. 'Let Mummy do that.'

She bent down to remove the wrapper from a sweet the child was about to put into her mouth and, as she straightened, tucked the back of her t-shirt into the loose waistband of the denim skirt. Barbara, who had yet to experience pregnancy and had been the same dress size for six years, wondered why she was wearing clothes that were clearly too large for her. She also wondered if Len was a father as well as a husband.

They crossed the road. 'It's just along here,' said Maggie, turning into a sidestreet. The houses were small redbrick terraces, not dissimilar to Len's, though more run down. They passed several that were actually boarded up.

'They were going to pull the lot down,' explained Maggie, gesticulating at the boards, 'so they could widen Princes Street. The council was using them for temporary accommodation. Then of course the scheme was dropped. I was lucky. Some of them are in a dreadful state because they've been empty so long, but it's not so bad our end. I decided to stay because I think it's nicer than an estate, and at least I'm not miles out of town.'

They stopped outside a house with a bright red front door and a pile of builders' rubble in the dirt strip between the pavement and the wall of the house.

'They've been fixing my roof,' Maggie said, as she manoeuvred the pushchair around it.

Barbara followed them into the house and waited in the doorway of what appeared to be a chaotically untidy sitting room.

'How old is Jacey?' she asked.

'Two and a half.' Maggie glanced at her daughter proudly. 'Big, isn't she?'

Barbara obeyed Maggie's waved instruction to enter the sitting room, removed a yellow plastic duck from the chair indicated, and murmured, 'I don't know much about babies, I'm afraid.'

'No, well you don't, do you,' nodded Maggie comfortably, dumping her shopping bag on the table, 'until you've had one.'

She went through to the kitchen to put the kettle on. The child pulled up another chair so she could stand on it to reach the table, and started unpacking the bag. She regarded each grocery purchase as she removed it and placed it with deliberation on one of several heaps in front of her. Maggie returned briefly to whip up a packet of fish fingers and a bag of frozen peas.

'I'll have those.' She grinned at Barbara. 'She's playing shops. I'll have to buy them all over again when you've gone.'

Barbara smiled. Of course this was more a playroom than a living room, she thought. And in fact although the chintz sofa under the window had holes in the covers and was in desperate need of restuffing, and the toy-scattered Indian carpet was more hessian than pattern, everything looked reasonably clean, under the mess. There were even some bookshelves here, on adjustable steel wall-brackets, incongruously contemporary-looking against the old-fashioned scruffiness of the rest. She guessed that Len had done rather better than Maggie, in terms of possessions, at the break up.

Maggie plonked a mug of coffee in front of her and cleared a space among the groceries for her own and the sugar bowl. 'I'm glad I bumped into you. I wanted to apologise for embarrassing you the other night. It was a defiance thing really. I was so surprised to see Len. I'm not usually that pushy.'

'You didn't embarrass anyone,' said Barbara, and then realised that although this was strictly true, it sounded unhelpful. 'At least,' she gave Maggie a quick smile, 'not really. We were surprised too. Neither of us knew Len had been married. Sorry if it seemed like that.'

'Your friend didn't seem to appreciate it. The other girl.'

'Oh, Sonia. Well, she's . . .' Barbara didn't know how to put it accurately. '. . . She's kind of Len's girlfriend.' She shrugged.

'Well of course I guessed she was, afterwards. I wasn't thinking. She must have thought me incredibly rude. Tell her I'm sorry, will you? She's a pretty girl.' She smiled at Barbara's cautious attempt to sip her coffee. 'How's the face?'

Barbara put the mug down and poked at her chin with a finger. 'Not too bad. My tongue's OK now.'

'So how do you know Len?'

Barbara explained her connection with Sonia, and how the bedsits were just around the corner from Len and Billy.

'Oh, Christ, Billy, yes.' Maggie snorted. 'I'm not sure I didn't put my foot in it there, too. He gave me such a funny look.' She shook her head, amused. 'That set-up surprised me. I really wouldn't have expected Len to be sharing with a kid like that, not at his age.'

'How old is he?' Barbara leant forward eagerly. 'He won't tell Sonia. We've both been wondering.'

Maggie chuckled. 'Vain old sod. God, that's typical. He's the same age as me. And Dave for that matter. Thirty-three.'

'Oh,' said Barbara. She wasn't sure if she was more surprised that Len was so old, or Maggie so young.

Maggie smiled at her ruefully. 'Puts years on you, being married to Len.'

Barbara laughed, which seemed the only possible response. The action felt lopsided, and she put a hand to her mouth.

The child scrambled down from her chair and tugged at Maggie, babbling something.

'Right, quick quick.' Maggie jumped to her feet. 'I won't be a minute,' she said.

She led the child through a door at the far end of the kitchen. Barbara heard it click shut. She sipped her coffee and then, because it was suddenly irresistible, rose quietly to inspect the rooms for signs of male occupation. Perhaps Maggie had remarried, or was living with someone. The child didn't have to be Len's.

There was an anorak tossed over the sidearm of the decrepit sofa; it was size thirty-six, however, so could well be Maggie's. And there was only one chair by the small table in the kitchen, apart from a trayless highchair, suggesting only one adult. She peeped round a half-open door by the fridge into an unrewarding broom cupboard.

'Careful of the straps, Jace,' said Maggie's voice, from the doorway behind her.

Barbara gave a guilty start away from the cupboard. 'Sorry,' she said in confusion, 'I was just . . . um.'

Maggie glanced at her with a smile. 'Come upstairs,' she said, as if blatant nosiness, far from being a crime, was a natural, even welcome, sign of interest. She waved a pair of children's knickers in her hand. 'I've got to take her up, she won't have a spot on them.'

'Oh,' said Barbara. 'Right.'

There were three bedrooms upstairs, two small and one tiny. They all had stains on the ceiling, but Maggie said the roof was fixed now, and she was going to decorate as soon as she could afford the paint. She rummaged through a chest of drawers in the tiny bedroom for knickers, while her daughter cavorted naked from the waist down on the unmade double bed in the front room.

Barbara could see nothing here that looked remotely masculine. She peered into the third bedroom, which had a single bed stacked on its side against the wall, and a table in the centre, bearing a sewing machine.

'That's supposed to be my money-making room,' Maggie told her, supervising her daughter dressing on the landing. 'I had all these great ideas about dressmaking, you know, starting a little business. But it's not really on. Everything's so cheap in the shops, you can't compete. And I don't have the time, now Jacey's stopped her afternoon naps. I still do a few party dresses and specials, but I'd never be able to make enough to risk losing my benefit. Hey, wrong way round.' She broke off to squat down beside Jacey and reverse the trousers the child was struggling into. 'It's a real problem, trying to think of something worthwhile to do. I even thought about childminding at one stage, you know, little ones, putting a couple of cots in here, but I think that's a non-starter too. Even if they OK'd the house, which they might now that the roof's done, I wouldn't be much better off, not unless I did it full time, and I don't fancy that. Still, the dressmaking helps, and it's cash in hand. My entertainment fund, I call it.'

Barbara saw her chance and asked, 'So what do you do with Jacey when you're out?' Maggie's reply, she hoped, would establish once and for all whether she lived alone.

Maggie jerked a thumb towards one of the party walls. 'I've got great neighbours, that side. They have Jacey Fridays, or the woman comes here, and on Saturdays I have their little boy. It works a treat. The husband's so keen on his Saturdays he bends over backwards to be neighbourly. I don't know what I'd do without them. You need people like that when you're on your own.'

Barbara smiled and nodded.

Coming slowly downstairs behind Maggie and Jacey, she took the opportunity to ask about Dave and Jane.

'Dave and Len go back a long way,' Maggie told her, as they re-entered the sitting room. 'They were at school together.'

'Do you like Dave?' Barbara made the question cautious. 'I mean I suppose I don't really know him, but . . .'

Maggie scratched her face, looking at Jacey. 'There's some squash on the kitchen table,' she said. 'Go and get it.'

She smiled at Barbara briefly. 'He's OK. When it comes to the crunch. Better than that wife of his, anyway. Or, whoops, have I done it again? D'you like her?'

'I hardly know her,' said Barbara. 'She doesn't seem to say much, except to Dave. She's very kind of . . . immaculate.'

'Isn't she just,' agreed Maggie scornfully, sitting down at the table and picking up her half-drunk coffee. 'You should see their house . . . or have you?' Barbara shook her head. 'When I went there last . . . well, it's years ago of course . . . but it was like something out of *Ideal Home*. You had to take your shoes off to go into the sitting room. Waist high in carpet. Ridiculous.'

Barbara had been surprised to hear Dave described as OK.

'Dave's horrible to Billy,' she said, frowning.

'Is he? That's interesting.' Maggie thought a moment, and then shrugged. 'Well, I said OK, not great. Not one for keeping his opinions to himself. He probably thinks Billy's a wimp. He's always had it in for wimps. So has Len for that matter. A bit short on human kindness is our Dave. You should hear him on the unemployed. But, on the other hand, if he's dealing with real people, he's pretty straight. And he's loyal. I mean, he still sees Len, he doesn't let Jane have it all her way.'

'You mean she'd like him not to?'

Maggie nodded. 'I'd have thought so. It's not really her scene, is it?' Her voice took on a spiteful edge. 'Although maybe she does get some sort of kick out of it. You know, la-di-da all week long, in her posh job and her posh house, and then at the weekends she thinks it would be fun to let her hair down and go slumming round the pubs with Dave. But I'm sure she wouldn't do it if he didn't want to. I suppose Dave's a bit like that himself, these days, but at least you're a real person to him while he's doing it, even if he doesn't like you. To Jane, you're just a spectator sport. She likes to think of herself as someone who smokes a bit of dope and all that, but she wouldn't let the stuff in her house. I mean – ' Maggie grinned, opening her eyes wide, 'she has dinner parties!'

Barbara laughed in anti-Jane solidarity, choosing to overlook the numerous dinner parties she and Peter had attended; often, it had to be said, held on fairly sumptuous carpets.

Maggie shook her head. 'I reckon if she'd had her way she'd have split Dave and Len up years ago – not that I blame her for that, mind – but Dave's no pushover, not on what he regards as the big things, so she compromises by treating it as a sideshow. I knew her for years and never really got close to her. I was just an appendage to Len, and pretty uninteresting at that. But Dave, well . . .' she laughed shortly, 'I have to admit to a soft spot for him. He was good to me when I was splitting up with Len, really good, which he needn't have been, considering they were mates. Still . . .' she waved the subject away, 'you don't want to hear about that.'

Barbara wouldn't in fact have minded at all, but knew it would sound excessively nosy to say so. She drained her coffee, watching Maggie staring through to the kitchen to Jacey, who had a chair up by the sink.

'I'd better go,' she said, standing up. 'They'll be wondering where I am.'

'Barbara.' Maggie turned to her abruptly. 'I don't want to sound as if I'm interfering . . . but is this Sonia serious about Len?'

Barbara hesitated. She wanted to know the reason for asking before replying.

'It's just that if she is . . .' Maggie saw her reluctance. 'I do think she ought to be careful.'

'What d'you mean?' Barbara sat down again.

Maggie lifted her shoulders awkwardly. 'Well, maybe he's changed . . . although I doubt it . . .' She sighed. 'This is going to sound dreadful . . . but he's really screwed up, that guy. Very possessive.' She paused, fiddling with the empty mug in front of her. 'He wants to possess things and, if he can't, he wants to smash them. And since you can't really possess people, they tend to end up getting smashed.' She smiled grimly, glancing up. 'It's just a warning. But, believe me, I know. I've been married to him.'

Barbara rubbed her nose. It was almost impossible to imagine this woman married to Len. Even less possible to imagine her smashed by him. Finally she said, 'I don't think Len wants to possess Sonia. I don't think he cares that much about her. And I don't think she cares for him that much either. She just fancies him. That's how I see it, anyway.'

'Oh, well, that's all right, then.' Maggie spoke briskly. 'Can't blame her, I suppose. He still looks good, bloody good. Sorry. Perhaps I shouldn't have said it.' She rose with Barbara, and touched her lightly on the arm. 'It's been nice seeing you. Next time you go to the dentist feel free to drop in.'

Barbara laughed, discomposed by the touch, but flattered too. Wanting to sound willing, she asked, 'Are you on the phone?'

''Fraid not. But I'm in most of the time. Any day, I mean it. I like droppers-in. I've enjoyed our chat, you're a nice girl.'

Barbara flushed and couldn't bring herself to say, 'You're a nice woman,' because it would have sounded ridiculous, although she thought it. She covered her embarrassment by calling 'Bye bye, Jacey,' through the door into the kitchen, and left Maggie rescuing china from the washing-up bowl.

'How's the teeth?' inquired Sonia, when she got back to work. 'Settled for a false set, have you, you've been long enough.'

'Two fillings,' said Barbara, and grimaced. Sonia laughed, baring her own teeth, which were perfect. Sonia had only ever had one filling, when she was nine.

'Guess who I met,' Barbara glanced around to make sure a conversation would be safe. 'That's why I've been so long. Maggie!'

'Who?'

'You know,' Barbara reminded her. 'Maggie. Len's wife. I met her at the bus stop and went back to her place for a coffee. She wanted to apologise for Friday. And, guess what, she's got a kid!'

Sonia blinked. 'What, Len's kid?'

Barbara gestured expressively. 'I don't know. A daughter. Two and a half. I was dying to ask.'

'Well, why didn't you?'

'I couldn't.'

''Course you could. I would have.'

'No, you wouldn't.'

'Yes, I would.'

Barbara sighed. 'All right, you would. But I couldn't.'

Sonia thought a moment. 'Has she got a new bloke?'

'No sign of one. She doesn't live with anyone. And she was with another woman in the pub, wasn't she? I bet it is Len's. D'you think he knows?'

'He must, if he's the father.'

'Not necessarily. Depends when she left.'

Sonia frowned over this, and then said, 'So what's her place like, then?'

'It's up behind the station. Little terrace. Pretty messy – toys and things all over the place.'

'What on earth did you talk about?'

'Oh, this and that. She doesn't like Jane, you'll be pleased to hear. Quite catty about her.'

'Great minds think alike.' Sonia breathed on her knuckles. 'Perhaps she's OK, after all.'

'And Len's thirty-three.' Barbara smiled. 'Thought you might be interested.'

'So what?' said Sonia, though failing quite to cover her surprise. 'Your Peter was thirty, wasn't he?'

'Well, yes,' Barbara conceded. 'Not that you'd have found him breaking into flats and stealing booze.'

'You said he was a stuffy old prune. You can't have it both ways.'

'And she said I was a nice girl,' Barbara said smugly. She giggled. 'Honestly, I didn't know where to look.'

'Yuk,' groaned Sonia. 'Introduce her to Miss Piggy.'

'Actually, I liked her. I did, really. It wasn't said gushingly. More as if she just says whatever she's thinking.'

'Told you you were modest too, did she?'

Barbara grinned. 'Ah, yes, and she wanted to warn you about Len.' She suddenly realised that she was going to say this flippantly too, there seemed no other way. 'Apparently he's liable to turn into a monster who wants to possess you until you are utterly destroyed. Something like that. I told her you were quite safe, because neither of you cared a toss about each other, which seemed to satisfy her.'

'Oh, thanks. You're a real friend.' Sonia sniffed. 'Honestly, wives always think they know best, don't they?'

'No idea,' said Barbara drily. 'I don't know many. Neither do you.'

'Ah, shut up and do some work,' said Sonia.

10

'What're you doing here?' Billy said in astonishment, looking up from his deckchair at four o'clock on Friday afternoon to see Len standing over him.

'Where's Springfield?' Len was in his blue work suit, tie loosened at the neck. He was staring over towards the funfair. 'His office said he was down here.'

'What d'you want him for?' Billy stood up, anxious. His supervisor and Len were old friends, but he'd never known Len seek him out like this before.

'Need a favour.' Len still wasn't looking at him directly. 'You seen him?'

Springfield's red estate car was just visible, parked on the lower prom beyond the dodgem stadium. Reluctantly Billy nodded towards it. 'His car's over there. Think he's at the shed with the deckchair boys. Been some fuss about gear being nicked.'

As he spoke a burly shirt-sleeved figure emerged from behind the stadium on to the road and started to walk towards the car. Billy pointed. 'There he is.'

'Right,' said Len, moving off quickly. 'See you in a minute.'

Billy called, 'What's going on?' after him, but got no reply. He watched Len stride across the concrete, pushing through a small crowd near the steps to the dodgems, to intercept Springfield by his car. The two men stood talking. Then Len jerked a thumb over his shoulder, towards the playground.

'Shit,' Billy whispered. Guiltily his mind raced over recent misdemeanours: late arrivals in the morning, evenings skipped off early, hut left unlocked overnight, first aid box lost . . . Springfield was staring across at him now. His expression was hard to make out, but he definitely wasn't smiling.

He was going to get the sack. Nothing less would have

brought Len here. Springfield had told Len first, as a courtesy to a friend, and Len had come down here to argue about it.

He snatched his eyes away and swung round to face the hut. The door was open; inside, draped on a folded deck-chair, were his towel and swimming trunks and, on a wall hook beside them, his bomber jacket. Below, on the wooden floorslats, were a *New Musical Express*, his tobacco tin and several Mars bar wrappers. His things, it came to him fiercely, in his hut. The sounds behind him seemed to grow louder, as if the disastrousness of what was taking place was exploding outwards, magnifying everything it touched. He clearly heard, above the clamour of music, voices and traffic, the sound of a car door slam, and an engine start up.

He turned round. Springfield's car had disappeared. Len was walking back towards him, adjusting his tie. He looked purposeful rather than pleased, or angry. Billy took a steadying breath, and waited.

'OK,' said Len as he drew close. He checked his watch. 'Get your things.'

'What's happened.' Billy's heart leapt. 'What's going on?'

'Nothing's happened,' said Len testily. 'I got you some time off, that's all. It's on the level, OK? Get your things.'

'Oh . . .' said Billy. He grappled with relief and confusion. 'Why?'

Len smiled. 'Just get them,' he said. He stuck his hands in his trouser pockets and transferred the smile to the sea.

Billy got his things. He didn't ask again why he was getting time off because he knew it was pointless. He locked the hut. 'I got to drop this off at the stores,' he said, holding the key out.

'Fine,' nodded Len. 'It's on our way.'

They set off towards the car. When they were almost there Billy couldn't stop himself asking, 'So where're we going, then?'

Len tapped the side of his nose, a gesture of pleasure and mystery. 'Wouldn't be a surprise if I told you, would it? Wait and see.'

*

'My God!' exclaimed Sonia, leaning out from her alcove seat to stare through the pub crowd to the door. 'Len's wearing a suit!'

Barbara muttered, 'Oh, bother,' concentrating on lowering drinks on to the table. They'd reached a compromise tonight: they'd come out early, and she'd stay for a quick Friday night drink, but be free to leave – with no complaints from Sonia – when the men arrived. Except they hadn't, for the past hour, and now she'd just bought another round.

She glanced back at the door. Len was indeed unusually dressed – a dark blue suit, over a pale blue shirt – but more startling was his expression, which was dauntingly disagreeable. He stopped for a moment just inside the door, the picture of impatient fury and, reaching back through it, hoiked Billy in after him.

'Christ,' she breathed, edging into her seat. 'What on earth's going on?'

Len strode towards them, pulling Billy along with him. Billy sat down quickly beside Barbara when he was released and rubbed at his eyes with the ball of his thumb.

'Shithead,' snarled Len, leaning over him. 'He's puked all over my car.' He stormed off to the bar.

Sonia and Barbara looked at each other, and then at Billy. Sonia recovered first.

'You all right?' she asked gently. 'You don't look so good.'

Billy put his palms between his thighs as if he was warming them, and rocked back and forth. 'I'm OK,' he murmured.

'Where've you been?' Sonia pressed. 'Why's Len in a suit?'

'Doesn't matter,' whispered Billy, shaking his head.

Len returned with a pint and slammed it down on the table. Barbara felt herself flinch.

'I'll have to sell the fucking car,' he fumed.

'Where've you been?' Sonia repeated. 'We thought you weren't turning up.'

Len eyed Billy grimly. Billy refused to look up. Len waved Sonia further into the alcove and sat down beside her.

'Been to see his mum,' he said.

'I thought you weren't going to?' Barbara said, to Billy. He shook his head again.

'They hadn't seen him for more than two years,' Len raged. 'Two fucking years. They didn't have three heads or anything. Nice couple. Nice, weren't they, Billy? Nothing wrong with them, is there? Is there?' he insisted loudly, reaching across the table to prod Billy in the shoulder.

'No,' whispered Billy, shifting away.

'I dunno what you were making such a fuss about.' He turned to Barbara and Sonia. 'So we get there and it's prodigal son and the rest of it, except he sits there like a dummy saying "yes" and "no" and not much else, ungrateful little sod, and then when I take him home he throws up the tea they gave us all over the fucking car.'

'He can't help being ill,' Sonia said reasonably.

'But I thought he didn't want to go,' said Barbara, at the same time.

'So what,' snapped Len, replying to Barbara. 'He bloody well ought to. They've got a right to see him.'

You sod, thought Barbara in sudden fury, since when have you cared a fig for anyone's rights. Judging from Len's suit, and Billy's flipflops, Len had whisked him there straight from work.

There was a short silence while Len gulped down his pint. Sonia glanced at the reducing level and threw her own drink down to match. Barbara still had nearly a full half-pint of cider in front of her. She wasn't leaving now, she was almost sure, but nor was she going to do anything so crass.

Len slammed the empty pint glass down on the table and dug out his wallet.

'Here,' he commanded, holding a tenner out to Billy. 'Make yourself useful. Get some drinks in.'

'Get them yourself,' replied Billy, most surprisingly, glancing up. He pushed the note away and rested his hands flat on the table.

'Fucking get them.' Len leant forward and stuffed the note under Billy's fingers.

Billy looked at him coldly and flicked it away.

'Shit. You puked over my car.' Len's voice was outraged. 'I'm not asking you to pay for them. Get a round.'

'I'll get them,' said Barbara, reaching for the note.

Len caught her outstretched hand and flung it back at her.

'Billy'll get them,' he said venomously. He picked up the little finger of Billy's left hand and wrapped his fist round it. 'Get them,' he said.

'No,' whispered Billy.

Sonia gave a nervous laugh. 'Give it a rest, Len. The car'll clean up.'

'Get them,' hissed Len, ignoring her, and pushed Billy's finger back. Billy blinked and said nothing.

'Oh, Christ, get the drinks, Billy,' said Barbara urgently. 'It's not worth fighting over.' He only had to pull his hands back to free himself, but she was very afraid he wouldn't.

'I'm not fighting,' Billy said, his face showing signs of strain.

'Billy,' she pleaded. 'Stop this.'

'I'm not doing anything,' Billy gasped. 'Len is.'

'Too right,' snarled Len, applying pressure. Billy lowered his eyes, which were watering.

Len's going to break Billy's finger, Barbara thought, appalled, and Billy's not going to do a thing to stop it. This is sick; not just late-night sick, but really sick.

She didn't dare throw her drink at Len, so she threw it at Billy instead. There was quite enough to make him splutter and snatch his hands away to scrape at his face. She grabbed the ten-pound note, pushed Billy's knees aside, and marched to the bar. I've done something, she thought, nervously triumphant. I'm not sure what, but something.

She bought two pints of beer and double gins and tonics for herself and Sonia, as private revenge, though she doubted Len would bother to check the change. When she returned with the tray he was sitting beside Billy, anger evaporated, helping him mop up.

'Why d'you make me do that?' he was saying, waving aside the sodden handkerchief Billy had borrowed to wipe his face and neck. 'What's eating you?'

He took the coins Barbara held out to him without comment. She guessed, from the way his eyes avoided hers, that he had been relieved by her solution. He couldn't have reckoned on having to break Billy's finger.

Billy pushed damp hair off his forehead. 'Sorry,' he said tightly.

Len slapped an arm round his shoulders. Billy swayed forward under the impact.

I don't know who's the sicker, Barbara thought despairingly; it's an unholy alliance.

Len didn't try to make Billy do anything else while they remained in the pub; wisely, in Barbara's opinion, since she doubted Billy would have obliged. Although he had said he was sorry, he didn't look sorry, and continued pointedly to ignore Len and everything he said. Len must have been aware of it, but let it pass; she guessed that having been pushed close to acceptable limits of behaviour – for a public place, anyway – he was wary of being forced to back down in a repetition. Sonia appeared to regard the episode as closed. Billy had said he was sorry, and Len had forgiven him, and that, her restored chirpiness seemed to suggest, was that. She leant forward at intervals to touch Billy's hand and smile, 'You OK now?' and seemed perfectly satisfied with the nods she received in reply.

Barbara, who could feel Billy trembling beside her, wasn't satisfied at all. She was furious with Len, not so much for the finger incident, which she knew he'd been caught out by, but for taking Billy to his parents. He'd done it, she was convinced, only because he knew it was something Billy sincerely didn't want to do. What does he want with him? she brooded savagely. Why should he want to hurt him like that? And as for Sonia – chattering stupidly away to Len as if all the suffering and cruelty in the world could be disposed of by refusing to acknowledge its existence – she wanted to hit her, somewhere extremely painful, and watch her dispose of that.

Most fervently of all, though, she wished that they would

both just go away, so she could ask Billy what the matter was. She resented being made to feel ashamed for not having the courage to stand up herself, express her outrage, and take him away from them.

Towards closing time, her imagination rioted. She saw Billy killing Len, perhaps stabbing him to death in the night; and just after that, Len killing Billy, almost accidentally, because he wouldn't back down over something.

At last orders the lights were dimmed. Billy flung his head back, features bloodless in the gloom, and closed his eyes. His face had read her thoughts, it seemed.

'You thinking of going yet?' hissed Sonia, after they had been back at Len's house an hour. A difficult hour even for her, it had turned out, now that there was only the four of them. Billy sat hunched over the table in the kitchen, pretending to read *Autocar*, scissoring the pages over at intervals. Len had had to deal with the stereo himself, and roll his own joints. He had just offered one to Billy, on his way out to the bathroom, and received a loud, 'No, thanks,' in reply.

'What?' said Barbara, pulling her eyes away from the archway, and Billy.

'You going soon?' Sonia's tone was unfriendly, as if she blamed Barbara, as much as anyone, for the present atmosphere.

'No,' said Barbara coolly, and then frowned, since Sonia didn't usually make enquiries about her movements. She lowered her voice to an aggressive whisper. 'I'm going to hang on till you've gone and have a word with Billy.'

She meant till Sonia and Len had gone upstairs. You're as bad as the others, she had been exhorting herself, if you don't at least try.

Sonia pulled a face. 'Suit yourself,' she said stiffly. 'I'm going now.' She stood up and reached for her jacket.

Barbara remembered, suddenly, that Sonia had her period and had told her on the walk to the pub that she wouldn't be staying. She said, 'Oh . . .' making Sonia turn to look at her. Before she could explain, Len reappeared.

'I'm off now,' said Sonia, putting on her jacket. She kissed him. 'Barbara's staying to have a word with Billy,' she added, making Barbara clench her teeth, 'but I think I'll go. See you tomorrow.'

Len returned the embrace absently, his eyes on Barbara. She nearly got up and said, 'No, wait, I'm coming too,' but anger at Sonia stopped her.

Len saw Sonia out and returned to the sitting room. He sat down, reached for the cigarette papers and started to roll a joint. Now and then he lifted his gaze; Barbara knew he was looking at her, and tried not to read anything into it.

In the kitchen Billy tossed *Autocar* away from him and slammed into the bathroom. Len lit the joint and came to sit on the arm of Barbara's chair.

'Want some?' He took a deep drag and held it out to her.

Barbara said, 'No, thanks,' feeling oppressed by his proximity. His thigh beside her looked enormous. She stared at the red and yellow squiggles in the black weave of her skirt; they crossed over and became briefly orange, she observed intently, before wriggling on again. You should have gone, a voice wailed somewhere in her head.

'Suit yourself,' murmured Len, echoing Sonia. He reached over and placed an experimental hand on her breast.

'No,' said Barbara, more firmly than she felt. The squiggles jumped and jerked. Below her chin a dangerous forest of strong black hairs rippled as his hand explored. For a terrible moment the dancing squiggles gave way to a picture of herself frantically fighting him off.

'OK,' he said, and withdrew his hand. Barbara realised she was trembling.

Len continued to smoke the joint next to her. Barbara could almost hear his mind, mulling over his next move. He's going to throw me out, she thought, and then: oh, God, he's going to make another pass. One rejection wouldn't deter him, he'd have seen it as obligatory, given her friendship with Sonia. Go upstairs, she begged him silently; please just go.

105

Billy returned from the bathroom and started clattering in the kitchen. Len rose and stubbed out the joint.

'Right,' he said. 'You'll see yourself out, then.' He smiled to himself. Barbara received the unpleasant impression that he hoped he was disappointing her. He stood a moment in the centre of the room, as if reminding himself that everything was happening with his permission, and left.

Barbara listened to his footsteps ascending the stairs and felt herself relax. After a moment Billy appeared in the archway. He looked surprised to see her, and not particularly pleased.

'Can't fucking leave me alone, can you,' he said viciously. 'Who asked you to stay?'

'No one,' Barbara snapped back, stung. 'I don't always do things because I'm asked.'

Billy's lips parted as if he were breathless. She wished she hadn't said it.

'What's wrong?' she said much more gently. 'I stayed because I could see something's wrong.'

Billy jerked his face away. He walked round the room, punching the lights off, until they were left with only the spillage from the strip in the kitchen. He kicked the sofa into a bed, snatched up the sleeping bag from under the table and with his back to her, started to wrench off his clothes.

'I'm sorry,' muttered Barbara, panicked into confusion, and got up to go. Through her dizziness an inner voice jeered 'Coward, coward,' at her, but her hands still groped for jacket and handbag.

At the door she stopped and swung round. Billy was standing rigidly by the bed in his underpants, thin and dark. He brushed a forearm across his eyes; then suddenly sat down on the side of the bed, put his face in his hands and began to weep.

Barbara felt her fear crumble. She had never seen a man cry – Peter had never cried – but she wasn't afraid of tears. She walked back, dropped her bag and jacket, and sat down beside him.

'Hey, Billy,' she said softly. 'C'mon.'

Billy made an ugly choking noise and twisted away from her.

'Hey,' she said again. She remembered twisting away herself, and how instinctive it was, but how much worse if your action was believed, and comfort withdrawn.

She put an arm across his shoulders. She felt them tense, but recognised that too.

'Billy,' she whispered. 'It's OK, Billy. C'mon.' His sobs were loud and gulping. She tried to pull him towards her, to muffle the sound – Len might hear, and return to investigate – but couldn't move him.

'What's wrong?' she murmured, stroking his back. 'You can tell me.'

But Billy only shook his head, as if in desperate disagreement, and buried his face deeper in his arms.

After a while he pulled away and lay back on the sofa, but turned away from her. She remained sitting, aware of nothing except the twilight room around her and the gasps of misery at her side. What am I doing here? she asked herself dimly. Why am I staying, he doesn't want me, why am I here? But then a moment later, with the questions still unanswered, found herself settling against his back and pulling the sleeping bag over them. She stared up at the ceiling. I'm just reacting, she acknowledged. It's instinct, it's what takes over when we don't know what to do.

The thought felt right, and comforting. She twisted towards Billy and rested a hand on his side. She felt his chest heave and slipped her arm over further. Because that felt right, too.

Some time in the night she was woken by him turning towards her. He ground his face into her armpit and screwed up the material of the t-shirt by her waist with his hand. Then he pulled away, and in the half-light from the kitchen she saw his closed eyes, damp and bruised-looking, and the corners of his mouth, tugged back into harsh creases down his cheeks. She watched his face until it relaxed and his body grew heavy against her.

Just as she was drifting off again, the room seemed to darken. She blinked her eyes wide and sensed something in the doorway behind her, blotting out the light.

She clung to Billy involuntarily, and then hastily released him, scared of waking him. She lay still, pretending to be asleep, her throat pounding. Through closed lids the room remained dark an age, until she thought she had imagined it; then suddenly it lightened and she heard soft footsteps mounting the stairs.

She was so thoroughly awake by now, and Billy looked so thoroughly asleep, that as soon as everything was quiet again she eased herself away from him, gathered up her jacket and handbag, and left.

11

'I don't know why you're being so bloody secretive about it,' Sonia complained, sprawled in cerise pyjamas across Barbara's armchair at half-past-eight the next morning. 'Something must have happened.'

Barbara was sitting at the table in her dressing gown, hands wrapped around a coffee mug. On a normal Saturday she wouldn't be awake at this time, never mind up and fighting.

'I told you,' she said wearily, 'nothing happened.' She had decided not to tell Sonia about Billy crying. It was a real part of him, she felt, it deserved respect.

She pushed her coffee mug away and clutched her forehead. A waking thickheadedness had refined to a persistent hammering. 'Christ,' she groaned. 'I must stop drinking Len's whisky.'

Sonia's expression said 'Serves you right.'

Barbara sighed. This was ridiculous. Sonia had been slightly mollified by explanation of the original misunderstanding, but it hadn't lessened her main complaint, which seemed to be that Barbara was getting above herself in her dealings with Len and Billy, and acting outside the agreed scope of operations. If, she thought bitterly, she had admitted staying on to have sex with Billy, Sonia would probably have been forgiving; maybe even congratulatory. It was the vague claim about staying on to keep him company she found so offensive. She seemed to think that either Barbara was lying – ashamed to confess the attraction perhaps – or if she wasn't, was being disloyal, even treacherous.

'I was just worried about him,' she repeated. 'I thought someone ought to stay.'

'God,' said Sonia, rolling her eyes.

'Oh, believe what you like,' Barbara said, suddenly losing

patience. 'You're obviously going to, anyway.' Sonia's attitude was astonishing, but the thought of treating her to the tongue-lashing of her life, which any defence would undoubtedly escalate into, was too exhausting to contemplate.

'I didn't want her to stay,' Billy mumbled, his head bent low over a bowl of Cocopops.

Len was standing behind him in blue boxer shorts, waiting for the hissing kettle to boil. ''Course you didn't,' he said.

'She just stayed,' Billy whispered. 'It wasn't my fault.'

'It's OK, kiddo.' Len's voice was low, almost soothing. 'I should've seen it coming. Interfering cow.'

He clicked off the kettle and filled two mugs. 'Here,' he said, passing one back to Billy. He ducked his head to see the clock on the cooker. 'Shit,' he muttered, and then, 'What the hell.' He sat down at the table next to Billy.

Billy understood that this was a friendly gesture, but still kept his head down. He had been to the bathroom a few minutes ago, and seen his face in the mirror. The eyes blinking back at him had looked grotesque, the lower rims scarlet and raw-looking, the lids swollen and bluish. Two minutes with his head in a basin of cold water had eased the gravelly discomfort, but not noticeably improved his appearance.

Len stretched across to a pile of magazines at the back of the table. He pushed aside the copy of *Autocar* that Billy had been reading last night and pulled a hi-fi catalogue towards him. Settling back in his chair, he started to turn the pages. Billy felt something pop in his sinuses and a torrent of catarrh poured down his throat. He took another spoonful of cereal and swallowed hard.

Len tapped one of the pages of the catalogue. 'You interested in these, then?'

Billy lifted his head far enough to see. Len had reached the personal stereo listings, several of which he'd circled in green felt-tip pen.

'Yeah,' he nodded. 'Gonna get one soon.' His voice, to

himself, sounded choked and thick. He coughed and swallowed again.

Len stared at the print, then at the photograph of the stereo and headphones on the facing page.

'You got twenty quid, then?' His voice was flat.

'I thought maybe . . .' Billy shot him a quick glance. Len was scratching an ear, apparently absorbed in the listings. 'If I bought it payday . . . then . . .'

Len gave a snort and looked up at him. As their eyes met the amusement in his expression faded to embarrassment. Billy dropped his gaze, ashamed.

'How're you going to eat, eh?' Len spoke gruffly, his eyes back on the catalogue. 'You giving up dope? Drink?'

'I'll manage,' said Billy awkwardly.

'I doubt it,' said Len. He continued to stare at the catalogue, then abruptly flicked it shut and scraped his chair back. 'I gotta get dressed,' he said, moving to the door.

While he was upstairs Billy finished his coffee, and cleared the table of breakfast things. He put Len's untouched mug to one side. His eyes began to smart again so he cupped his hands under the cold tap and splashed water into them. As he was drying his face on a tea-towel Len reappeared, tieless, but otherwise dressed for work.

Billy put the tea-towel down quickly. 'Your coffee's there,' he said.

'You have it.' Len dug in the inside pocket of his suit jacket and took out his wallet. 'Here,' he said. He removed three brown banknotes and slapped them on the work surface. 'Get your stereo. My treat.'

Billy stared at the banknotes, then at Len, replacing his wallet with a frown, then at the notes again.

'Shit, Len,' he breathed, moving towards them. 'Hey, shit.'

'Get a decent one,' Len said sternly. He checked in his outside pocket for his tie. 'No cheap crap, OK?'

'Right,' Billy nodded. He picked up the notes. Thirty quid. *Thirty quid.*

Len stabbed a finger at him. 'And you get it today, right, before you blow it.'

Billy nodded again, vigorously. Of course he'd get it today. He lifted his eyes to Len. 'Wow,' he said. 'Thanks.'

'Save it,' muttered Len, turning to go. 'It's only thirty fucking quid.'

See, what did I tell you? Sonia's eyes flashed at Barbara triumphantly, on several occasions on Saturday night. *I don't know what you were making such a ridiculous fuss about.*

Barbara ignored the looks. She was only at the pub this time – this very last time – out of a sense of duty. Not to Sonia – bugger her, and her peculiar demands of friendship – but to Billy. Obviously, she'd told herself, she had to see him again, to make sure he was all right. You couldn't witness what she had last night and then simply disappear. But she wasn't going to pretend it was anything other than duty and had refused to dress up, to make the point visible. She wore jeans, sweatshirt and ancient flatties, and had then been infuriated when Sonia had complimented her on the sweatshirt motif on the walk to the pub, saying that actually she suited the casual look; it went with her hair. It was only on entering the pub that it occurred to her that if Billy wasn't all right, he might not be there.

As it had turned out, however, he was there, and fine, and she needn't have bothered. They were at the same pub as last night, but the atmosphere couldn't have been more different. Billy appeared completely recovered; indeed in some respects improved. He'd brought himself a personal stereo during the day, a purchase that clearly gave him enormous pleasure, so much so that he was still wearing it, the cassette player attached to his belt, the headphones draped round his neck. At intervals he put the headphones on and grinned around inanely, nodding time to inaudible music. Barbara thought it made him look like a disabled person – one of her great aunts had a hearing aid that looked remarkably similar – but his delight was touching, all the same. Len was in ebullient mood too, giving a convincing performance of a friend keen to show off repaired bridges, resting his arm affectionately on Billy's shoulder when he wasn't directing remarks at him, and shaking or clouting him playfully when he was, all of which met with Billy's grinning approval.

Everybody, it seemed, was conspiring to convince her that last night hadn't happened. She felt frustrated, seeing Sonia's told-you-so smiles and, obscurely, a little hurt.

Only once, just before she left (at well before eleven, to offend Sonia as much as anything) did she glimpse a chink in the conspiratorial wall.

'Glad you're better,' she whispered to Billy, while Len was at the bar. 'I was worried about you last night.'

Billy smiled, looking towards Len, and said loudly, 'Christ, you do take things serious, don't you?'

But as she regarded him reproachfully, he dropped his gaze and when it lifted again it had lost everything to do with Len and was almost shy, though he was still smiling.

In their Monday morning coffee break Barbara and Sonia argued about Billy and Len. Billy's recovery was raised.

'All it shows,' Barbara said, 'is how dependent Billy is on Len being nice to him. And it doesn't alter my general point.' Her general point, put tactfully (though evidently not tactfully enough), had been that Len was bad for Billy, and he ought to leave. Sonia's general reply – put without a vestige of tact – had been that it was none of Barbara's business and if she was that interested it proved she must really fancy him, and that was her actual reason for staying behind Friday night, whether she was woman enough to admit it or not.

Barbara had been so irritated by this that she had almost told her about Len making a pass at her, but at the last minute hadn't. Indeed Len's name had been scarcely mentioned at all in the specific context of her staying the night, though the question of his presence (or otherwise) had hung unavoidably over it.

'Honestly,' snapped Sonia, 'I don't know what's got into you. A few weeks ago you couldn't have cared less. You don't have to poke your nose in, you know. They've been getting on fine without you for a year or more. Jesus, I thought you'd got enough problems of your own, without wanting to take on everybody else's. Do give it a rest.'

Barbara screwed the lid on the coffee jar viciously, wishing it was Sonia's neck. Sonia had been quite happy to listen to her problems in the past and yet now, when she wanted to discuss Billy's – not because she cared, of course, in a personal sense, but because they were interesting, dammit – she was behaving as if most of them were products of her imagination, and the rest a matter of dismissive tedium. Sonia wasn't interested in why Billy had run away from home, or got himself kicked out, or anything. All she'd say was, 'Why don't you ask him, if you really want to know?' and point out that hundreds of young people didn't get on with their parents and escaped from them as soon as possible, that the town was crawling with them, in fact, and it was only because Barbara had had such a sheltered upbringing herself that she was making such a fuss about it.

Barbara had mulled this over for elements of truth, but come to the conclusion that just because a problem wasn't unique, it didn't make it less of one. The individual distress was the same however many were suffering. All it did was encourage others who were luckier (i.e. Sonia) to gloss over them. Much like Mr Watson's battered women, she reflected, whose affidavits lost much of their impact simply because there were so many of them. She returned to this argument now.

'Just because something happens all the time,' she said crossly, 'doesn't make it any better.'

'You can't move him into the bedsit,' Sonia said pointedly, as if getting at the nub of her motives.

'Christ!' exclaimed Barbara. 'Don't be stupid! Imagine living with Billy!'

'Well, then.' Sonia's voice was sour. 'If you've got no solutions I should just leave it, if I were you. It's up to Billy and Len, isn't it?'

12

It was Billy who made the first move.

At eleven o'clock on Wednesday night, just after Barbara had changed into her nightdress to read *Cosmopolitan* from the comfort of bed, her doorbell rang. The bedsits had separate bells, like proper flats; hers operated an old-fashioned brass contraption above the door courtesy of the previous tenant, who had disliked buzzers. She cursed, and padded downstairs.

'Who is it?' she asked through the closed front door, drawing her dressing gown around her and envisaging drunks or rapists.

'It's me,' said Billy's voice.

She opened the door a crack.

'Hi,' said Billy. 'I'm locked out.' It was raining steadily. He was hopping from one foot to the other, shoulders hunched, clearly hoping to be invited in.

Barbara stood her ground. 'Thought you had a back door key?' she said suspiciously.

'Well, I have, normally,' Billy agreed, 'but I've left it in the house. I can't get in.'

'Where's Len?'

'Over at Dave's. I dunno when he'll be back. Maybe not at all.' He glanced upwards. 'It's raining,' he added.

'If you didn't have the key to lock it behind you,' Barbara asked aggressively, 'how come it's locked now?'

'I went out the front door.' Billy looked aggrieved. 'Come and see for yourself if you don't believe me.' He regarded her dressing gown, and then the rain.

'Ha,' snorted Barbara, and then wondered what she was making such a fuss about. He didn't appear uncontrollably drunk and, after all, she'd stayed at his place twice, uninvited.

'Oh, come on in, then,' she sighed, and opened the door wide.

Billy shot in and bounded up the stairs. She plodded after him, debating, if this was contrived, whether he was doing it because he genuinely wanted to see her, or to punish Len for abandoning him.

Up in the room she found him sitting on the bed. He had turned the television on and had *Cosmopolitan* on his lap, along with several cigarette papers, which he was in the process of gluing together.

'Stop that,' she ordered. 'I don't want the place stunk out. This is my bedroom, not yours.'

Billy screwed up the papers and put the magazine to one side.

'Look,' she said severely. 'I was just going to bed. If you want to lark around I suggest you go somewhere else. I've got work tomorrow.'

'It's my day off, Thursday,' Billy offered.

'Bully for you. I have to be up at eight.' She viewed her bed. Although it was almost as wide as Billy's sofa sharing it seemed a quite different proposition, because it was a proper bed, and because it was hers. The armchair had removable cushions, but there was no spare bedding.

She reached for her sponge bag. 'The bathroom's the second door down,' she said, still thinking. 'You can borrow my toothbrush as long as you rinse it afterwards.'

'Oh, right,' nodded Billy, and took the brush. He disappeared, banging the door behind him, and reappeared seconds later, as if anxious not to let his absence grow attractive to her. Then he wandered round the room inspecting things, waiting for instructions.

'Well, don't stand there looking spare,' said Barbara, brushing her hair ferociously in front of the dressing table mirror, 'I told you, I'm going to bed. Turn the telly off.'

'Right.' Billy switched the portable off and sat on the side of the bed to unlace his trainers. Barbara walked round to the other side, discarded her dressing gown and got under the duvet. She banged the pillows into place.

Billy glanced over his shoulder at her. 'You want to screw?' he asked.

'Christ, Billy,' Barbara snapped, concentrating on the pillows. 'Don't overdo the romance.'

Billy grinned. 'You're not romantic.'

'Aren't I really.' Barbara gave up with the pillows and folded her arms in front of her. She watched him pull off his t-shirt. There were sparkling waves of salt along the sides of his back. She settled herself a little lower in the bed.

'So how do you see me, then?' she asked, less belligerently. 'Go on, I'm interested. Be truthful.'

Billy shrugged and turned to look at her, smiling.

'Well, you're not romantic. And you're not . . . you know . . . the dolly bird type . . .'

'Come on,' Barbara interrupted. 'I don't want to know what I'm not. What am I?'

Billy thought. 'Um . . . kind of tough. Sensible tough,' he amended hastily, catching her expression. '. . . like you could be a teacher or something.'

'Bossy, perhaps?' Barbara inquired.

'Well . . .' said Billy, giving it consideration.

'God,' sighed Barbara. 'Is that really how you see me? No wonder Len doesn't like me.'

'I like you,' Billy said quickly. 'I feel you'd always do the right thing, kind of.'

'Sort of steady and reliable?'

'Sort of,' admitted Billy. 'Nothing wrong with that.'

'But not very romantic?'

Billy didn't reply.

'Do you actually want to have sex with me?' Barbara asked acidly, feeling steadier and more reliable with each minute, 'or were you just being polite?'

'Sure.' He lifted his shoulders again. 'If you want to.'

'Well then, no,' pronounced Barbara. 'I shall be sensible. I'm not on the pill and I don't suppose you've got anything on you, have you?'

Billy shook his head, as if the idea was a new one on him.

'In that case,' she continued, 'looking at it sensibly, I don't

117

think we should.' She sniffed. In fact in more conducive company she might have risked it. Her period was due the next day – she could already feel a vague cramping sensation – but he wasn't to know.

'Oh, Barb,' smiled Billy. 'Don't be like that. There's nothing wrong with sensible.'

'You make me feel about ninety,' she grumbled. 'Get into bed. Anyone would seem sensible compared to you.'

Billy stood up and took off his jeans, but left his red underpants on. Barbara recognised them from Friday night, and hoped he had more than one pair.

He climbed in beside her and wriggled down the bed. There was no way they could share the bed without touching, so they just had to touch. Barbara turned her head to say goodnight.

'You've got a funny lump on your ear,' she said.

'Mmm.' He reached up and tugged at the lobe. Barbara realised she had seen him do it as a mannerism, when he was agitated.

'Had an infection a year or more back,' he said. 'Just before Len. Found this really nice earring, and a guy in the house I was in said he could do it, you know, with a needle. He burnt it and everything, but something must have gone wrong 'cos it all swelled up and I couldn't get the ring out again. It kind of disappeared. It was weird. All the side of my head went stiff.'

'Typical,' groaned Barbara. 'Don't tell me it's still in there?'

Billy shook his head. 'That's just the scarring. They took it out in the hospital. I was in for two weeks.'

'Goodness.' She looked at him, taking it seriously. 'It must have been bad. You poor thing.'

Billy smiled at the ceiling. 'It was OK. Most of it was like a dream. A nice dream. You know the best bit?' He tilted his head to hers. '. . . when they bathed you in bed. You weren't meant to help . . . you know . . . just lie there and relax. They'd pick up your arm and wash it, and then put it down again, all cool and clean. Fantastic. They were great, the nurses.'

'Billy,' said Barbara, not unkindly. 'You are a baby. Turn the light off.'

Billy reached out and switched the table lamp off. She felt him lie back. The blackness was absolute.

'Hey, Barb?' he whispered, after a minute or two. 'It's really dark.'

'Oh, Christ,' she mumbled. 'Of course it's dark. Close your eyes and you won't notice it. Nothing's going to go bump in the night, I promise.'

Billy dutifully closed his eyes. He expected a long wait; unless he was heavily drugged he was a poor sleeper. He felt Barbara shift position on to her side, her buttocks coming to rest against his hip. He wondered if she had really wanted to have sex, and whether he should have made more effort, but it seemed too late to suggest it again now.

The thought made the hand on his chest creep up to finger his ear; there was a real connection. The infection, and his time in hospital, had closed the active chapter in his life, sexually speaking. An inglorious and depressing chapter at that. It was a time when his body had seemed his only asset and he'd exploited it indiscriminately, to survive. He'd slept with anyone, male or female. The men hadn't usually wanted him around long, but most were unalarming and some were even kind. He never asked for money, but always got it – they seemed to understand the transaction better than he – plus occasionally a meal and, once or twice, a bed for the night. The women were more unpredictable. Sometimes he spent longer with them – a week or two – but they were often drunkards or worse, and they didn't pay with money, and some of them stole.

Really, until he'd met the blindfolder, he'd felt safer with the men. But the blindfolder had been a terrible mistake. After a night of horror which he'd endured unprotestingly, unsure of his body's right to protection whilst on hire to someone else, he had considered walking into the sea, but in the end even that seemed too much effort. However he was already feverish with the ear infection, and two days later

119

got the rest he needed when he passed out on the seafront and was taken to hospital. His stay there was the happiest two weeks he'd known since leaving home. He didn't have any visitors so the nurses made a great fuss of him, and because he was never bored or difficult, like some of the other men, they called him a model patient, and one of them even baked him a cake for his nineteenth birthday.

Towards the end he'd been taken to see an unfamiliar doctor who wrote all the time and asked a lot of questions, most of which seemed to have nothing to do with his ear. He tried to answer them, but it didn't make much sense, not even when he grasped that the doctor wasn't interested so much in his ear as in the slow-healing cigarette burns on his arms. He appeared to think Billy had done them himself, and Billy hadn't liked to contradict him as it would have meant explaining so many other things as well and, anyway, he decided, in a sense the doctor might be right.

When the doctor had finished he gave Billy an appointment to come and see him again, and afterwards another younger man with a beard came up to the ward to say he had been found a place in a hostel, and told him how lucky he was because they were like gold dust. Billy, though, had memories of another hostel, not very golden ones, and since he was still flush with money (delighted with the combination of unwillingness and co-operation, his torturer had paid exceptionally well), he never turned up, and the appointment card got torn into filters for at least three joints.

But he had avoided the station, which was where he'd met the man – he didn't trust himself to be able to say no – and then he'd met Mal, and Len, who used to have quite a crowd back in the evenings in those days. He found he could stay the night, and one night stretched to several, and he became good at making himself scarce when he wasn't wanted and in evidence when he could be useful. He was impressed by Len, and Len's place, and wasn't going to lose either of them if he could help it. It meant being selectively deaf and blind in the days before Len came to appreciate his company, but the rewards were worth the insults. Len had possessions, things that actually worked: a stereo, a proper cooker, and a toilet that flushed. If anything stopped working it was mended and from time to time new things appeared, without fuss or celebration, just because they were wanted, or needed. Billy treasured these things; it was only right that if Len allowed him to use them – for which he demanded no payment, nothing at all – he should be repaid with obedience and loyalty. And if Len sometimes hurt him and made him unhappy, it was a small price to pay, he felt, for the other things.

Nor was he frightened of Len; at least, not like he was frightened of Dave. Len only wanted control and, mostly, that was fine by him. Dave, though, wanted to judge him, and that wasn't. When he was with Dave he saw himself as the sort of person he knew Dave thought he was: manipulative and parasitic, toadying and pathetic. He knew Dave despised him for making a fool of Len, his friend, and resented being forced to think less of Len, for being made a fool. He accepted that Len felt the need to be nastier to him in Dave's presence, as Len's loyalty to Dave was longer-standing and altogether worthier than his attachment to himself. In fact, till now, he'd accepted everything Len dished out; he'd had no choice.

Now, though, he had discovered someone else who seemed to care about him a bit. Barbara had a nice place and nice things, and, maybe, might not want to make him so unhappy.

And lying beside her now, with his eyes closed against the blackness, he found that the achievement of being here, near her, surrounded by her nice place and nice things, acted almost like a drug. It filled the same inner space with the same comforting fuzz, pushing out conscious thought.

He let go, sank back into it, and drifted into sleep.

13

Some time in the night Barbara changed her mind. Or, rather, she discovered her body taking an initiative which her mind found expedient to approve, given the success of the initiative. Just to show him, she thought dozily, justifying it to herself, and hoping it was arousal that made it so easy, and she wasn't a day out and had already started her period. She didn't expect much – which was just as well – but it allowed her to wrap her arms around someone warm and male and naked, and have his drowsy weight pressed against her. In the darkness Billy's body felt young and artless, and gritty in places because of the salt: beautiful, really, though she knew it wasn't. I've never behaved like this before, she thought in the middle of it. Billy thinks I'm in control, if only he knew.

As he lay collapsed on top of her afterwards she couldn't help comparing their languor with how it had been with Peter: him pulling back after he had come, reaching for the tissue, then moving aside to fold himself around her. He never lay heavily on her like this; gentlemen used their elbows and showed consideration.

But now, bearing Billy's abandoned weight, it crossed her mind that maybe gentlemen had got it wrong, and there was something questionable about their kind of consideration. She thought back to the times she had said, 'That was nice,' – which it had been – and Peter had murmured, 'Good,' and left lingering in the air was the feeling that her enjoyment was his success. For all its selfishness, Billy's technique – or lack of it – felt momentarily liberating. I don't have to take responsibility for this, it seemed to be saying, since it's for you as much as me. With him the physical pleasure was less, but at least it felt like – was forced to be – her own achievement.

In the blackness she smiled to herself over Billy's shoulder, smelling his salty sticky hair, and acknowledged that she was being unfair. It wasn't all Peter's fault; she had given him the responsibility. All along the line, she thought; the flat, her job . . . why hadn't she had thoughts like this then?

She couldn't sleep with Billy on top of her. 'Get off,' she murmured, and groped for his hips to push him away.

The regular breathing in her ear faltered and, as he rolled away, was expelled in a groan. Feeling suddenly deprived she reached for his arm to put it around her, then changed course, deciding to match action to sentiment, and drew his head to her shoulder instead. Holding Peter like that had always felt odd, as if she were babying him, though she had enjoyed doing it. But he did it to me, she thought, and I liked it, and why shouldn't men feel safe and comforted too; especially Billy, she added with an inner tremor, when what he really wants is a nurse to give him blanket baths.

'Thought you didn't want to do it?' Billy said the next morning with his arms behind his head on the pillow, watching Barbara get dressed. He liked watching her; her movements were brisk and economical, as if she always knew exactly what she was doing.

'Sheer lust,' sighed Barbara. She grinned at him. This morning she was even prepared to regard him as pretty – well, he was, lying there naked in her bed, looking so disgracefully at home.

Billy regarded her owlishly. 'Thought you said . . . you know . . .'

'It's OK,' she said, vexed that she was going to have to admit to being fairly sensible after all. 'I'm due today. I can feel it.'

Billy pulled a squeamish face. Barbara rolled her eyes.

'It doesn't change anything,' she said. 'It didn't mean anything.'

'OK,' said Billy, defensively.

'Just friends, that's all.'

'Fine,' agreed Billy, thinking that sounded all right.

'I don't want you laying any claims.'

'No.' Billy wondered what she meant. He had been rather hoping that Barbara was going to be the one laying claims.

Barbara looked at her watch. 'You'd better get up. I'm off in ten minutes.'

'I don't have to go to work today,' he reminded her.

'I couldn't care less. You're not lounging round here all day. You go when I do. That's what I meant.' She reached out and jerked at the quilt. 'Come on. And don't get yourself locked out again, OK?'

'I like being here,' Billy muttered. Barbara wasn't sure if it was a compliment or a complaint. He swung his legs out of bed and scratched his head. For a moment she thought he was wearing white underpants, the rest of him was so brown.

'Well, I didn't mind this time either,' she said. 'But I don't want to be kidded into anything. Just a one-off, OK?' God, I sound hard, she thought, this isn't me. It must be something to do with Billy.

'Do you have to go to work?' He yawned.

'Yes, I do. Move it.'

He rummaged for his underpants at the bottom of the bed. Barbara smiled, thinking how unselfconscious he looked. She remembered the first time she had seen Peter undressed and how intensely aware of his body she had been, and her own. Billy just seemed naked, and profoundly safe.

'How 'bout a drink at lunchtime?' he suggested. He pulled the underpants on. 'You get a lunch hour, don't you?'

'I don't like drinking in the middle of the day. It sends me to sleep.'

Billy looked disappointed.

Do I want to go out with him? Barbara thought. Has he made me feel good, or did I do it myself? She realised she was still smiling at him. She relented.

'We could go for a walk if you like.' He was leaning forward, reaching for his socks.

'Christ, Billy,' she sighed, viewing the tangle at the back of his head. 'Look at you. Don't you ever brush your hair?'

Billy tugged fingers through the clumps, 'Where d'you work, then?' he asked.

Barbara explained. 'It'll take you about twenty minutes to walk from your place,' she added. 'I'll meet you outside, one o'clock. If you're late you'll find us on the front. Sonia and me. Billy . . .' She sighed kindly. 'Why don't you spend the morning washing your hair? You can't wear it that long and ignore it. Give it a treat.'

'OK,' said Billy.

Sonia tapped on the door at twenty to nine, as usual. Billy opened it.

'Hi!' cried Sonia, converting her surprise into a smile, and flashing it at Barbara.

'He got himself locked out,' Barbara explained, busying herself with her handbag.

'Fancy that.' Sonia grinned at Billy, who grinned back.

'It's nothing to be embarrassed about,' insisted Sonia, clattering beside Barbara, who was setting a very fast pace this morning.

'It wasn't like that,' Barbara said fretfully. 'He really did get himself locked out. At least that's what he told me.'

She stopped suddenly and sighed. Sonia stopped too and looked back at her.

'All right, it was like that,' she confessed, walking on. 'But I didn't intend it to be. I think Billy may have, but I didn't. It just happened.'

'Fine,' said Sonia. 'It happens to the best of us.'

'You did enjoy yourself, though,' she asked cautiously, a hundred yards further on.

'Yes,' nodded Barbara. 'As a matter of fact I did.'

'Well, that's all right, then,' murmured Sonia.

During the morning Barbara thought about all the things she could do to improve Billy. Since he'd sought her out, and apparently viewed her as some kind of teacher figure . . . well, why not? Maybe all he needs, she thought, is a firm, stabilising hand; someone to look at his life objectively and suggest positive, constructive changes to it. A permanent, more challenging job . . . more settled accommodation . . . more care with his appearance . . . less drinking . . .

By lunchtime she had compiled quite a list.

She was also visited from time to time, between ideas for improvements to Billy, by thoughts of how easy sex with him had been, and how pleasurable. Because certain doubts followed from these thoughts, regarding another's faithlessness, she was at pains to point out to herself that of course her adventure was quite different. She was not living with anyone at the time to whom she owed loyalty. It was definitely a one-off event, foisted on her by force of circumstance. And it had taken place with someone to whom she felt no emotional attachment of any significance, indeed scarcely knew at all.

However, since, apart from the first, these excuses came disconcertingly close to those she had only recently disallowed as quite irrelevant and mere proof of the inherent promiscuity of the male species – who apparently couldn't survive a week in a strange town without resort to casual sex with the first female who flung herself at them – she didn't pursue the line of reasoning longer than she had to. She found it more comfortable to view her behaviour as an eye-for-eye revenge, accepting that both acts were promiscuous, but that his was worse because it had happened first, and hers wouldn't have happened at all if it hadn't been for his. She apologised mentally to Billy for calling it revenge because it seemed an offensive description of what had in fact felt spontaneous and essentially innocent, and told herself that there must be such a thing as subconscious revenge. She gave up thinking about it altogether a short while later, lest her conclusions permanently depress her good mood.

Sonia, luckily, understood the priority of the male assignation over the female – even a male like Billy – and gave Barbara no more than an indulgent shrug when she apologised for deserting her at lunchtime. Sonia was in an excellent mood too, with attractions out in the open, nobody kidding themselves anymore, and herself proved right.

Billy was on time, indeed, may even have been early, judging by his relieved, 'Ah,' as he pushed himself away from the wall of the building. And he had washed his hair, although he still seemed to have forgotten about brushing the back.

'That's a start,' she said approvingly. 'You ought to get in the habit of doing it after you go swimming. It's awfully bad for hair to be salty all the time.' He really ought to have a haircut too, she thought, and wondered if she could do it herself.

Billy found the subject of his hair uninteresting.

'Where d'you want to go, then?' He stared around.

'Let's go on the pier and laugh at the tourists,' Barbara proposed. 'That always makes me feel good.'

Billy saw tourists all day and didn't find them especially funny.

'How 'bout a drink first,' he suggested, noticing a pub on the corner.

'You drink too much,' Barbara said sternly, and led him in the opposite direction. 'And you smoke too much. I know it's only dope, but you shouldn't smoke it all the time. Don't you ever want to be normal? You don't use anything else, do you?' She might as well ask, she thought, establish the extent of the task ahead of her.

'Nope,' said Billy, thinking all this sounded quite hopeful, despite her earlier remarks about claims. People didn't usually offer unsolicited advice without reason. Also he was aware that Barbara was kind of high, and thought he might have something to do with it, which was encouraging too.

'Len uses speed sometimes,' he offered.

'But you don't?'

'No . . . well . . . tried it, 'course. But I don't like it.' He had to give a skip to keep up with Barbara, after being distracted by a display of children's paintings in a building society window. 'It makes me feel kind of jumpy. As if I should be doing things.'

Barbara snorted. 'No, I can see that wouldn't be your style.'

'I like dope, though,' Billy said. 'Len uses it too.'

'Not as much as you.'

'He drinks more.'

'He can handle it. You don't see him passing out at the end of an evening.' He has enough energy left for his exercises and Sonia too, she thought. 'He's bigger than you and he's had years more practice.' She took Billy's arm and jiggled it. 'It's more the pointlessness of it. I mean, what else do you do, except sit around all day at work smoking your head off, then sit around in pubs all evening drinking yourself stupid. It's not a very active sort of life.'

'I go swimming,' objected Billy. 'Nearly every day.'

'What, even when it's raining?'

'Sure. Rain doesn't matter. I don't go when it's too rough, and not in the winter, 'course, but otherwise . . . well, nearly every day. I'm a good swimmer, really good. Next year I might try for lifeguard. I didn't think of it this year. Yeah, I could do that, easy.'

'Well, that's something,' conceded Barbara. 'They always say swimming's good exercise.' Doubts about Billy's powers of vigilance as a lifeguard entered her mind, but she refrained from expressing them.

'And I play chess with Len,' Billy said, feeling Barbara was making rather sweeping assertions about his life when she only saw him at times he was least likely to be active, as she put it.

'You play chess?' echoed Barbara.

'Yeah,' said Billy, a little hurt by her tone.

'Who wins?'

'Oh, Len does. He taught me.'

'Is he any good?'

'Dunno,' shrugged Billy. 'Better than me.'

Barbara made no comment on this. 'Have you ever won?'

'No,' he admitted. 'But it takes him longer to beat me now. I can stay out of trouble, for a bit, anyway, but I can't seem to get it together to attack. He kind of hustles all the time, you're having to deal with that. I never seem to have any moves left over to do much myself. It's a good game, though.' He nodded approvingly.

Barbara wasn't a bad player herself. Peter had once said she hustled too. 'How long does a game last?' she asked.

Billy shrugged. 'An hour, say. Used to be all over in ten minutes. He plays fast. Most of the time's waiting for me. I need time to think.'

'Ah,' said Barbara.

On the pier Barbara rested her back against the metal guard rail to admire the lurid cascades of tourist tat shrouding the souvenir kiosk in the centre of the walkway. Her eye was particularly taken by the Prince Charles plastic ears, whose massed and disembodied appearance lent a surreal – almost artistically significant – dimension to the view. The spectacles with pop-out dangly eyeballs the other side of the hatch offered minor competition, but failed to achieve the transcendence from tastelessness into Art. Billy was walking slowly back and forth in front of her, gazing down at the boards. Ahead, the walkway was blocked by nylon-clad trippers waiting their turn for the tourist launch. Screeches and wails emanated from the nearby ghost train, interspersed with thumps and explosions from the machine emporium beyond.

'My,' said Barbara, smiling broadly. 'Doesn't it all look gloriously tacky. I do like this place.'

Billy lifted his head from the boards. He had been enjoying the little disorientating jolts of glimpsing the shifting sea far below, through the cracks. He stared around. 'You want an ice-cream?' he said, seeing the display card at the kiosk and fancying one himself.

'Why not,' nodded Barbara. 'Something really disgusting, with flaky bars and ripple.'

Billy wasn't sure how serious she was being, but nevertheless bought two double ripple choc-o-nuts.

'Did Len wonder where you were last night?' Barbara asked when they'd finished the ice-creams and were strolling back towards the turnstiles.

'Dunno.' Billy shrugged. 'I missed him this morning.'

'But the back door was mysteriously open, was it?'

'Yeah,' Billy lied. 'Len must have done it.' In fact the hardboard had got punched in as usual, but he had had time to refix it properly, so he was unlikely to get into trouble.

'That's lucky,' grinned Barbara.

Billy stuck his hands in his pockets and frowned.

The other side of the turnstile she moved closer to him.

'Sorry,' she said quietly. 'I'm only teasing. Don't take me seriously. Actually this is me in a good mood. I didn't mind you coming round last night, honestly. Not just that once. I feel good this morning.' She tugged at his arm. 'C'mon. I'm going to be late. I'll show you my short cut.'

They crossed the coast road. She led him towards the entrance of a narrow lane that wound up behind the city bus station to the rear entrances of the townhouse offices. As they entered the lane the noise of traffic and crowds was instantly cut off.

Halfway up, Billy slipped his arm around Barbara's waist. She glanced at him with a surprised smile; then looked sharply up the lane, seeing his attention occupied not by her, but by two men approaching from the other end. The arm suddenly felt protective rather than affectionate. The two men looked large and hard and were staring at them, or rather, at Billy. One of them was smiling; not, Barbara thought, very reassuringly.

'Hello, Billy,' said the older man as they drew level, and caught his free arm, drawing them to a halt. The action suggested he was accustomed to laying hands on people and expected no fuss about it. His companion offered Barbara an excuse-me-this-won't-take-a-moment smile, and made some pantomime with his hands, to which Billy responded by turning out his pockets. The younger man received the contents, which weren't much, with minimal interest and then patted Billy's jeans front and rear.

Barbara stood to one side of the group feeling frightened, and excluded. Billy didn't seem worried; more patiently resigned.

'He's clean,' said the younger man.

The older man put a hand under Billy's chin to hold his face still, looked into his eyes, and asked if he was OK.

'Yeah,' said Billy, shaking him off. The man made a small negative gesture to his partner.

'You got an address, Billy?' the younger man asked.

Billy mumbled something that wasn't Len's address. The older man looked disbelieving, but wasn't going to make anything of it.

'Take care then, Billy,' he smiled, and they moved off, tipping their heads to Barbara as they passed.

Billy stared them out of sight, then reached into the far pocket of Barbara's linen jacket and removed a small foil-wrapped nugget. He stuffed it back in his jeans. Barbara watched him with her mouth open.

'Jesus Christ, Billy!' she exploded. 'They might have searched me!'

'Na,' said Billy. 'Not two blokes.'

Barbara thought he looked unrepentent. She clamped her lips shut and walked on furiously. She had actually been touched by what she'd thought was his embrace.

Billy caught her up. 'Hey,' he murmured. 'Everybody does it. It's standard practice.'

'There might have been a policewoman round the corner,' she snapped, striding on. 'You couldn't be sure.'

Billy shrugged, conceding it. 'You could have said it was mine.'

'And you'd have backed me up, would you?' She pulled a savage face.

'Sure,' said Billy, after a regrettable delay.

'I don't think I like you,' she hissed, walking faster.

Billy said nothing, but kept pace.

'Don't you ever do that again,' she said, relenting a little.

'No,' agreed Billy.

Barbara stopped. 'They knew you.' She regarded him grimly. 'How?'

'I been around a bit,' he said evasively. 'Nothing special.'

She couldn't get anything more out of him.

*

Barbara's day was spoilt. For at least an hour back at work her hands actually trembled: the correction ribbon on her typewriter had never sustained such use. I wasn't the one to get searched, she kept telling herself, this is stupid; but somehow she doubted Billy's hands were trembling, and it was that much more than the incident itself, which was upsetting her. He hadn't been angry, or frightened, or shocked. To him it had been nothing more than a routine inconvenience, requiring a 'standard practice' response. It probably wouldn't even have worried him if he'd been arrested, or if she had, for that matter; just a natural hazard – along with Christ knows what others – of his delinquent way of life. She didn't see how she could ever get to know someone like that, let alone improve them. Even the policemen seemed to know him better than she did. They had looked in his eyes for mysterious messages and asked him if he was OK; they made her feel the outsider. He belongs to a different world, she thought despairingly, we only overlap at the edges. What am I playing at?

She gave up and took her afternoon tea-break early; and remembered breaking into that house, how funny she had thought it, how she had imagined calling Mr Fiddick out in the middle of the night.

She closed her eyes and rubbed her temples. Sonia's right, she thought unhappily, I am half clever and half incredibly stupid. She doesn't want to get involved and I can see why. It's only the surface that's fun, the irresponsible froth we skim off the top; underneath it's real and it's not fun any more, and it might even be dangerous.

She sighed, propping her chin on her elbows, and took a moment to brood deeper on her failings and how they had led her here. Why do I always overreact, she wondered bleakly, thinking of Peter, and university, and lots of other things, stretching back into the past. Why do I let myself get so angry and do such stupid things, when all I end up hurting is myself?

14

Len wasn't too angry on Thursday evening when Billy told him about staying over at Barbara's. Instinct told Billy how to put it. He said, 'Went over and screwed Barbara last night.' Len was annoyed, but more, it seemed, at the deceitfulness of the initiative than at what had actually happened. Indeed the thought of Barbara getting screwed appeared to give him minor satisfaction. Billy got off with a lecture about ball-breaking females, and heavy reminders over a couple of hours of his incompetence and uselessness, and Len's own long-suffering tolerance and generosity. However Billy felt he had gained an unassailable advantage by confessing voluntarily in the first place, rather than having it bullied out of him – Len hadn't stayed all night at Dave's and knew he had been somewhere – and ended up feeling more smugly pleased with himself than chastised.

On Friday morning, just before he set off for the playground, a sudden doubt – because of how they'd parted – made him ring Barbara. Fiddick and Watson's number was printed in bold type in the telephone book.

'Coming out tonight, aren't you?' he asked, after Sonia had put him through.

There was a long silence. 'Barb?' he said.

'I don't know,' she said.

He fiddled with the pages of the phone book. 'You said you would.'

'I did not.' Her tone was tart.

'Well . . .' He suddenly remembered her saying they'd be friends. Friends saw each other, didn't they? He spoke with more insistence. 'You kind of said it.'

He heard her sigh. There was another silence. Maybe she

was remembering things too. Finally she said, 'You're not staying at my place again,' and he knew it was all right.

Len drove them all to a bar near the seafront.

Barbara regretted, almost immediately, agreeing to come. It was a hotel bar – the staff wore maroon jackets with velvet lapels and dickey bows and looked ridiculously formal to be serving such a scrum – low-ceilinged and dark, eye-watering smoky, insufferably hot and, Barbara thought, astonishingly ill-designed. The bar filled the middle of the room so that the drinking area was confined to a rectangular corridor around it. It was obviously used as a meeting place and the clientele – mostly loud-mouthed casually dressed young men – were in perpetual motion in one direction or another, engaged in a ceaseless quest for acquaintances they could shout 'Hey, what yer doing, mate!' at, and slop one of several pints of beer they were carrying over.

'What are we doing here?' she complained, when they had been there an hour. 'This is ghastly. I'm going to fall over in a minute.'

She was melting beside Sonia in the only unjostled space they had been able to find, squeezed between the jutting corner of a mantelpiece above a brass-filled fireplace and the backs of a group huddled on tiny stools at the bar. She couldn't imagine why the place was so popular.

'I think Len wants to score,' said Sonia, pushing her face close. It was noisy as well. Tiny beads of perspiration sparkled through the make-up on her nose.

Len was standing by a side door about twelve feet away, talking to a group who could have been mufti-clad businessmen. Billy had got into the swing of the place and already made two circuits, the first to deliver their drinks, but had then disappeared the main-door-side of the bar. Barbara hadn't been sorry to see him go, since earlier he had been behaving in an infuriating manner, addressing pointlessly provocative remarks to her and Len, and soliciting unnecessary opinions from each of them ('Len thinks this place is great, what d'you think, Barb?') for no other reason, as far as she could see, than to incite conflict. She couldn't decide who he imagined he was getting at, and thought the performance pitifully infantile and annoying, and likely only to rebound on himself. Len had looked quite as irritated as she felt and, for once, had her sympathy and almost her allegiance, as one of the played-off parties. She assumed Billy had told him about Wednesday night and that in some perverse and counterproductive way, this was the result. It was hopeless, she had just decided. However much anyone pleaded – Billy, Sonia, anyone – she wasn't, absolutely wasn't, coming out again.

She rubbed the back of her hand down her nose to confirm it was suffering the same fate as Sonia's, and regarded the throng.

'What? Score in here?' She frowned, thinking a less likely crowd of drug pushers would be hard to find.

Sonia winked knowingly. 'You'd be surprised,' she said. 'They're not going to hang out with the pill-heads and freaks now, are they? Not the together ones.'

'Well, I wish he'd hurry up about it.' Barbara stared at what little she could see of the men Len was talking to. She wondered if Len's style of scoring meant putting an order in, for delivery perhaps, or if surreptitious packages were going to be exchanged in the Gents.

'And where's Billy?' she muttered. 'He bloody suggested this.' Christ, she sighed inwardly, what am I doing here?

She sipped her drink, felt the flesh round her mouth grow cold and prickly, and realised that her remark about falling over was no longer a joke. The combination of prolonged standing, stuffy heat and the wrong time of the month was suddenly overwhelming.

'I feel dizzy,' she said urgently, thrusting her glass out to Sonia. 'I've got to go outside.' She viewed the way out with dismay, and prayed she could make it.

'Use the door behind Len,' said Sonia quickly, grabbing the glass. 'Someone's closed it, that's why it's so hot. Christ, you've gone all white. Can you manage?'

Barbara nodded and pushed her way towards Len. She

gasped, 'Excuse me,' to a man blocking the door and obeyed the printed instructions to Pull.

Cool fresh air slapped her in the face. She gulped it in, stepping out into a dark alley at the side of the hotel. The door swung shut behind her.

It took her a couple of seconds to realise that she was not alone in the darkness, and a couple more to grasp that what she was looking at was a fight. Or rather, a beating up. The victim, whom she took a second or so longer to identify, was being held by his arms from behind, and was wriggling frantically against his captor. The man in front of him had his back to her, but she could see his elbows working, pumping in the blows. The whole scene was oddly silent – or maybe just seemed silent, compared with inside.

'Len!' she shrieked, struggling with the door to get back in. 'Len!' she screeched again, meeting the fug. 'Someone's beating up Billy!'

Len stared at her briefly, his eyes wide, then wordlessly brushed past. Before the door swung to again she saw the men he'd been talking to turn away, blank-eyed, as if fights were definitely not their business.

She pressed herself against the side of the doorway, hand to her mouth; and thought Len looked magnificent. His determined approach was enough to break things up. The man doing the punching got in one last jab, but distractedly, glancing over his shoulder, then muttered, 'Shit!' in alarm, and danced swiftly out of range.

The other man realised Len was making for him. In a panic of self-protection he hurled Billy sideways, into his path. Billy, disabled and off-balance from the blow and with his arms only released at the last moment, fell heavily against the wall opposite. Barbara winced as she saw – and heard – his head strike the concrete.

Len raced down the alley, shouted, 'Fucking do you if I see you again!' after the retreating figures, and then strode back. Billy was lying crumpled on the ground, his legs jerking feebly.

'Leave him a second,' Barbara gabbled. 'He hit his head.'

Len took no notice. He hauled Billy to his feet, dusting him down and patting him into shape as if he were a wobbly doll that only had to be positioned correctly to stay upright.

'He's OK,' he grunted. 'Just a bit shook up.' He realigned Billy, whose legs were buckling. 'It was those bastards from the party, wasn't it? Why d'you let them take you outside, Billy?' He shook him lightly. 'You got no pride, why d'you let them take you?'

In answer Billy sagged against him and rested his head on his shoulder.

'He's concussed,' Barbara wailed. Sonia appeared at the doorway beside her, handbag over her wrist, a glass in each hand, like a vision from a garden party. 'He hit his head really hard,' she insisted, glancing from Sonia back to Len. 'He ought to go to hospital.'

Sonia was staring at Billy and Len. 'What's happened?' she gasped. She looked as if she thought they were embracing.

'The sea'll do it,' announced Len, ignoring both of them. He draped one of Billy's arms round his shoulder. 'C'mon, Billy.' He started walking him down the alley. Barbara stared after them, aghast.

Sonia put the glasses down on the sill of one of the pub windows.

'But what happened?' she hissed, grabbing Barbara's arm and tugging her on.

'I think it was two of the blokes from the party,' fretted Barbara, watching Billy's legs stumbling beside Len's. She could hear him mumbling something. 'Where Billy stole the tapes . . . you know. They were beating Billy up. He fell and hit his head on the wall. Really hard.' And now Len's going to dunk him in the sea, she thought desperately, as if it were a horse trough and we were in some bloody cowboy film.

'It's madness,' she moaned breathlessly as they dashed across the coast road. Len and Billy had caught an earlier gap in the traffic and were already descending the steps to the beach. No one was going to stop them, she realised despairingly; Billy just looked drunk. It was a Friday night, there must be drunks all along the front that no one took any notice of.

They scrambled down the steep steps into a shadowy, pungent, unpopulated world. The sea was visible from the first bank of pebbles: the tide was in, the water oily and insidious-looking. The reflections of the prom lights started some way out; if it hadn't been for a shifting glimmer of white surf at the water's edge you could have walked straight into it without realising. In the distance the pier illuminations stretched out into the blackness. They looked disconnected and unreal, like runway lights into an alien, frivolous kingdom.

Len was waiting impatiently for them at the water's edge.

'Here,' he said, and tossed his wallet and keys to Sonia. She flailed around, retrieving them. He went through Billy's pockets and hurled the contents in the same direction.

Billy mumbled, 'Sod off,' petulantly as he was searched, and tried to sit down. Len yanked him up, grasped him firmly round the chest, and waded off with him into the sea. When the water was up to his waist he put his hands on Billy's shoulders and forced him under.

Barbara tripped over a plastic jerry can in the gloom, trying to keep her eyes on them, and sat down heavily. Sonia sat down too, patting the pebbles beneath her first to make sure they were free from tar. Billy was thrashing around in front of Len, who was allowing his head to surface at intervals.

This is how it ends, thought Barbara hopelessly, in drunkenness and stupidity. Billy's struggles became feebler. She put a hand over her mouth.

'He'll be all right,' ventured Sonia. 'Len'll look after him. It's OK.'

Barbara felt like the only adult in a crowd of kids.

'He might have a fractured skull,' she moaned. 'He shouldn't be doing that, I know he shouldn't.'

Len started to drag Billy shorewards. At least he's still alive, Barbara thought, hearing a succession of spluttering coughs.

Len pulled him a few yards clear of the water and laid him

on his front. Billy spat prolifically on to the pebbles and rolled over. Streams of water poured from the pair of them.

'Billy?' called Barbara, scrambling towards him. 'Billy?'

'Hi,' mumbled Billy, waving a hand drunkenly in the air. 'I'm cold.'

'He's cold,' repeated Barbara, looking up at Len. 'He's cold.'

'Of course he's cold,' snapped Len. 'I'm fucking cold.'

'Barb?' rambled Billy, groping around and sounding anxious. 'You still there?'

'I'm here,' said Barbara, immediately convinced that he must be blind since she was sitting within a yard of him.

'Come on,' said Len impatiently. 'You gotta walk home.' He stepped across Billy's body, crunching the pebbles until he had a firm foothold, and bent over him to pick him up.

'Mummy!' Billy suddenly screamed, sounding terrified.

'Oh, my God,' gasped Barbara, so shocked it came out as a laugh.

Billy tried to fight Len off, making whimpering noises. Len grabbed his wrists and held them tightly. Billy sobbed frustratedly, twisting to get into a sitting position; then went limp and fell back.

'Let's get this lunatic out of here,' muttered Len. He sounded shocked too, under his embarrassment. Billy let himself be pulled to his feet and buried his face in Len's shoulder. Len put an arm round his waist and set off up the beach.

'Can't we get a cab?' asked Sonia, eyeing Billy anxiously as they approached the steps.

'You must be joking,' replied Len scornfully, not having to explain why.

It took nearly an hour to walk back to the house, a distance of less than a mile. Billy tried to sit down every hundred yards or so, and at one point was violently sick into someone's front garden. Barbara was convinced that vomiting meant brain damage at the very least. Both men were shivering, Billy so alarmingly that at times it looked as if he were having a fit. Every few minutes he said jerkily, 'Shit,

Len, I'm fucking soaked!' or alternatively, 'Shit, Len, you're fucking soaked!' each time with a note of astonished discovery in his voice. Len did most of the work, letting him walk when he seemed willing and supporting his full weight when he lost interest.

Christ, he must be strong, Barbara thought, after having her and Sonia's help refused, or else he's out to prove a very important point. All the same, she found herself admiring him again, simply for his decisiveness, even if they were the wrong decisions.

'It's worse because he's drunk,' reassured Sonia, as they neared the house. 'It's always worse when they're drunk.'

Barbara doubted that Sonia had any experience on which to base this assertion, but prayed she was right.

'Keys,' said Len imperiously outside the house.

Sonia scrabbled in her handbag. Len snatched his wallet and motioned for her to open the front door.

'Out the way,' he ordered, and hauled Billy through. Released in the narrow hallway Billy promptly slid down the wall to his haunches and started to rub the back of his head. Len spread his arms in a shielding gesture, blocking the entrance way.

'I'll deal with him,' he said, flicking his fingers for Billy's possessions, which Sonia was holding. 'You can go.'

He can't mean it, thought Barbara, outraged, knowing he did. It wasn't you he called for, he was frightened of you, she shouted silently as the door banged in their faces. But there didn't seem anything to be done about it. It was his house, and he had stolen the responsibility.

Walking home she wondered drearily if it was all her fault. Would Billy have stolen the tapes if he hadn't been kidnapped by her and in need of something to make it up to Len?

'I'm going round there first thing tomorrow,' she told Sonia grimly before they parted. 'Bugger Len.'

15

Billy woke to the smell of coffee and a thunderous clanking rushing noise. Above it was another, high-pitched tuneless sound, but he wasn't sure if that was real or inside his head.

He became aware that he was lying on his front, his cheek on the very edge of the sofa. He tried to roll away, on to his back, but found he couldn't. His left arm was hanging over the side of the sofa, and something out of sight was tugging at his wrist, preventing him. There was a foul taste in his mouth and his head hurt. He lay still, trying to work things out.

The rushing noise stopped abruptly. He heard two metallic clanks. He suddenly recognised the sound: someone had run a bath. And the high-pitched noise was real: a whistle, growing louder. It stopped.

'You awake, then?' The lower half of Len's body came into view, clad in black tracksuit. Billy tried to roll over again, and again failed.

'Hang on,' said Len, and squatted down beside him. He fiddled with something by the leg of the sofa. Billy felt the brush of fabric being slipped off his wrist.

'OK,' said Len, and stood up. Billy pushed himself over. A throbbing weight slid from the front of his head to the back. For a moment the room seemed to pulsate. Len was standing beside him, holding a knotted tie in his hand.

'Had to keep you on your front,' he said, tossing the tie into the armchair. There was a rumpled blanket over the arm of the chair too, a green one, from upstairs.

Billy gazed at the blanket, and the tie. A flicker of fear rose in him, and then died. He was with Len. But something had happened. It looked as if Len had been sleeping down here.

He tried to locate himself. He was naked and in bed. It was

morning. What morning? He pushed his mind back, looking for something to fix on, and found nothing.

'Am I ill?' he asked.

'Got yourself knocked stupid last night.' Len picked up a blue bowl – the kitchen washing-up bowl – from the floor by the sofa. 'You need this any more?'

'Don't think so.' Len was saying he'd been knocked out, and he'd been sick. Suddenly a chunk of memory returned. It was Saturday morning, because last night had been Friday. They'd gone to the hotel and he'd met those men. His stomach hurt.

'Shift yourself,' said Len, and tugged at something clear and crinkly sticking out from under the sleeping bag. With difficulty Billy lifted his hips. Len withdrew a sheet of polythene. It was the sheet he used to cover his windscreen in winter. Billy took a moment to comprehend why it had been there, and then was greatly relieved to see it was dry.

'Was it those blokes?' he asked. 'I remember them.'

'Kind of. You hit your head on a wall.' Len rolled up the sheet and propped it next to the fireplace. He jerked a thumb towards the archway. 'I've run you a bath. You stink of puke.'

Billy sat up slowly. He had to use his arms, his stomach muscles were so sore. His head felt heavy and enormous. Gingerly he explored it. There was a large tender lump, as big as an egg, above his left ear. And Len was right, he did smell.

He looked around for his underpants. He couldn't see anything belonging to him. 'Where're my clothes?' he asked.

'In the sink,' said Len. 'They're wet.'

'Oh,' said Billy, faintly. He hoped that had no connection with the plastic sheet.

'So're mine.' Len gave him an amused look. 'We had a dip in the sea.'

Billy stared at him. 'Shit, Len.'

'Have your bath,' said Len, smiling. 'I'll tell you about it.'

Billy realised that Len was expecting him to walk to the bathroom naked; then that he was ill and Len was enjoying looking after him, and that he didn't mind. He swung his legs over the side of the sofa. The room swayed.

'Here,' said Len. 'I'll give you a hand.' He grasped Billy's elbow and helped him to his feet.

Billy took a couple of steps. It was OK; he thought he could probably manage on his own, but didn't say so. Len's grip was strong and reassuring. He glanced sideways at him and said, 'You're not going to work today, are you?' hearing his voice come out small. It should be Len's Saturday off.

'Not going anywhere,' said Len soothingly. 'Careful.' He steered him through the archway and across the kitchen. He pushed the bathroom door open with his foot. Steam billowed over them.

They reached the side of the bath. 'Gotta have a slash,' said Billy suddenly, looking down at the water.

'Right,' said Len, and led him on to the pan. He released his elbow and stood back.

Billy relieved himself, and managed it back to the bath unaided. The steamy atmosphere felt good; the throbbing in his head was quieter already. He climbed over the side and lowered himself cautiously into the water.

'Think I'd better stay,' said Len. He removed a pile of towels from the back of the bathroom chair and pulled it up. 'Don't want you drowning, do we?'

The chair creaked as he sat down. Billy stretched out in the water. He doubted he was in danger of drowning, but quite liked the idea of Len worrying about it and staying to watch over him.

Warmth soaked into his stomach muscles. A comfortable sense of security enveloped him.

'Go on, then,' he said drowsily, closing his eyes. 'Tell us what happened.'

Sonia insisted on accompanying Barbara round to the house, reassuring her on the short walk there that of course everything would be fine, but at the same time obviously not wanting to miss any of the action, just in case it wasn't.

The moment Len opened the front door, however, it was

clear she was right. He flung it open expansively, as if their appearance was not only anticipated, but positively welcome.

'Cup of tea?' he suggested smugly, waving them inside.

'Great,' said Sonia, flashing a smile at Barbara. 'You're not dashing off to work, then?'

'No,' said Len. He made it sound like a decision, not a fact of life. He pushed the sitting room door wide and ushered them through.

Billy was lying on the opened-out sofa, the unzipped sleeping bag covering him to the waist. He looked remarkably unscathed, Barbara thought, everything considered. The only conspicuous signs of damage were clusters of purple finger marks on his upper arms, which could have been the fight, or Len carrying him home. The room smelt of bathroom steam, fried breakfast and clean male bodies.

'How are you, then?' she asked. She sat down at the end of the sofa, by his feet.

Billy grinned at her. 'Got a headache,' he said, almost proudly. 'Want to feel my lump?' He leant forward, proffering the side of his head.

She giggled, mostly from relief, and inspected it. 'Very impressive,' she agreed.

He lay back. 'Stomach hurts a bit, too.' He ran a hand lightly across his midriff and peered down at himself. 'Looks OK, though. Funny that.'

'People don't bruise on their stomachs,' Sonia said knowledgeably.

'I'm not surprised it hurts,' said Barbara. 'Don't you remember?'

'Not really,' Billy admitted. 'I remember those guys hustling me outside.' He frowned. 'Then it's kind of hazy. Len says he dunked me in the sea.' He twisted to face the archway and called loudly, 'Fucking maniac!'

Len walked into the room bearing mugs, still looking excessively pleased with himself. Barbara put a hand on Billy's forehead. It felt quite cool. He looked at her with bright eyes and then at Len, placing the mugs on the coffee table, and smiled.

He's enjoying himself, the creep, Barbara thought, not unaffectionately; everybody gathered round, the centre of attention at last.

Len held a mug out to Billy. As he shifted position to receive it, the sleeping bag slipped sideways, exposing his naked hip bone. Len reached down and tugged it up again. A disturbing image of Len stripping Billy while he lay semi-conscious flashed into Barbara's mind. Christ, she thought, dismissing it hurriedly, he was wet, of course he had to, what is the matter with me?

'Better lay off the booze tonight,' said Sonia, tucking her feet up beside her in the armchair.

'Billy's not going anywhere tonight,' pronounced Len, in chief nursing officer tones. He leant an officious elbow on the mantelpiece.

'Aw c'mon, Len,' complained Billy. 'It'll be OK by tonight.'

'You're not going out.' Len turned deliberately to Barbara. 'What d'you think?'

'I think Len's probably right,' she said. She wished she didn't have to agree, but was relieved not to have to disagree all the same.

Billy batted his eyelids at her sulkily, then winced, as if his headache had suddenly got a lot worse. Barbara sighed inwardly. Len gave everyone a complacent smile and drained his tea. The action seemed to say, Well, you can see he's OK, so drink up and get out. He walked into the kitchen with the empty mug and made splashing noises in the sink.

While he was out of sight Barbara leant forward and whispered, 'I'll come round and keep you company tonight, OK?'

Billy perked up and glanced at Sonia, who inspected her nails.

Len returned in time to catch the end of the exchange. He frowned and looked at Barbara sharply. She concentrated on drinking her tea, thinking how silly she had been to say it when she could simply have done it.

'Are Dave and Jane coming out tonight?' Sonia asked brightly, through the tension.

Len stepped back against the mantelpiece again. He had switched his gaze to Billy and didn't appear to hear.

Barbara rose and murmured, 'We'd better let Billy get some rest.' She gave Sonia a brief smile.

'Oh, right,' said Sonia. 'Of course.' She got to her feet hastily, looking relieved to pretend they were merely over-staying guests.

Len saw them out. Billy folded his arms behind his head and half closed his eyes. Through his lashes he saw Len return, his face darkly thoughtful. He watched him cross to the fireplace and swing round.

'I don't want that cow Barbara round here again,' he said forcefully.

Billy kept his lids down and didn't reply.

'Fucking ball-breaker,' Len swore. 'She hasn't even got decent tits.'

Billy opened his eyes fractionally. 'Her tits are OK.' He smiled, sure he was safe, and added, 'Anyway, you haven't seen them.'

Len's body tensed. For a terrible moment Billy thought he'd got it wrong and Len was going to lunge at him. The muscles in his stomach cramped. Then gradually relaxed as nothing happened.

After a minute he said, 'You gonna ring Springfield, then?' making his voice normal and inquiring. 'He'll be wondering where I am.'

Len rubbed his nose violently. It occurred to Billy that Len could make him lose his job; but then that he probably wouldn't, because he'd lose by it too.

'Yeah,' Len grunted, and strode across to the phone.

16

Barbara spent the afternoon with her parents. It was her father's fifty-fifth birthday. As a present she had bought him a bottle-green sweatshirt with the words *Naughty . . . but nice* in white on the front. Not her ideal choice, but at least it wasn't an executive toy to gather dust with the others on top of his study desk, nor a cricketing cartoon book to join the stack on the bottom shelf in the sitting room. And she thought the message conveyed a jokily teasing affection, and that he would probably wear it with amusement in the garden at weekends. He looked delighted with it, but then he would have, anyway, whatever it had been.

Both her parents asked after Billy. Her father called him 'your young friend' and her mother referred to him as 'that funny boy'. Barbara replied to both enquiries – made separately – with an offhand, 'Oh, he's fine,' because she couldn't think what else to say. She definitely couldn't imagine saying, 'Actually he got beaten up yesterday but he's OK now, and I'm going to see him tonight but I'm a bit nervous about it because the man he lives with doesn't want me to.' It was extraordinary enough thinking it.

Her mother followed up her enquiry after Billy with, 'Peter rang again this week, dear, I wish you'd let me give him your phone number,' exasperating Barbara so much – her mother made the association so transparent – that she was even more scornfully dismissive of the idea than usual.

She caught the six o'clock bus back into town, ate a yoghurt and a hunk of chocolate cake at seven-thirty and then at eight-forty-five, quarter of an hour after she had heard Sonia leave – and telling herself as she closed the bedsit door that there was absolutely no reason to feel so furtive – set off for Len's house.

Billy let her in, looking ludicrous in sweater, underpants

and socks. On the coffee table in the sitting room were the headphones and cassette player of his personal stereo, and a half-rolled joint.

She frowned at the latter. 'D'you think you should?'

'Don't you start,' Billy said testily. 'Len's even locked the whisky in his car.'

Barbara pursed her lips and sat down in the armchair. Billy eased himself back on to the sofa.

'Stomach still sore, is it?' she asked.

'Bit,' he said grudgingly. 'It's OK.' He applied himself to the joint. After a moment he glanced up at her.

'Len doesn't want you round no more.' He returned his gaze to the table. 'And he thinks you've got lousy tits. I stuck up for them.' He smiled to himself.

'Oh, Christ,' she sighed. 'D'you want me to leave?'

'Nope,' said Billy. 'Just telling you what he said. Probably didn't mean it.'

I bet he did, she thought, and looked at her watch. She gave herself two hours, maximum.

Billy was rubbing his thighs.

'Why don't you get dressed properly if you're cold,' she said, still thinking about it.

'Jeans aren't dry yet. Can't find my other trousers.' He stared at the box under the table and shook his head. 'I reckon Len's nicked them.'

'You're joking.'

He shrugged. 'They're not in the box. They were yesterday.'

Barbara studied him, and decided he was unconcerned. She replaced 'You're in terrible danger and must leave immediately,' which had flickered, quite unheralded, across her mind, with 'How incredibly childish.' She felt the situation was galloping beyond her comprehension, and wondered how extraordinary it had to become before an inkling of its oddness registered with Billy.

'Billy,' she said at last, 'd'you like living here?'

Billy settled back on the sofa, pulled the sleeping bag around him and lit up. 'Sure,' he said, inhaling deeply.

She frowned. 'How did it start . . . I mean, you moving in . . .?'

He shrugged. 'Just happened. Accident, really. I was around and came back a few times and just kind of stayed. Used to be Mal and lots of them. Len was on his own, you know. Don't see so much of them now, though, just Dave and Jane mostly, and Sonia.'

'Have you ever thought of leaving? Moving on somewhere else?'

Billy stared at her, not sure if this was an invitation or was leading to more unsolicited advice. 'What d'you mean?'

'Well, finding a place of your own. Or getting a flat-share. You know. What other people do.'

He laughed shortly, disappointed. 'Fat chance. You gotta know people to get a flat-share. I don't know people like that. Can't afford a bedsit. Anyway, no one'd rent me a place with my job. They always ask. Everyone knows it's summer work. It's OK here, anyway.'

'If you found a proper job you could get your own place. Well, you might be able to,' she amended, having had recent occasion to appreciate the shortage of rented accommodation, and the likely unpopularity of twenty-year-old males as tenants.

'I did get a job once,' he said, stretching out on the sofa. 'Back in March. I didn't take it, but I was offered it. At MFI. You know, the furniture place. The job centre gave me an appointment and I went along and they said I could have it. Permanent too.'

'So what happened?'

He flicked ash in the general direction of the coffee table. 'Len said I wouldn't like it. He rang Springfield instead and got me this one.' He caught Barbara's expression and added defensively, 'It's nearer and I can walk to work. I like it. It's nice.'

'Why did Len think you wouldn't like the other one?' Sodding Len, she thought, he can't keep his nose out of anything.

'Well . . .' Billy hesitated. 'Not so much I wouldn't like it.

149

More . . . he said there'd be other people there, you know, workmates . . . and I'd probably make a mess of it and get the push. He thought it'd be better if I worked on my own, no one hanging over my shoulder, sort of.'

'D'you think you'd have made a mess of it?' Barbara asked grimly.

'Dunno,' he shrugged. 'Maybe. Anyhow, I like the play-ground job.'

'Billy,' Barbara said. 'I worry about you.'

'Do you?' he said, pleased.

Barbara sighed. After a minute she said, 'Shall I tell you something about myself?' She reckoned she knew something about dependency.

'Sure.' Billy settled himself lower on the sofa to listen. He was pretty certain she was working round to why she worried about him.

'Right,' she said. 'Well, when I was twenty I moved in with this man. A really nice man, I thought. Yes. He was nice. Then. Anyway, I moved in with him, and it was his place, his things – he was older, twenty-six then – and I even worked for him. He was my boss. I didn't force myself on him, most of it was his idea, but I didn't argue about it either, and while we were getting on OK it was great. I'd always thought of myself as strong, in my personality, so I suppose I thought the other things didn't matter.' She hesitated. 'Well, to be quite honest I didn't think at all, and I doubt he did either. We just wanted to be together. But you see these things do matter. They really do. He was carrying every-thing. Through his own choice, but still. And I didn't have anything, not a thing. So in the end we had a big bust up, it doesn't matter over what, but the point is we had it and everything collapsed. I had to go because everything I had was his. Everything. I didn't have anywhere I could even stop and think about it. I was furious and hurt, and he was feeling hemmed in by me, and there was nothing else I could do. I could see what we'd done, then, and that made me furious too, because everything had been his idea and it was all being flung back at me, and it seemed so horrible and unfair. I'd thought he'd known what he was doing, you see, and I don't think he did. I don't think he'd thought anything through. But in the end, well, it was me who suffered. I had to pack in my job and leave the flat. I just had to. I had to go back to my parents and start over again. And all because I didn't have anything of my own. It's the same with you. You haven't got anything either. It's all Len's.'

Billy stared at her. 'Shit, Barb,' he said. 'That's not the same.' You're a girl, he meant.

'Well,' she said, retreating slightly, since she could see he was insulted and there were significant differences, 'of course it's not exactly the same, but the dangers are still there. What happens if Len gets fed up with you? Or you get fed up with him? You're not settled in a job, you've got no rights here. You haven't got anything except a box of clothes. Who's going to be the one to suffer? It can't go on for ever.'

'It's OK at the moment,' Billy said stubbornly. 'Len likes me being here.'

'Yes,' she said.

'And I like being here.'

'Do you?' she said bleakly, thinking of Len stamping on his hand, and bullying him with Dave, and forcing him to see his parents. 'Have you ever wondered what Len gets out of it?'

Billy shook his head. 'He must like it. He'd throw me out if he didn't.'

'Well, is it for the rent? How much d'you pay him?' Billy was silent. 'You don't pay him anything, do you? Billy, what the hell do you think he gets out of it? Just think, for once in your life. Have you ever wondered why he doesn't like me? And about the way he treats you? Christ, all along the line. You ought to watch out, Billy. It's really weird, honestly, you ought to watch it.'

Billy thought she was criticising him, without offering any solutions. She was also frightening him.

'What d'you expect me to do, then?' he asked bitterly. 'It's OK you warning me off. What am I supposed to do about it? You tell me.'

Barbara lifted her shoulders. 'I don't know. What you did before, I suppose. I mean you managed then. Before you met Len.'

'I didn't manage,' he said shortly. 'I didn't manage at all.'

'Well, you could go back to your parents, couldn't you? Just for a little while, to get yourself sorted out?'

'You're joking.' Billy looked away.

'Why?' asked Barbara. What was his problem?

Billy shook his head. He took a last drag on the joint and stubbed it out violently in the ashtray. 'Put something on,' he said, indicating the stereo and the end of the conversation.

Barbara got up with a sigh and grabbed the first tape she came to. One of the stolen ones, doubtless. She rammed it into the machine. Billy pulled *Autocar* towards him and started to roll another joint.

She sat thinking for ten minutes. Then asked, 'Billy? When did your dad die?'

'When I was four,' he replied, without hesitation. Barbara knew she'd miss-hit, but carried on anyway.

'How did he die? Was he ill or something?'

'Nope. He had a smash-up on the way to work. On a motorbike.'

'What did he do?'

'He was a teacher. Well, sort of. He did craft stuff at a special school. Maladjusted kids. I don't remember him much. He had a beard. I'm pretty sure I remember that, not just from photographs. Kind of wiry, with orange bits in it. And he liked the Stones. We got all these old records. Mum doesn't play them, but she kept them. Loads of them.'

Barbara smiled, reminded of the Everly Brothers records hoarded by her mother.

'Your dad dying . . . does that have anything to do with you leaving home?'

'Nope,' said Billy, very firmly.

'I'm sorry,' she murmured, after a moment. 'I shouldn't pry.'

Billy swung his legs off the sofa and sat with his elbows on his knees. He slowly started to join cigarette papers together.

He'd never told anyone his secret, but didn't necessarily object to someone knowing. In fact, although he hadn't told anyone, he had yearned, for almost as long as he could remember, for it not to be a secret any more. It was just that the only people who had ever questioned him about it had been people who were dangerous, who might act on what he told them and blow the world apart. He'd never had a friend who'd simply sat him down and asked him what the matter was. He'd never had a friend who'd cared that much. The friend would have to be very persistent too, because it wasn't something that would be easy to get started on and, if he did tell, he would have to be absolutely sure that they were listening properly because it was too enormous to be glossed over, or moved on from. And he had to be believed. He could feel his mind seizing up, just contemplating it.

'I can't tell you,' he said, aware of Barbara's eyes on him.

She thought this sounded ambiguous. 'I might be able to help,' she said cautiously.

'How?' He looked up.

'Well, I don't know,' she shrugged, 'unless you tell me.'

The idea of help appealed to Billy, though he didn't see how she could achieve it. On the other hand she was cleverer than he was, and what he couldn't see, maybe she could. He sighed.

'I wouldn't mind you knowing,' he said slowly. 'But I can't tell you.'

Barbara thought about this. After a while she asked, 'Would you like me to know?'

Billy fiddled with the tobacco.

'Maybe,' he said at last. He frowned.

Barbara pondered how they could get around the problem.

'Shall I ask you things,' she suggested. 'And you don't have to answer if you don't want to?'

Billy considered, and then nodded. He thought he was thirsty, and went into the kitchen to get a glass of water. While he was getting it Barbara tried to think of intelligent questions she could ask, faced with twenty years of unknown.

'Do you have any brothers or sisters?' she asked, when he was sitting down again.

'No,' said Billy.

'But your mother married again. How old were you then?'

'Nine,' he said, concentrating on the joint.

'Was it a shock?' Barbara asked. 'I mean some children get upset . . . you know . . .'

'No,' said Billy steadily. 'I liked him.'

'What, you liked him already?'

'Yeah.' He nodded. 'He was a friend of my dad's. Worked at the same place.' His head was getting lower.

'It is something to do with your stepfather, though, isn't it?' Barbara had been watching him and knew she was close. Really, it wasn't so difficult. It had to be mother or stepfather, nothing less would do.

Billy nodded minutely, without looking up.

'You don't like him now, then,' she said. 'For some reason?'

Billy didn't reply. His head was roaring; they had got here much too fast.

Barbara took his silence as assent. She frowned, unclear where to go, when she was sure she was so near the mark.

'Did he like you?' she asked, more as a filler until she had sorted something better out.

Billy stopped what he was doing and rubbed his eyes. He took his hands away and looked at her with desperation.

Barbara knew she'd scored a bull's eye and, with sudden horror, exactly what he was going to say.

'Yes,' he whispered. 'He liked me.'

She stared at him. She knew she knew, but couldn't say it outright, to confirm it, in case she was wrong, or right.

'Is that it?' she managed finally.

'Yes,' he whispered. 'That's it.'

The front door slammed.

'Oh, Christ,' she gasped, and glanced at her watch. It wasn't even half-ten. Billy blew out and swung his legs on to the sofa. He lit the joint. Barbara's mind juggled with guilt and shock.

Len burst into the room with a so-I've-caught-you-at-it expression on his face. Sonia slipped in behind, tight-faced.

'Thought I'd come and keep Billy company,' Barbara said bravely.

'So I see,' said Len. He slammed a half-full bottle of whisky down on the table and marched through to the kitchen. He returned with a glass; one glass, Barbara noted dimly. Billy smiled at her and then glanced expectantly up at Len. Barbara frowned back at him, feeling hopeless. She decided he honestly didn't know what he was doing most of the time.

Len took the joint off him, and with his other hand grabbed a fistful of his hair, wrenching his head sideways.

'Shit,' gasped Billy, with an edge of panic.

'Like a fucking girl,' Len hissed, twisting his grip. 'Get it cut.'

'Billy's hair's all right,' Barbara said stoutly, her heart leaping.

'For Christ's sake, Len,' snapped Sonia at the same time.

'Get it cut,' repeated Len, eyeing Barbara savagely, 'or I'll fucking do it myself.' He released Billy's head with a jerk. A tangle of brown hairs drifted down from his fingers to the coffee table.

Billy blinked rapidly, looking from him to Barbara. 'OK,' he breathed, almost excitedly. 'It's only hair.'

Barbara got up. 'I think I'd better go.' Len was only going to take it out on Billy if she stayed, and Billy was going to make it worse.

'I'm coming too,' said Sonia quietly beside her.

The slam of the door behind them sounded very final.

'I didn't tell him,' Sonia insisted, as soon as they were on the pavement. 'He guessed when you weren't in the pub. He's been foul all evening.'

Barbara started to walk, chewing her lip. She didn't know what to think about first.

'He hit me,' continued Sonia, falling into step beside her. 'Right in the street. He told me to shut up and I asked why, and he hit me. On the shoulder.'

'I'm sorry,' said Barbara, suddenly hearing Sonia's words,

155

and suspecting that she was being blamed as well as Len. 'Did he hurt you?'

'Not really,' Sonia admitted. 'But that's not the point. It was right in the street. I'm not having that. Told him so, too.'

'No,' said Barbara. She hoped Sonia wouldn't have had it if it had been in the privacy of Len's room, but could see how she would find a public blow the more humiliating.

'Honestly,' went on Sonia. 'I don't know what you've stirred up. Len really doesn't like you.'

'It's not me,' Barbara complained. 'I haven't done anything wrong. It's Len. He frightens me.'

'I think you ought to leave them alone. I don't want to see Len again. Let's call it a day. Harvey'll be back soon. I really didn't like Len tonight.'

But Billy's just told me something awful, Barbara wanted to scream, and I can't leave him alone, not if he doesn't want to be left alone. She had offered to help. *Billy's stepfather had 'liked' him.* God, how could you help?

'I think Billy should be frightened, too,' she whispered. 'I wish I could make him see that.'

'Just leave them alone,' Sonia begged. 'They were all right till you came along.'

'No, they weren't,' Barbara said fiercely. 'Len may have been, but Billy wasn't. It's not my fault.' It isn't, she told herself desperately; but I'm not going round there again. Billy can't expect that.

Billy thought Len was going to hit him, the way he strode back into the room.

'I told her,' he said hastily. 'She hasn't been here long. I told her she wasn't to come again.' He made himself very small as Len passed by to snatch up the whisky bottle.

Len collapsed into the armchair and filled his glass to the brim.

'Stupid cow.' He jerked his head furiously over the glass. 'Fucking brainless cow. Should have stopped her sodding mouth.' He threw the whisky down.

Billy couldn't connect this to Barbara.

'Fucking lectured me,' Len said. 'Yabber yabber yabber.'

Billy suddenly realised he was talking about Sonia.

'Cows, the lot of them.' Len grabbed the whisky bottle and refilled his glass.

'Len?' Billy asked nervously. 'Where're my trousers?'

Len stared at him. 'You'd have gone out, wouldn't you? Knew I couldn't trust you. In the oven.'

'Oh,' said Billy. 'Right.'

'You can take stuff down the launderette tomorrow morning. You'll have to use the dryer for your jeans, anyway.'

'OK,' said Billy. He wouldn't be going to work; Len had got him the weekend off, sick.

'And you can get back sharpish. I'm going down to Comet in the afternoon. You can come too.'

'Great,' said Billy. 'What're you going to get?' The Comet stores sold electrical and hi-fi equipment. He wondered if Len had forgotten tomorrow was Sunday.

Len swung his head from side to side. 'Dave says they've got some new stuff in,' he muttered vaguely. 'We'll have a scout round, see what we're missing.'

Billy realised that, far from incurring punishment, he was being offered a treat. He hoped the store was open. 'Great,' he smiled, meaning it.

It took him a long time to get to sleep. He felt powerful, because he knew Len and Barbara were fighting over him, but scared too, because someone had to lose, and whoever lost, he lost as well. He wanted Barbara to win, because she had said she would be his friend, and he was at the beginning of telling her something terribly important and now she had started him off he had to tell her more; but he needed Len, because without Len he didn't have anything. He didn't think Barbara could take over from Len now. She wasn't fighting for him, he realised, but on his behalf, which was quite different. He dwelt on this for a while, and discovered he was impressed by it: it meant she was doing it just for him, without standing to gain anything herself. And from this thought a conviction grew – a hopeful glimmer at first, welling to an excited rush – that he had done something tremendous in telling her, and that he mustn't lose her. But that was frightening as well, because he didn't think she would come round to the house again, which would mean him visiting her. And that was going to be very difficult, if Len wasn't to know.

17

Barbara was halfway to Maggie's house on Sunday afternoon – walking, since the day was fine and fresh – before she acknowledged that the main reason she was going was not because she wanted to help Billy and had hit on an inspired solution to some of his problems, but because she was in a panic and wanted to offload him on to someone more competent to cope. The thought that some of the burden would be shared had lodged in the back of her mind while she was in the bath that morning; but it didn't assume its true predominance until she was near enough to start running through dialogue in her head, trying to work out the best way of convincing someone who had a room to spare and wanted to make money from it that the obvious answer would be to let it, and that Billy would make a deeply deserving tenant, oh please.

But it was guilt that brought the acknowledgement home to her, for what she was trying to offload. Because she had been forced to recognise last night, with Billy's secret clamouring in her mind, that it wasn't only Len she was frightened of now, but, in a different way, Billy too. Of course it was terribly unfair, when she had encouraged him to confide in her, and when to have a reason for his oddness should have made it less not more alarming, but it didn't; all it did was make it impossible to ignore. The abrupt cut-off made it worse too, as it left the extent of Billy's stepfather's 'liking' for him unknown. The worst possibilities were so horrific that her imagination kept roaring off to places she would rather not have gone, and conjuring up all sorts of repellent images that somehow ended up contaminating Billy too, even as victim. She had told herself that of course it probably wasn't like that; maybe he had always been odd and it was all in his mind, part of a fantasy that had got out of control and assumed a false reality of its own. Or maybe, just conceivably, it was a downright and deliberate lie.

But these thoughts didn't stop others crowding in as well, because everything was possible and although she knew very little about it – and perhaps the images were worse, accordingly – she knew it did happen. She had been trying to tell herself that even if her most awful imaginings were true, he was still the same Billy as a day ago, and for her to turn round after he had trusted her enough to tell her and decide she couldn't trust him – and was *scared* of him because now she was forced to see him as undeniably damaged – was worse than unfair, it was treacherous.

But it was these thoughts that made her feel guilty about attempting to foist him on Maggie. It seemed like saying: here, I'm scared of him and don't want the responsibility, but you can have him, and you'll be all right, because you don't know and I was all right when I didn't know. She found herself wishing now not that Len had come back later, to allow time for Billy to tell her what had happened, but that he had returned sooner, so she wouldn't have had to hear anything at all and could have come up with the same solution – and a solution would still have been needed – with a clear conscience.

And Maggie had a child. The sudden thought made her literally stop in her tracks, and only proceed when more rational and realistic arguments intervened, such as that Maggie was hardly likely to make any instant decisions, however well-disposed to the idea she was; that Billy had never to her knowledge harmed anyone, or indeed shown an ounce of aggression; and that, anyway, Maggie might have already rejected the idea of taking a lodger for reasons of her own, and if this became immediately obvious the visit might well pass off with no mention of the idea at all.

This last thought depressed her a little because it had only just occurred to her and seemed, now she considered it, increasingly possible. On the other hand, she consoled herself, Maggie was a good person to go to if only for advice, since she knew Len and had lived with him herself, and although there were a few things she couldn't be told, there was a lot she could, and it was really those that Billy needed practical help with.

As Barbara approached the house she reflected how fortunate it was that she had decided to walk, rather than take the bus, or she would never have had time to think all this through and would probably have made a terrible hash of it.

'Hi there!' Maggie exclaimed as she opened the door, looking genuinely pleased.

She was wearing jeans and a bright red sweatshirt, blotched down the front, Barbara couldn't help noticing, with what looked like foodstains. She smiled, feeling slightly guiltier, and let herself be ushered into the sitting room. This looked, if anything, untidier than last time. Jacey was playing at the large table top; in front of her were numerous low-rise constructions in wooden bricks and, scattered among them, dozens of plastic farm animals.

'Bet you don't spend your Sunday afternoons playing farms,' said Maggie cheerfully. 'I'll put the kettle on.'

Barbara said, 'Hello,' politely to the child; she wasn't sure at what age it became rude not to acknowledge their presence.

''llo,' said Jacey without looking up, but tilting her head to rub her ear on her shoulder, which gave a squirmish impression of greeting.

'One sugar, is it?' called Maggie from the kitchen.

'Thanks.' Barbara wondered where to sit down. She filled the wait by studying the bookshelves, crammed with dog-eared paperbacks. A detective novel at the end of the lowest shelf had a twenty-five pence sticker on it, clearly second hand.

'Well,' said Maggie, returning with two mugs. 'This is nice.' She nodded towards the sofa by the window. 'Over there, I should.' She hoiked a smaller table out from under the larger with her foot and placed the mugs on it.

'There,' she said, and sat down with a contented groan. She pushed one of the mugs towards Barbara. 'I am pleased. I didn't think you'd come, to tell the truth.'

Barbara decided she would start with the problem and see if Maggie came up with the solution unprompted, which would save a lot of trouble.

She stirred her coffee. 'Actually,' she said, 'I've come to ask your advice.'

'Really?' smiled Maggie. 'Wow. Are you sure I'm qualified?'

'Well, yes.' Barbara nodded. 'I think you are. It's about Len.'

'Oh,' said Maggie, with a significant lowering of tone.

Barbara ploughed on. 'You know what you said last time, about warning Sonia?'

'Yes.' Maggie frowned. 'But I thought you said it was all right. That it was just casual.'

'Yes, it is. It's not Sonia I'm worried about. I think she's packed him in, anyway. It's Billy. You know . . .' she said, since Maggie was looking blank, '. . . who shares with Len. You saw him in the pub.'

Maggie nodded comprehension. Barbara experienced a disturbing shift in consciousness. Suddenly the prospect of speaking her thoughts aloud – and to someone to whom Billy was a complete stranger – seemed utterly daunting. She had to force herself, and it came out rather rushed.

'Len's dreadfully possessive about him, honestly, it's really weird. The whole set-up's peculiar. He's possessive about him, and not very nice to him, and I don't think Billy's very good at looking after himself. Len seems to want to control him, and Billy lets him, but at the same time Len's hurting him, quite deliberately sometimes, and really nastily. It's frightening. And I've made things worse by getting friendly with Billy, and, well . . . now Len won't let me in the house. He's actually said he doesn't want me round there again. I'm worried for Billy. I think he ought to leave.'

She stopped. Maggie was frowning down at the coffee table. With an air of taking first things first, she looked up and said, 'So what's he like, this Billy?'

'Um . . .' Barbara was aware of needing to strike a balance between appealing to Maggie's sympathy and presenting him as completely hopeless. 'He seems very young for his age. A bit dependent . . . well . . .' she admitted, '. . . very dependent, actually. He lets Len organise his life for him, literally everything. But I quite like him . . . and he's harmless, I'm sure of that. Lost, really. He doesn't have a very happy background, doesn't see anything of his parents, hasn't for years and he's only twenty. He says he doesn't have any other family, and he doesn't have any friends of his own, well . . . he doesn't have any friends at all, in fact, except me.'

'Dear me,' said Maggie. 'He's not gay, is he?'

'Oh, no,' Barbara said immediately, and then hesitated, realising she'd never seriously considered what Billy was. 'At least,' she continued uncertainly, '. . . not obviously.' She felt herself blush. 'Christ, I don't know. It never occurred to me. He's not like that. I mean, he doesn't seem to be noticeably anything. Why? Len isn't gay, is he? Surely not?' She glanced at the child, suddenly remembering she was in the room, and then back at Maggie, confused.

'Not that I'm aware.' Maggie grinned and leant forward. 'Don't worry, we're quite safe. She's only two.' She shook her head, then went on more seriously. 'Look, I'm sure you're right to be worried because it does sound depressingly familiar, but I really don't see where I come in. My advice to anyone living with Len would be don't, but you've already come to that conclusion. If Billy doesn't want to leave no one can force him. Some people just don't know what's good for them.'

'But . . . I think it's sick. It is sick, the way Len's treating him. . . It's like a man and a woman.'

Maggie snorted. 'Is that really what you meant to say?'

Barbara waved at her impatiently. 'Oh, you know what I mean. But it is. You should see some of the affidavits we get at work. All the things men do to their wives. You know, trapping them, cutting them off from their family and friends, telling them they're useless all the time, honestly, reducing them to zombies . . . dreadful things.'

'Barbara,' said Maggie. 'You don't need to tell me abou
things like that. I've been married to him, remember?'

'But Len and Billy are like *that*,' insisted Barbara. 'And,
mean, it seems worse when it's a bloke.'

Maggie gave a bitter laugh. 'Perhaps that says somethin
too.'

'Oh, Christ, I didn't mean that,' Barbara said hastily. She
groaned. 'Oh, I don't know what I mean, I'm putting it al
wrong. Of course it's all sick. It's just that you kind of accep
that things like that happen to women, don't you? Even
though they shouldn't.' She caught Maggie's eye again and
winced. She collected her thoughts. 'What I'm really gettin
at is that I don't think Billy properly understands. He seem
to treat it as a game, almost, or else he doesn't care. He's
mess, quite honestly.'

Maggie gave her a tired smile. Quietly she said, 'You can'
live other people's lives for them. It has to be up to him
Presumably if he wanted to leave badly enough, he'd leave.'

'But he can't,' Barbara said quickly, relieved they were
getting back on course again. 'That's the problem. I think he
might, if he could. I think he's beginning to realise that it'
not safe with Len. But he's got nowhere else to go. He's go
a job, but only a summer one on the front that Len found fo
him, and it doesn't bring in much and won't bring in
anything after September. Not enough for a bedsit, even i
anyone would rent him one. He doesn't have any friends he
could go to, and the only people he sees are people like Dave
and Jane, who despise him, or people who can't be bothered
like Sonia. Then I come along, and Len takes an instan
dislike to me and banishes me from the place as soon as he
sees we're getting friendly. It's like dealing with a jealou
husband. I've begun to feel quite furtive about seeing him.
mean . . .' she emphasised, coming to the point, 'he can'
come to live with me. I've only got a bedsit myself, and my
landlady wouldn't allow it, even if I did want it, which
don't. I can't think of an answer. The council aren't going t
be interested, and he can't go back to his parents . . . he'
got nowhere except Len's and he knows it.'

'So what's wrong with his parents? Where do they live?'

'Not far away. But he can't go back there. I don't think he would, however bad things got. He doesn't get on with his stepfather. It's a big thing in his life.'

Maggie looked perplexed. 'Well,' she agreed slowly, 'I can see he's got himself in a bit of a jam, with Len's help, no doubt. But you seem to have thought of all the angles. I'm sorry, I really don't think I can come up with any magic solution.' She scratched her face, frowning over it.

Barbara waited, hopefully. She could see Maggie was still thinking.

Maggie removed her hand. She shook her head.

'I'm afraid I'm not going to be much use to you. There really isn't an easy answer. When I left I went to Dave's. It sounds crazy, but I couldn't think of any other way of doing it. Not of ending it, permanently. I couldn't face spending the rest of my life looking over my shoulder. It was either Dave's, or jump off the pier.' She laughed shortly. 'Funny how when you're desperate the choices turn out to be either exactly right, or exactly wrong, and you can't tell which is which till afterwards.'

Barbara glanced at her, startled, both by her words – was she really saying that she'd contemplated jumping off the pier? – and by a sense that some misunderstanding had taken place. The conversation seemed to have turned an unexpected corner, leaving Billy behind. Oh, God, she thought suddenly, grasping it: she thinks I'm asking her how *she* did it.

Maggie leant back with a sigh. 'Looking back, I don't know how I had the nerve, to dump myself on them like that, but there you are. I suppose forcing the issue's sometimes the only way. And it turned out to be the right decision. I told you Dave's OK when it comes to the crunch. It was only for a few days, and Jane humphed around disapprovingly, but he played it straight and I'll always be grateful to him. He went round to sort things out with Len – obviously I'd put him in a very awkward position, what with work, and them being friends . . .' She smiled humourlessly. 'I say "sort things out", in fact they got blind drunk, went to see a Clint Eastwood film, and decided to settle it with a shoot-out at the clock tower. They were both arrested for threatening behaviour and obstructing the traffic. Jane had to collect Dave from the police station . . . she was livid, I can tell you. Though they'd talked their way out of it, by then. She left Len holding arm-wrestling competitions with a queue of policemen.' She paused, and added grudgingly. 'Actually I'm being unfair to Jane. It's a bad habit with me. She's OK too, when it comes to practicalities. A godsend if you need organising, which I'm afraid I did. She helped me find a bedsit out by the cemetery. And at least I'd still got a job, because Len hadn't quite got round to screwing that up for me, like he had the last, and I was nearly thirty and a woman, which is a much better proposition for a landlord than a boy of twenty. Billy's not going to find many who'll rent to him, even if he could afford it, not when they can pick and choose. There's masses sleeping under the pier every night, you seen them? Half of them kids. It's a scandal.'

Barbara knew she was going to have to put her solution to Maggie herself, and now, or it was going to get lost altogether. It felt uneasily – though obscurely – misplaced already.

'I'm not sure a bedsit would be the best place for him, anyway,' she said, trying to put a mental finger on her unease. 'Too lonely. What would really suit him would be to lodge, you know, somewhere he could have his own room, but wasn't all on his own. He'd be better off with other people around.' She smiled and tipped her head in the direction of the stairs. 'I don't suppose you've ever thought of it? I mean, taking a lodger?'

'What?' said Maggie.

Her expression made Barbara immediately backtrack. 'It was only an idea,' she said hurriedly. 'I remembered what you said about the room, and wanting to make some money . . .'

'Oh, Barbara.' Maggie looked shocked. She glanced across

166

at Jacey, still absorbed over the table. 'You haven't discussed this with Billy, have you? Oh, my God.'

'No, no,' said Barbara, sensing she had made a terrible mistake, but unable to work out how. 'It only just occurred to me . . . well . . . this morning, actually,' she admitted, not wanting to compound her guilt by lying. Maggie put a hand to her chest in relief. 'It was just a thought,' she stressed. 'Obviously he doesn't know you, and you don't know him . . . but I thought I'd come and see what you said . . . I needed to talk to someone . . . oh, dear . . . it's not a good idea, is it?'

Maggie put her fingers to her lips as if to stop words issuing from them before she was ready, then shook her head.

'I'm not saying it's a bad idea,' she said carefully. 'I mean, the idea of letting the room. In fact it's quite a good idea. A woman down the road has a lodger, and I know she makes a fair bit on it. It's one of the few things you can do without it being stopped from your social security. Although he's an older bloke, it's not so simple when they're young. There are all these new rules above moving them on if they're on the dole, and things like that. But even if I did decide to take someone in, I couldn't have Billy.'

'Oh,' said Barbara.

'I couldn't. I couldn't risk it. You say the only person he's got is Len . . . suppose he still wanted to see him? Even if I asked him not to, could you guarantee he'd stick to it? You couldn't, could you? He might get fed up, or change his mind, even ask Len round. Or Len might find out where he was and come round anyway. It's unthinkable.' She shook her head vehemently. 'Sorry, it's out of the question.'

Barbara was silent, and ashamed, because she could hear reproach in Maggie's voice and knew she deserved it. Maggie had been telling her how out of the question it was all along; she hadn't been listening.

'You don't know what you're asking,' said Maggie insistently. 'Len isn't just an ex-husband, he's the man who tried to destroy me. I was frightened of him . . . more than that, terrified. You look at me now and you see someone reasonably bright and together, or at least I hope you do, but, Christ, I wasn't then. If you haven't experienced it, you can't imagine what it's like. Jesus . . . sorry, I must have a cigarette . . .'

She got up quickly and rummaged in the pocket of a jacket hanging from the back of the door. Barbara, seeing the urgency of her movements and with no memory of her smoking during the last visit, was mortifyingly aware of having driven someone into an uncustomary vice.

Maggie lit up, still at the door, and then returned to her seat. She tossed the matches on to the table and exhaled deeply.

'You don't know Len,' she said, more calmly. 'You might think you do, but you don't. He's got no brakes, that man, and no shame. He's capable of anything because he doesn't draw any lines. He can't see them. He's from a hard family, well, both he and Dave are, but at least Dave's had rules. I'll give you an example, I told it to Dave once . . . If they ran you over on a dark night in a deserted street neither would panic, and they'd both deal with it efficiently. Dave would do all the right things and get you rushed to hospital and probably save your life into the bargain, but he wouldn't come and see you in hospital and he'd insist it was all your fault and screw you for every penny you'd got for the damage to his car.' She grimaced, reaching behind her for an ashtray from the window sill. 'If it was Len, he'd probably finish you off with his bare hands to avoid any inconvenience to himself at all, and make a first-class job of disposing of the body. They both like to think they're hard men and complete shits, and they both were when they were younger, but Dave's grown up and Len hasn't. I used to go around with both of them when we were young and, my God, I thought it was exciting. Len seemed so brave and reckless – which he is in fact, because of the lack of brakes – and he was so good-looking. I should have realised then that men like him are better kept as wild company. You can't *live* with them. He's got charisma and he can make things happen, and a weird kind of honesty too, because he doesn't try to kid himself, or you . . . but he's got no sense of give and take. If you can't stand up to him, like Dave can, you're fair game, and there's nothing to stop him walking all over you. I thought I was dirt because that's how he treated me. It's a kind of brainwashing. He tried to make me believe that I was hopeless and couldn't live without him, and he damn near succeeded. I had no one to talk to, because he'd made sure of that, and I couldn't understand why anyone should want to do what he was doing to me unless there was something wrong with me. Once I'd left I couldn't think why I'd put up with it for so long, but that's it; when you're out, you can see it. When you're in, you're too far gone to see anything. And of course he detests women, it's obvious now. They're just something else to be defeated. I tell you, there's nothing like a good scrap to turn Len on. Sex is definitely an aggressive act with him . . . I expect it is for a lot of men, underneath, only with him it's on the surface, because he's not ashamed of it.'

Barbara glanced over to the child, wondering if this was her father Maggie was describing. She was beginning to think it couldn't be.

'You know what that bastard did before I left? I'll tell you. He raped me, that's what he did. I know we were married, but it was still rape, whatever they say. It was the worst thing he could think of doing to me. Gives you some idea how his mind works. He thinks that what he's got between his legs is some kind of deadly weapon that can reduce anything to dirt. That's how he views it. I didn't fight him, because he'd have loved every minute and I wouldn't have won, but I've never forgiven him for it.'

Barbara blinked at her furiously. She had never heard anyone confess to being raped, and had frantically to remind herself that they had been married, so it couldn't have been as bad as proper rape. Not with someone you'd done it with lots of times before, willingly.

Jacey climbed down from her chair and tottered toward them, her thumb crammed into her mouth. She leant across

169

Maggie's lap and ground her face into her stomach as if she were trying to bore her way inside.

Maggie stroked her back. 'It's all right, poppet. We're not arguing. I'm sorry,' she said to Barbara, looking a little depressed by her speechlessness. 'But I'm only trying to explain. And I don't see why I should be ashamed of something that wasn't my fault. It's him who should be ashamed. I've told lots of people – it's the only way to deal with it. You can't come to grips with anything until you've said it. I don't know why, but you can't. I just want you to understand why I can't have anything to do with Len any more. I won't have him near me, nor near Jacey, and Billy would just be too much of a risk. You must see that.'

Barbara cleared her throat. 'I'm sorry. I didn't think. You seemed so strong. I didn't realise. You went up to him in the pub and everything.'

'Yes, well, perhaps I am now,' agreed Maggie. 'And I'm not even saying I couldn't cope. What I'm saying is that I don't want to have to cope. I don't want any complications in my life, and I don't want to sacrifice anything for anyone any more.'

'Oh, dear,' sighed Barbara. 'I feel so awful.'

'Well, don't. You weren't to know.' Maggie gave her a pat on the arm. 'There's no harm done. And perhaps you are taking this all a bit personally. You aren't responsible for Billy. You're just a friend. Anyway, he's going to have to learn to stand on his own two feet some day, and how's he ever going to learn if other people keep doing it all for him? It has to come from him. I spent years waiting for Len to do something about me, until I realised I'd got to do it myself. I've done a lot of thinking about how I could ever have let myself be taken over like that, and how I could ever have thought I wanted someone, just because they were exciting and powerful, and they wanted me. I'll look after myself and Jacey, and I'll help my friends, but I won't be responsible for them. They can damn well be responsible for themselves.'

She shook her daughter's body, eliciting muffled giggles. 'Even with her, actually. I decided that when we were still in the hospital. You're my kid, I told her – I really did, anyone listening must have thought I was mad – but you're not mine. You're yours, and you've got to work at it too. She's never going to want to belong to someone, not if I can help it.'

Barbara knew Maggie was making a deliberate effort to lighten and broaden the conversation for her sake. She felt in the presence of someone of superior integrity, and because of the divide in age and circumstance could admire her wholeheartedly for it.

'I'm a fool,' she said. 'And you're awfully nice not to be angry with me. I'm an idiot.'

'No, you're not,' Maggie said. 'You were just trying to help a friend. Nothing wrong with that. I agree with everything you've said, and I'm sure you're right about it all. I just can't have him here, that's all.'

'I can see that.'

'Well,' said Maggie, 'Forget it now and have another coffee.' She set the child on her feet and picked up the empty mugs.

Barbara stayed until Jacey started asking about tea.

At the door on her way out she hesitated, saw the child hadn't followed them into the hall, and said, 'So Jacey's not Len's, then?'

'No,' said Maggie. 'She's not. I've got nothing to remind me of him, thank God. Jacey's dad is a friend, a common or garden friend. In fact I don't think Len can have children. I never used anything with him because I wanted a kid, and he convinced me that was my fault as well. That's how I got caught with Jacey. No complaints, mind.' She let Barbara pass her before adding with a grim laugh, 'I don't think Len's is good for anything except as a deadly weapon. I wish I could have told him.'

Barbara took the bus home. She sat upstairs, right at the front, and as the bus lurched and swayed on its twisting route scowled at her reflection in the glass. That's exactly what happens, she berated her vibrating ghost, mutilating the paper ticket between savage fingers, when you kid yourself about who you're trying to help.

Approaching the clock tower the phrase 'You're a spectator sport to her' entered her mind, jeeringly. This caused prickles of alarm, because she could hear the words being spoken, until she recalled – with a flood of guilty relief – that they had been Maggie's, about Jane. But it could be me, she sighed. Look at Billy: he's stopped being a project and become a real person, and all I'm doing is trying to get rid of him.

Passing the hospital she became momentarily humble. I'm not a very nice person, she explained mournfully – though silently – to a tiny Indian gentleman slipped into the seat next to her; only I'm clever at hiding it, and other people think I'm nicer than I am.

Just before she got off the bus she was startled by the notion that she had got the whole thing the wrong way round: that she was the unreal one, from an unreal, super-ficial world, where, because everything was more civilised and nothing terrible happened – or appeared to happen – a lot of fuss had to be made about events that on the scale of human suffering would scarcely register at all.

Is that what Sonia meant? she thought. Why am I so shocked, anyway, when I know these things happen, and that the people they happen to must be real people, like Peter and myself, because there isn't any other kind of person, and nobody can wave a disaster pass in the air and shout *Stop, this isn't allowed to happen to me*.

And this led her to realise that of course terrible things must happen everywhere, and it was only her perceptions at fault for assuming otherwise. Which meant that the real world was in fact one world, encompassing all others, and that at any time the artificial walls of the civilised world could collapse, and the occupants be jolted into the real thing. Barbara felt, for a few moments as she stepped off the bus, very jolted.

18

'Harvey's coming back on Thursday,' Sonia announced smugly, over coffee in the office on Monday.

'Is he?' said Barbara. 'How d'you know?'

'Saw Mrs Barnstaple. He's rung. And he told her to tell me specially.' Sonia grinned.

'Does that mean it's definitely over with Len?' Barbara sensed that the return of Harvey was going to mean changes for herself as well as Sonia: from what she had picked up he didn't sound the type to welcome Sonia's girlfriends trailing around on dates too.

'Yup. Brilliant timing, isn't it? I expect we'll still see them around, you know . . . but I don't think Harvey and Len would hit it off too well, really.' She waved her coffee mug at Barbara. 'What about you and Billy?'

'What about me and Billy?'

'Well, you know . . . are you going to see him again?'

Barbara sighed. 'I think that rather depends on Billy. I'm not going round there again, not after last time.'

Sonia shrugged. 'You could always see him at lunchtime. I'm not recommending it, mind, but you could.'

'Mmm,' said Barbara. Sonia, she guessed, was also aware of impending changes and wouldn't have minded seeing her fixed up elsewhere. 'I know. But I don't think I will. I don't want to push anything. If he wants to see me he knows where to find me. I think I'll leave it at that.' She had half expected to see him yesterday, on her return from Maggie's, and had been relieved when he hadn't shown up. But she was almost sure he would, when he could get away from Len.

'You'll like Harvey,' said Sonia apologetically. 'He's got really nice manners. I'll introduce you.'

This, Barbara thought, was Sonia as good as saying that

this was all she could do, and was sorry about it. She felt oppressed by the mess of Len and Billy, which Sonia was copping out of; or perhaps had never copped into.

'I'm very glad for you,' she said, making the effort. Still, she supposed, Harvey had to be an improvement on Len; he was bound to be safer, and recollection of yesterday's conversation with Maggie spurred her to sound more enthusiastic. 'I think you're very wise,' she added emphatically. 'I really do. And I'm sure I'll like him.'

During the afternoon Barbara remembered something else Maggie had said yesterday, something that had got lost at the time. She waited until Mr Fiddick was closeted with a client, and then rang the Citizen's Advice Bureau. Yes, a helpful female voice confirmed, her information was correct. Board and lodging payment was now only payable for a limited period to the young unemployed: two weeks locally, because it was a seaside town, and this would apply to anyone under the age of twenty-six.

'Twenty-six!' cried Barbara, outraged, realising she would fall into this net too, if she were unemployed and in digs. 'Are you seriously telling me that no one under twenty-six and on the dole, or likely to go on the dole, can become a lodger?'

'Effectively,' said the woman, after a pause. 'The ruling's only just come out. We're all finding our feet at the moment, and there may be some test cases. But, yes, as it stands at the moment.'

'This is the government's contribution to International Youth Year, is it?' inquired Barbara, recalling an image of Prince Charles gyrating at some inner city youth club from the television last night. 'Christ, there must be thousands of young people in digs. Where on earth are they all meant to go?'

'We've been asking that ourselves,' the woman replied, a trifle stiffly. 'There certainly aren't enough cheap bedsits to go round. The thinking is that they'd be better off at home, I understand.'

'Till twenty-six!' screeched Barbara, and then moderated

174

her tone, since she appreciated that it wasn't the woman's fault. 'And what if they haven't got a home?'

'Oh, there are exceptions of course,' said the woman, easing back into helpful. 'If they're orphans, or if they've been in custody, or if they can produce very good reasons why they couldn't live with their families.'

'Oh, great,' said Barbara. 'Thanks.'

She banged the phone down and slumped back in her chair. Brilliant, she congratulated the powers-that-be bitterly; and what if the reasons are so good that no one could possibly want to produce them?

'Yes?' inquired Barbara to an unfamiliar male back as she opened the front door, only minutes after getting home on Monday evening. 'Goodness!' she cried as he turned. 'Billy! You actually did it!'

Billy ran a hand over his shorn head – his hair was less than an inch long all over – and smiled at her shyly. He was in combat trousers and khaki again; the military impersonation was almost convincing.

'It's all fluffy!' she exclaimed, coming out on to the pavement to inspect him. 'My, doesn't it look dark now? You've lost all the fair bits. It's sweet . . .' She realised she was gabbling and made herself slow down. 'Come in,' she said, much more quietly, and touched his arm. 'Do come in.'

'Got it done at the Greyhound,' said Billy, as she closed the front door. 'Yesterday lunchtime. They do it in the upstairs bar on Sundays. Len says it makes me look like a convict.'

'Well, there's no pleasing some people.' She followed him up the stairs. 'At least he won't be able to pull any more of it out.' The back of his neck was very white, where the sun hadn't reached it. She felt her chest tighten.

'I've come straight from work,' said Billy. 'I can't stay long.'

'No,' said Barbara, pushing the bedsit door to.

Billy sat down on the edge of the bed and pulled at his ear.

Barbara walked over to the sink and rummaged beneath it for pots and pans.

'D'you want anything to eat while you're here?' she asked brightly, over her shoulder. 'I'm starving.'

'No, thanks,' said Billy.

'Well, you'll have a cup of tea, anyway, won't you.' She stood up. It was like emerging through a fog. She wasn't starving at all; what had she been doing with pots and pans? She bit her bottom lip, frowning, and plugged in the electric kettle. Billy was watching her anxiously. She opened a cupboard for teabags, and then again for sugar. She snapped open her coolbox for milk. Then rattled in the cutlery stand for teaspoons.

She heard Billy sigh. He had switched his gaze to the window.

'Saw an ad for a room today.' He said it as if it wasn't what he really wanted to talk about, but he was starting anywhere.

'Yes?' She suspended the pint of milk she was holding above the mugs.

'Yeah. In the newsagents. It was for the room above the shop. I asked them about it.'

'Oh, wonderful!' Barbara heard her voice surge with enthusiasm. 'Well done!' She handed him the mug of tea. 'So what happened? Have you got it?'

Billy shook his head and pulled at his ear again. The mannerism was much more noticeable with his hair so short. 'It was really small, and a lot of money. He wanted a deposit too. Sixty quid.' He sighed again. 'I don't think he would have given it to me anyway, but he asked for my address and phone number. For references, I think. Or maybe to let me know.' He glanced up at Barbara. 'I said I wasn't interested. I didn't know what else to say.'

'Oh, Billy,' said Barbara, and sat down beside him. 'Would you have taken it otherwise, if he had offered it?'

He shrugged, and stared at his mug. 'I don't have sixty quid.'

'But if you could have afforded it. What I mean is, are you saying you've made up your mind to go?'

'Well . . .' said Billy awkwardly. 'Dunno . . . maybe . . . if I could find somewhere . . .'

Barbara stared at him. Finding him somewhere to live suddenly seemed the important issue. And something she wasn't frightened of helping him with.

'Listen,' she said, making her voice practical. 'You've made a start. But why don't you tell Len now? If you've made up your mind, that is. Don't make it a big thing, just say you're thinking about it. And not because of me or anything. Just getting a place of your own, and you'll still see him and be his friend and whatever else he wants. It's not unreasonable. And even if he was unreasonable about it the worst he could do is throw you out, and I don't see why he should do that. He might even help, I mean, if you said you needed it, you know, involved him. He knows a few people, he might come up trumps. Anything would be better than trying to do it behind his back, if you've really decided. It's ridiculous that you can't give people your address and phone number because you're scared of him finding out.'

Billy's eyes were still fixed on the mug in his lap. After a moment he raised them and stared bleakly at the blank screen of the portable television.

Barbara realised her words had missed him completely. And that they'd been the wrong words. He hadn't come here to talk about leaving Len. He hadn't made any decisions. He'd just been trying to start things off. Oh, God, she thought with an inner wail, he's probably been gearing himself up for this all day.

Billy sipped at his tea. In an agony of shame she stood up and walked over to the cooker. With her back to him, appalled at what she was doing but unable to stop herself, she picked up the bread knife and started to hack slices off a loaf.

After a minute or two Billy's voice, low and shaky, said, 'Can I come round tomorrow? Please?'

She turned to look at him. He'd written this evening off. She was suddenly disgusted with herself. She put the knife down.

177

'Of course you can,' she said huskily, walking back to him. 'I'm sorry, I'm so sorry.' She nearly said 'It's because I'm nervous,' but stopped herself in time. Having nearly said it made her throat tremble.

Billy looked away, as if he were scared she might embrace him.

'You said you'd help,' he muttered, blinking at the window. 'You said . . .'

But you ought to be talking to a grown-up about it, Barbara cried silently, not me. She briefly imagined taking him to her mother; a problem too big for daughters but within the competence of parents. But then shook her mind clear because it was only cowardice. She sat down on the bed again.

'I'll be here, Billy,' she said, resting a hand on his arm. 'I promise. But . . .' – she couldn't stop herself – 'I'm only me. I could help you find someone else, if you wanted . . . someone who might be better . . .' A doctor, she thought desperately, or . . . Christ, there must be someone.

Billy was looking panic-stricken.

'I don't want anyone else,' he whispered. 'I want you.'

'Fine, then,' Barbara said, her heart sinking, reminding herself that he was the one who was suffering, not she. 'Fine,' she repeated, squeezing his arm. 'I'll be here.'

Billy stood up abruptly, as if he couldn't bear to be with her any longer, with this hanging over them. 'I gotta go,' he said.

'OK,' said Barbara. 'I'm home by five-twenty. As early as you like.'

Billy nodded, and left.

On the way down he stopped off at the bathroom to wet his hair, so he could say he'd been swimming, if Len asked.

19

Barbara was ashamed she wasn't a better listener. It took Billy three evenings to tell her what he wanted her to know – he daren't stay long – and the first evening, Tuesday, she felt so anxious and inadequate she was scarcely capable of listening at all.

The first fifteen minutes felt actually dangerous. She was used to a different kind of listening. When she and Sonia talked – or she and Peter, in the past – they sat close and the listener was expected to participate, even in serious, intimate conversations: to help things along, fill gaps, make the right noises. 'How dreadful,' you could say, or 'My God, you poor thing' or 'I don't know how anybody could be so awful.'

But Billy didn't seem to want her to tell him how dreadful or awful it must have been. Her words seemed to block him, making his gaps even longer, as if he were having to unseize his mind before continuing. It was as if some of the bits that were awful to her, weren't so awful to him, and the discrepancy frightened him. It frightened her too, which made it worse. He didn't even want her beside him on the bed. When she touched him he shifted away, as if he couldn't bear the invasion of her sympathy. She felt incompetent and useless, to have even her silent compassion rejected, until she reminded herself that it was *his* need she was attempting to satisfy.

She sat for a moment with her trembling hands in her lap, and then moved to the armchair. Billy stretched himself out on the bed. And gradually the sense of danger passed.

That first night she learnt that Billy's mother had been a nurse, and that after her marriage to Billy's stepfather she'd gone back to full-time work. And that when she worked nightshifts Billy's stepfather had taken him into his bed.

Billy said he'd liked it, at first.

'He said it was in case I had nightmares. I used to have them, sometimes. He was nice. Mum was out, it was a game, sort of.

'I remember . . . I'd go to bed, and he'd say good night and turn the light off . . . but then after a while he'd come up again and ask if I was all right. And I'd say no, because it was part of the game, and he'd come in . . . He'd sit on the bed in the dark and we'd talk and play around, and he'd say Mum would be cross if she knew how late I was staying up. And then he'd say I wouldn't have nightmares in their bed, and I'd better sleep there. So I did. I liked it. It was OK, at first . . .'

It took Billy a long time to move on from there. But after Barbara had retreated to the armchair he managed it. He spoke with his eyes closed.

'It was like he became someone else. Like I *made* him become someone else. It would be all dark, and to begin with he'd be normal . . . but then he'd touch me, and his breathing would come fast like it suddenly wasn't him any more. I'd say I was frightened, but he'd say I wasn't. And he'd take off my pyjamas and I'd say, no, I didn't like it . . . but he'd say it was all right, and it was because he loved me . . .'

Barbara sat with her eyes closed too, through this, and with her hand across her mouth.

Billy said he played music in his head, to obliterate what was happening.

'He told me I sang sometimes. I don't remember. I just imagined all these instruments and made them play. Really loud. So everything kind of disappeared into the music.'

And his stepfather had started warning him then not to tell anyone. Not aggressively, Billy said, but as if it were for his own benefit.

'He said Mum could be arrested. For leaving me alone at night. I believed him at first. He said lots of things like that. But they were different things, they couldn't all have been true. He once said they'd put my name in the papers. I dunno why he kept on about it. He knew I wouldn't tell.'

Only once, he said, had he sought help. It was from the toothfairy.

'I remember that,' he said. 'I thought I could stop him. It sounds stupid now. I lost a tooth and, before she went to work, Mum said to put it under my pillow. So I did, and I told him. I was sure it would stop him. He'd have to put the money there . . . and I thought he couldn't, you know, do that, and be the other person as well . . .

'But he was. He put the ten pence under my pillow, and then he screwed me. It was the first time . . . I thought he was killing me. And the next day I put the ten pence into the boiler hopper to make the house explode. They always said never put things in the hopper, it blocked the pipes, and the tank would blow up. But it didn't. Nothing happened. Everything just went on.'

The burden of 'everything' seemed to include the secret of what his stepfather was doing, as much as the night-time acts themselves. And Billy made it sound as if the secret was a secret from everyone, even his stepfather.

'Because he was always OK in the daytime. Like nothing was going on. He was the same as he'd always been. It was weird, like it was all on me. I felt . . . if I said anything, it might shock him too . . .'

He was silent for a long time after that, as if what he'd said had become suddenly inexplicable.

He never sounded angry. The nearest he came to it was when he talked about his mother.

'She was with him. She must have known. And she asked me about it once, I remember. I scorched my hand over a bunsen burner in chemistry, and I said it was an accident but there was a fuss and she had to go up to the school. And when she came back we had a talk in my room and she asked me if I liked my stepdad. Her face looked sort of funny, as if she was frightened too, and I knew I had to say the right thing. So I said yes, and I could see she was relieved. She knew.'

Barbara couldn't see that this necessarily followed, but was still too scared to speak. So there was no way of arguing it, or pursuing it.

And then Billy had to leave. Barbara was appalled, and imagined him walking straight into the sea. But Billy, oddly, didn't seem to mind the cut off.

'It's OK,' he said, 'It's better, really, knowing you gotta stop.'

He found it exhausting, she realised later. And then also remembered that he knew everything already, and had been living with his distress for years.

On the Wednesday night he told her how it ended.

'It went on until Mum got ill. She had this operation and she was off work for ages. More than a year. I was in the third year at school by then. And he had to stop. But I didn't know if it was really over. So it was still there in my mind.

'And then she went back to work. She started on nights. The first evening my stepdad and I had supper, only I couldn't eat anything, and he was fine, but all the time I was waiting, to see if he was going to change. But then he went out, some evening class. I didn't know what to do. So I carried all the pills from the bathroom down to the kitchen, and started taking them. Dunno why. I watched the kitchen clock, and took them, one of each kind, like I was counting. And then he came back. He'd forgotten something. He stood in the doorway, and he could see all the pills and I knew then that he knew, and it wasn't just me. He made me drink salt until I was sick – '

'He made you drink what?'

'Salt. Salt water,' said Billy. He carried on. '. . . and he made me stay awake all night. I felt peculiar, but I don't know if it was the pills, or being with him like that. Then in the morning he said it must be all right, and I was very stupid, and there was no need to have done that. And I knew then that he wouldn't do it again, because he was frightened too. It had to be his fault as well, or he'd have called a doctor, wouldn't he? He never once asked me why. Just said I was stupid, and there was no need.'

Barbara, throughout this last speech, had been grappling with the fact that she had spoken – asked him a simple, neutral question – and it hadn't thrown him. Speech was possible. As long as she was careful, she could ask questions.

During the rest of the evening she used the discovery to straighten Billy's story out. She hoped she might even be helping him, by turning his attention to timespan and sequence.

'How old were you?' she asked him at one point, 'when your mum first went out to work?'

'It was right after they married,' Billy said. 'I was nine.'

'And how old were you when she had her operation?'

Billy had to think about this, but he didn't look fazed.

'Um . . . second year. Twelve. No. Thirteen.'

'So the er . . . thing with your stepfather – ' she fluffed, unable to think of a safe word for it, 'started when you were nine and ended when you were thirteen?'

Billy took a moment to answer. Barbara winced, guessing her error.

'Didn't feel like it ended,' he said.

'No,' she said, ashamed. 'I'm sorry.'

But she went on to ask about his mother then; just little things, where she worked, about her illness. She'd had a hysterectomy, Billy said. Somehow it was easier to talk about his mother than his stepfather because neither of them were sure about her. And she could see that, as Billy talked about her, he became less convinced she did know. He worked out he hadn't told her, though he'd thought he had, and doubted his stepfather had either, else why the warnings not to tell? It made him pull his ear for quite a while. Barbara thought his mother could be innocent, but remained silent, suspecting it might be a rather enormous discovery, if it were true.

She avoided talking about his stepfather. She thought he was wicked but was scared of saying so, because Billy seemed unable to see it. It was as if his own sense of guilt eclipsed his stepfather's. She wanted to shake him by the shoulders and shout 'He was evil, can't you understand?' but guessed he couldn't, because he was looking in the wrong direction.

'You were a child,' she pointed out several times, getting as close as she dared. 'It couldn't have been your fault.'

But his expression told her he didn't agree.

'So when did you leave home?' Barbara asked, towards the end of Thursday's visit, as the story was being brought up to date. This whole session had been easier; she had been surprised how quickly, after a minute or two's acute awkwardness, they had slotted back into the mood they had left the night before, as if the day between hadn't existed.

She was more relaxed too. His story no longer came across as a demand on her. It was he who had to deal with it, she'd realised – only he could – and she just had to be there, as the person he was telling it to.

'When I left school,' said Billy. He wasn't going to tell Barbara all that had happened since leaving home, it wasn't necessary. He'd left school at sixteen, after failing everything. He couldn't concentrate, they'd said.

The gaps after Billy's answers were beginning to sound almost conversational. Barbara sensed the finish. She asked him where he had gone, how he had managed, at sixteen, simply to disappear.

He told her he hadn't at first, how he had gone home if he couldn't find anywhere to stay, or it was too cold. But that after a while he had gravitated to the right places, and the right people.

'It weren't very good, though,' he admitted. 'I didn't have much dough and when I did it got ripped off. And I got in trouble with the cops because they kept busting the places I was staying. They didn't do me but they took me home a couple of times. Said I was too young to be on my own and I was in moral danger.' He smiled faintly at the ceiling. 'Until Harris, that is. He's one of the cops who stopped us in the street. He guessed something was going on at home because I wouldn't stay there. He came in to see me one time I was in the police station and sent the other copper away. I was scared because I knew he was pissed off with me and I thought he was going to thump me or something. But he just started asking about my family and why I kept leaving home, and when I said I didn't know he asked me if it was my stepdad, if he was knocking me around, and I said, no, and then he said, well, had he been fooling around with me, just came right out with it, and I was so surprised I didn't say no straight away and he guessed. I asked him how he knew, because I was so surprised . . . and kind of worried too . . .' – Billy realised he had actually been anxious in case it showed, that he was marked in some way, though it sounded too irrational to say aloud – 'But he just said he'd been a copper twenty years and I'd be amazed what he knew.'

He glanced across at Barbara. He, too, felt they were winding down tonight and didn't mind looking at her. 'Funny, isn't it? I mean as if it wasn't such a big thing? Anyway, he said it was OK and I didn't have to go back and he'd fix something up, which was good of him really, because he was drugs and he could have just busted me. He found me a place in this hostel out by the General, only it was a dump. It's closed now. It was all kids, mostly junkies and freaks. The blankets stunk of glue. I felt swallowed up, as if this might be normal, life could really be like this. I was nearly eighteen by then, so I lit out.'

He frowned at the ceiling. He could barely remember it now, except in the snap-shot imagery of a distant dream. A bad dream: it had been the other boys who'd frightened him, in case they were reflections of himself. A ginger-haired boy with sores round his mouth and a wicked knife in his sock had had the next bed. He thought Billy needed educating, and said he'd teach him how to fleece the homos. He helped him choose a knife and took him to the station. 'Just wait until they put a paw on you,' he told him, 'then pull out the knife and get the money. If they argue, stick 'em in the hand or something. They don't want no fuss, it's illegal, see, 'cos you're a kid. S'easy.'

But Billy's homo had been young and friendly and kinder than the ginger-haired boy. He was a Welshman from Cardiff and called him 'flower' jokingly, which Billy had never heard before but didn't mind. They went to a pub and the man laughed a lot and said he was a sweet kid, and he had affectionate, generous hands, not paws. Billy dumped the knife in the Gents and, when they got back to his digs, let the man seduce him because he was drunk and grateful and wanted the man to like him. It wasn't frightening and he felt liked, and he was pleased when the man said he'd look him up next time he was in town, though he never did.

He left the following year blank, until he met Len, because although it merely depressed him he knew it would shock Barbara, and she didn't press him to fill it.

Barbara thought, later that Thursday night, that it was incredible Billy was still alive and had survived long enough to tell her about it. She was assailed by images of him, maimed and desperate, groping his way through his teenage years, miraculously avoiding drug addiction, incarceration, suicide. (It astonished her that someone could attempt suicide without appreciating that was what it was.) Of course that's what he is, she told herself, a survivor; there are probably hundreds who don't make it this far. She could understand now why he thought living with Len was all right: anything would seem all right, after that. Grudgingly, she found herself grateful to Len, who had taken him in for the wrong reasons, and was misusing someone who had no choice, but had very likely saved him from something worse, all the same.

Later still, lying in bed, she totted up all the people she could go to if something terrible happened to her and she was desperate. Her parents – she wouldn't like it but they would; her brother in Milton Keynes, who wouldn't be keen but would put up with it; even, in an emergency, her father's sister in Bristol, or one of her old schoolfriends like Anne in Yorkshire. She tried to imagine what it would be like to have no one, to feel the need to be untraceable, and on top of that to be crippled by a secret that cut you off from anyone you might get to know.

And for a moment, as she imagined it, the maimed Billy was replaced by an identical but unpitiable figure: a carefree, optimistic, energetic young man, likeable and self-liking, the ghost of the unfairly murdered Billy – Billy as he should have been. She pressed her cheek into the pillow and thought about his stepfather, and what he was responsible for, and decided that if anyone in the world deserved to be angry, it was Billy.

And that led her to think about anger generally, and how some anger might be therapeutic and some destructive, and how some might start out as one and end up the other.

On Friday evening Billy had nothing left to say, but still went to see Barbara. He liked lying on her bed, amongst her things; the room, and her presence, had assumed the security of a home. Anything that was going to happen to him – and he was haunted by a sense that something might happen, either to or within him – would be all right if it happened here, where he had nothing to hide. Barbara had left him reading *Cosmopolitan* while she went out to do the shopping she'd put off from the day before.

'You still here?' she asked when she got back. It was after half-seven; he was usually gone by now.

Billy muttered, 'Off in a minute,' although he made no preparation to leave. He'd enjoyed being in the room alone for a short while. It had allowed him to swell and fill it completely, and discover that it was safe, even without Barbara.

He dropped the magazine to the floor and watched her unpack. She removed the contents of the bags briskly, thumping things into the cupboard, or under the sink, or on to the shelf by the kettle. She was humming a tune under her breath; he saw her become aware of it, frown, and stop.

'What're you looking like that for?' she asked, without breaking her rhythm, but flicking her eyes at him.

He hadn't been conscious of looking like anything. He put his hands behind his head and smiled. 'Nothing. Just . . . how you do things. Kind of organised.'

'You'll have to be organised too, if you get your own place.' She tore the string netting from a bag of oranges and tipped them into the fruit bowl. It felt odd mentioning practicalities, almost tactless: they rattled in an atmosphere that was suddenly empty, now the intensity and concentration were gone. She had to keep reminding herself that it was over; that there were no decisions to be made, no action to be taken; at least, not by her.

She collected up the paper bags and wedged them into a bin below the sink.

'I don't suppose you've said anything to Len about leaving, have you?'

Billy shook his head. He watched her screw up the empty carrier bags and stuff them into a canvas holdall hanging from the back of the door. He felt pleasantly tired.

Barbara walked over to the bed and stood over it, studying him. He smiled up at her peaceably. She thought he looked as if he would probably never do anything, ever again. Frowning, she sat on the edge of the bed and pulled one of his hands from under his head.

'Hold my wrist,' she said.

He enfolded her wrist loosely with his fingers.

'Properly,' she insisted. 'Hold it steady.' She jerked her arm, and his grip gave.

'Hold it, blast you,' she hissed.

Billy adjusted his position on the bed, realising she was serious about something.

'What're you doing?' he asked.

'Just hold it,' Barbara repeated. 'Hold it so I can't move it.'

Billy braced himself for the jerk, and held her easily. Barbara nodded. She shook his hand off and pushed him sideways, so she could lie on the bed beside him.

'What was that about?' asked Billy, after a moment.

Barbara stared at the ceiling, then twisted her head to answer him. 'I'm not sure,' she said, and turned back. 'I'm really not sure.'

They lay beside each other for a few minutes. Billy wished he could stay here for ever, just like this.

'I think you're very brave,' Barbara said eventually, and reached for his hand to squeeze it. 'Very brave.'

Billy returned the squeeze, although he would really have preferred to be held properly, so he could disappear inside her. He liked the collapsing sensation when she touched him, now there was nothing to stay intact for.

'You're a nice person,' he murmured, shifting his head so her hair brushed his cheek. 'I'm glad you're such a nice person. It's OK here.'

Barbara wondered whether she should warn him not to trust her too much, and that there were limits to the weights she could be expected to carry – even his arm felt heavy, if it fell across her she might never rise again – but didn't want to destroy anything for him just now, so stayed silent.

'How d'you feel?' she asked, after the silence. Though she guessed it was an impossible question.

Billy hesitated. 'I don't feel anything much,' he said at last. He meant not that there were no feelings, but that there wasn't much of them. They were very small and muted, whatever they were; resting perhaps, or waiting.

'Perhaps it's too soon,' Barbara said reassuringly. 'I expect they'll come. I'm sure they will.'

Billy was a little frightened because she was saying what he sensed, that there was something to come. He wished he could guarantee that it would come while he was here, but knew he couldn't.

'You'd better go,' said Barbara quietly, confirming it.

On his way out Billy stopped off at the bathroom, as usual.

'Why's your hair wet?' Len demanded, back at the house. He was propped against the kitchen worksurface, arms folded across his chest.

'Been swimming,' Billy muttered, and turned his back to open the wall cupboard. He stared at the contents and couldn't remember what he wanted to get out. He tugged a sliced loaf down.

'Liar,' observed Len. 'You've been round at Barbara's.'

'Who says?' asked Billy, not looking round and having no success with the plastic tag on the loaf.

'I do,' snapped Len. Billy gave up with the wrapper and

waited, chewing the inside of his mouth. 'I saw you,' Len said.

Billy turned round. 'What d'you mean?'

Len tapped his eyes, as if speaking to an idiot. 'I saw you. You never went swimming at all. You went straight from work.'

'I didn't see you,' said Billy, disorientated. Len was meant to be at work, twenty minutes' drive in the opposite direction, till half-five.

'No, you didn't, did you,' agreed Len.

'We were just talking,' Billy murmured. He didn't like the idea of being watched one little bit. Len must have left work early, specially. 'You said you didn't want her round here,' he said quickly. 'You didn't say anything else.'

Len smiled triumphantly. 'So why d'you pretend you've been swimming?'

Billy couldn't think of an answer to this. A tight lump formed in his throat.

'You moving out then, Billy?' Len's voice was almost conversational.

''Course not,' said Billy breathlessly. 'She's only got a bedsit. We was just talking. I like it here, anyway,' he added hastily, suddenly realising that should have come first.

'Do you,' nodded Len. 'Do you now.'

'Shit, Len,' said Billy. 'Where d'you think I'd be moving to? I got nowhere else to go.'

Len nodded again and pursed his lips. Neutrally he said, 'You going round there again?'

'I like her,' said Billy. 'She's just a friend.' It strengthened him to say this, though he knew it was a mistake. Len would have been much more forgiving of 'She's just a screw'.

Len settled his backside more firmly on the worksurface.

'She's a friend, is she?' He raised his eyes, as if reviewing the notion of friendship and its application to Billy. 'But who'd want to be friends with you, Billy? You tell me that.' He pondered some more, and then wagged his finger in the air. 'You know what, I reckon I've got her number. Yeah. I got it. She's using you.'

'For what?' Billy said blankly.

Len shrugged. 'For entertainment.' He smiled. 'Interesting specimen, you are, Billy. I bet she and Sonia have a real laugh about you.'

'I don't think so,' Billy said steadily.

'Don't you now.' Len's voice sharpened. 'Try asking them. Ask Sonia.'

Billy didn't believe him. Len detected it and changed tack slightly.

'I told you she was a ball-breaker,' he said patiently. 'Didn't I? Only she doesn't have to break yours, does she? Come on, what d'you think she likes about you, Billy? What d'you think you've got?'

Billy took a step towards the sitting room. Len pushed himself away from the worksurface to block his path.

'There's a lot of cunts like her, you know,' he went on fiercely. 'They get a real kick out of someone like you. Makes them feel all big and strong, a real turn-on. They like to see you hurting. They come on all soft and sympathetic and all the time they're loving it, getting their knickers wet.' He reached out and flicked at Billy's chest. 'And you're a gift, aren't you, a real gift. She doesn't even have to knock you down first. She's got you on a plate. You're being had, boy, one big turn on.'

'I don't believe you,' said Billy, very faintly.

'You don't know anything,' hissed Len, moving closer. 'That's your trouble, nothing. What brings her running here, eh? You think about it. It's not your big brown eyes, I'll tell you that. You think she cares, she feels sorry for you? Poor little Billy, all alone with big bad Len, is that the line she spins you?' He prodded Billy twice in the chest. 'Why should she fucking care? Shit, she doesn't know you. She just likes you all pathetic, you're something she can maul around, get a big buzz from.'

'She's not like that,' whispered Billy. The world seemed to be filled with Len, he couldn't see Barbara at all. The choking lump in his throat broke audibly, gushing liquid into his eyes. He twisted his face away.

Len stood motionless, watching him. Then reached out, grabbed Billy's chin, and jerked his head back. He pushed his own face close.

'You stop blubbing and listen to me now, Billy,' he said softly. 'And listen good. You go round there again and I promise you, boy, I'll kick your fucking head in.'

20

Billy was in hospital to begin with, in his dream. He was lying on a bed in a room he recognised, surrounded by the calm figures of nurses. One of them was standing by the window with her back to him and, when she turned, he saw she was his mother. She was wearing a white mask like an operating mask, only it was bigger and covered her eyes as well, but she didn't seem to notice the obstruction and nor did anyone else: they were moving around and talking in low voices as if everything was normal. There was a drugs trolley by the bed with bottles on it, full of pills, and he was sure he needed some of them, but no one went near it, not even his mother. Then a nurse started to unwind the dressing round his ear, smiling at him kindly, and brown pieces of cake fell out, all over the bed.

Then it wasn't the hopsital any more but the sitting room at home, and he was naked – in fact he had been all the time, but it hadn't seemed odd in the hospital – and a man, a large man, was standing behind him, holding his upper arms. Although Billy was facing his mother, he could somehow see the man too, and that the man was smiling. His mother was still wearing her uniform and her mask, but the gauze was very fine; he could see her face behind it, and she appeared to be able to see him. He was ashamed to be naked in front of her and to be in the arms of a man, but she didn't look shocked; she was shaking her head resignedly and saying in a tired voice, 'Well, I don't know, Billy, I really don't know,' and it seemed to him that she thought they were alone, that although the man behind him felt enormous, somehow his shape was hidden from her by his own body. He wanted to move towards her, but the hands were holding him too fiercely. He tried to say something, but the effort felt so great he knew that if he was going to produce any sound at all he was going to have to scream, and the scream would be heard by everybody, and something terrible would happen.

And then he saw the smile on the man's face behind him widen. So wide it began to tear at the sides. His face split open and peeled back as the figure inside emerged. He had thrown off his stepfather's skin at last, and Billy wasn't even surprised to realise it was Len underneath, all the time.

Harvey turned out to be black. The young man who banged on Barbara's door on Saturday evening to tell her she was wanted on the telephone was everything Sonia had led her to expect – unmistakably American, tall, slender and elegantly good-looking – but he was also black. As she trotted down the stairs behind him – it would be her mother, who always rang minutes after six even at weekends because she forgot it was cheap all day – Barbara thought this omission of Sonia's typically surprising and couldn't help admiring her for it. They'd make a stunning couple, she thought, him so dark, her so fair; and then immediately had to suppress the unworthy suspicions aroused.

'Hello?' she said to the mouthpiece, and returned the dazzling smile Harvey gave her as he disappeared into his room. A definite improvement on Len.

'Barbara?' the voice said. It was male, rather thin and cautious.

'Who's that?' she asked, frowning, feeling she should know it.

'It's Peter.' There was reproach in it now.

'Peter!' Something invisible punched her in the stomach. 'How did you get this number?' She pulled an agonised face, hearing the accusation in her voice.

'Your mother agreed to give it to me. I thought I'd give you a ring, see how you are.'

Barbara bit off 'But I told her not to, the cow,' which vied with 'And why didn't you get it out of her a month ago?' and finally settled for, 'I'm fine. I'm working for a firm of solicitors. I've got quite a nice bedsit.'

'Yes,' said Peter. 'Your mother told me. Are you sure

194

you're all right?' He sounded puzzled, as if he might have received a different impression elsewhere.

'I'm fine,' she repeated, through clenched teeth. 'What about you?'

'Oh . . . well . . . fine . . . I just wanted to make sure, you know . . .'

'Well, no need to worry,' she said briskly, then sighed and added less briskly, 'It was nice of you to ring, though. Thanks.'

'Barbara?' His voice became thinner and more urgent. 'I wanted to say . . . I didn't behave very well. I'm sorry.'

Barbara swallowed back 'No, you bloody didn't, did you.' Instead she said tightly, 'It's OK. Water under the bridge and all that. And you weren't so wrong about some things. I can see that now. It wasn't all your fault.'

There was a short silence. She strained her ears and heard the faint sound of his breathing. He's working up to something, she thought. She saw his expression: the furrows over his blue eyes, his lips tremulous with effort. Oh, why did you ring? she begged silently, do say something.

He managed it at last. 'I haven't seen Marie again,' he squeezed out. 'I've missed you.'

Barbara held the receiver away from her ear as if it had attacked her. She stared at it, thought she heard a feeble 'Barbara?' issuing from it, then replaced it with a bang on the handset.

Creep creep creep, she mouthed as she hurtled upstairs. *O parasite, leech, millstone, drag on the market, he misses you.* She slammed the door of her room shut and leant against it. How does he have the nerve? she screamed inwardly. How can he do it?

She switched on the television and flopped across the bed. Sodding man, she told the screen, the sounds and pictures meaningless. She waited for the telephone to ring again, but it didn't. She saw his face as he put the phone down, defensively blank because he hated showing hurt. She imagined him and her mother earlier, conspiring. 'She'll have

195

calmed down by now,' she heard her mother say. 'Just be patient, she's always been like this.'

She closed her eyes and groaned. She thought of ringing her mother and screaming at her, someone who would forgive later and understand how evaporating targets could make you even angrier. If only he had written rather than rung, so she wouldn't have had to hear his voice and be reminded of last time, and be jolted back to all that fury.

After an hour or so, when she had calmed down a bit and the telephone still hadn't rung again, she made herself a toasted cheese sandwich. As she ate it she remembered it was Saturday night, and thought about Sonia and Harvey out there somewhere enjoying themselves, and then Len and Billy out there somewhere else, hurting each other, and finally herself and Peter, not out anywhere and not enjoying themselves, and still managing to hurt each other.

In the end she wrote him a letter because it was all so stupid. An adult, restrained letter, setting out all the things she knew they had done wrong, but imparting no blame. She described her feelings of hurt but acknowledged that there were worse things than sexual infidelity, and that she understood this now. But, she wrote, she could never go back to live with him like before, because it was the wrong footing and it would only happen again, and she hoped he understood this and didn't take it personally. She apologised for slamming the phone down on him and reminded him how unsuitable the instrument was for matters like this, and explained that that was why she was writing, to set the record straight. Then she signed her name.

She stared at the letter a while and wondered if he would sense what she was saying between the lines so she wouldn't have to swallow her pride and write it, but in the end decided that the implicit words were invisible and it would probably just look like a letter to him, and not a hand, outstretched. So underneath her name she wrote, *I did love you, and I know you loved me, and we were happy. I miss you too and I'd still like to be your friend.* She folded the letter quickly and sealed it in the envelope so she wouldn't reread it and be tempted to tidy it into something different.

Then she went to bed. It was much too early, but she felt a great angry weight had slipped from her and didn't want to replace it with anything else just yet. She read two chapters of her book and turned the light off well before eleven.

'Well, he must have got it by now,' Sonia said on Tuesday lunchtime. They were on their municipal bench on the seafront as usual.

'Mmm,' nodded Barbara. She had told Sonia that Peter had rung, and she had written back to him. Sonia had breathed, 'Oh, I am glad,' with a note of relieved satisfaction in her voice, as if she, along with everyone else (i.e. Barbara's mother), had been privy to some essential truth about the real state of affairs unavailable to the main parties. She was grateful that Sonia wasn't turning round and reproaching her with 'but you said . . .' although at the same time it was vexing to look back on previous conversations and suspect her words hadn't been believed then, when she had meant them, and a lot of what she'd said felt truer than ever, now she knew what real wickedness was. It was just that it didn't apply to Peter, because he wasn't wicked, and never had been.

'Perhaps he'll ring tonight,' suggested Sonia.

'Not if he's got any sense. He's hopeless on the phone.'

'Well, maybe you'll get a letter tomorrow. Or Thursday.'

'Maybe,' said Barbara. Her thoughts were only vaguely on Peter. She knew he would write whether he still loved her or not, because he was a decent person and wouldn't dream of ignoring a personal letter from anyone.

'Billy didn't come round last night,' she said, staring in the direction of the funfair. 'I haven't seen him since Friday. I hope he's all right.' She blinked away the sense of deceit. Sonia had had to be advised of Billy's visits last week and allowed to presume more carnal intimacies in progress. Although grotesque, this had seemed the simplest way of guaranteeing privacy.

'You don't still want to see him, do you?' said Sonia incredulously. 'Not now, surely?'

Barbara wondered if she ought to go and find him, to put her mind at rest. Or whether that counted as selfish, when he was the one under pressure. She was very aware, after a morning devoted less to work than intense thought, of where decisions had to come from. At one point it had crossed her mind, as an explanation of his non-appearance, that he might be deliberately avoiding her. She hoped she was wrong, but could understand the logic in recoiling from someone who held your secrets.

'Billy's nothing to do with Peter,' she said impatiently, as Sonia's words registered. 'I'm still going to see him if he wants to see me. In fact . . .' She threw the debris from her lunch into the litter bin and dug in her handbag. 'I want to read you something.' She took out a folded sheet of typed paper and smoothed it flat. 'About Billy. I wrote it this morning.'

'You did what?' Sonia laughed. 'Oh, Barbara, really!'

'Just shut up and listen. It's important. I only typed it because I wanted to get it straight in my head. It's what I've been thinking for ages only I hadn't tied it all together. It's very short.'

'Right.' Sonia sighed and assumed an attentive expression.

Barbara stared at the typescript in her hand, glanced at Sonia, and then read: 'Len is jealous of me and Billy. He wants Billy for himself, or at least he doesn't want him to have anyone else. He wants to control Billy's life. He wants Billy to stay with him and show obedience, and in return he will keep him and protect him but if he steps out of line he will be hurt, and he may well be hurt anyway, to keep him in his place and demonstrate his dependence, and maybe even to punish him for it. Len is treating Billy like a lot of men treat their women, and I don't know if it's more shocking that he's treating Billy like a woman, or that it's not so shocking when it really is a woman.'

She looked up at Sonia, whose face was blank. 'There,' she said, a little embarrassed, and waited.

'Come again?' frowned Sonia.

Barbara read it again.

Sonia put a finger to her lips. 'Do you really think a lot of men are like Len?'

'I didn't actually say that,' said Barbara, thinking how typical it was of Sonia to sidestep the issue. 'But since you ask, yes. Enough. Underneath. Or at home. That wasn't the point I was making, though.'

Sonia stroked her lip. 'Well . . . if you're right . . .' she laboured the 'if', '. . . *if* you're right, it's more shocking how he's treating Billy. Obviously some men do that to women.'

Barbara sighed. 'Yes,' she said tiredly. 'That was exactly my point: it's shocking that it isn't shocking when it's done to a woman.'

Sonia shook her head. 'You've lost me now.' She smiled. 'Sorry.'

Barbara expelled air through her teeth and looked away. Sonia squeezed her arm.

'Listen, Barbara,' she said kindly. 'I think this is becoming an obsession. You don't have to treat it as anything bigger than it is. Not with me. It's probably only because you feel guilty.' She caught a dangerous glimmer in Barbara's eye and, provoked, added, 'And even if there is something funny between Len and Billy, it's private. Perhaps you shouldn't poke your nose in.'

'I expect people say that all the time,' said Barbara grimly, thinking of the women.

'And, anyway,' continued Sonia. 'If Billy didn't like it he wouldn't stay with Len, would he? It stands to reason. He could just go, couldn't he? He must like it.'

'I expect they say that too,' nodded Barbara.

'He must want someone to look after him. I don't see that it's all Len's fault. He must want it.'

'Or have believed he needed it,' sighed Barbara, still on her parallel train of thought. 'For some reason.'

'There you are, then,' said Sonia. 'Just stay out of it. Nobody else can do anything.'

'No,' Barbara agreed bleakly. 'They can't. You're right there. It's terrible.'

21

When Barbara's doorbell rang early Wednesday evening she assumed it would be Billy. She ran downstairs and flung the front door wide.

'Hi,' she said welcomingly, and then saw it was Dave. 'Oh, hi,' she said again, confused.

Dave shifted his gaze from down the street to her, and removed his hands from his suit trouser pockets.

'Sorry to bother you,' he said, looking reluctantly determined. 'But can I have a word?'

'What's happened?' she said, instantly alarmed.

'Nothing's happened.' He frowned. 'That's what I wanted to talk to you about.' He nodded over her shoulder. 'Could we . . .?'

'Oh, sure,' said Barbara hastily, backing into the hall. 'Come in.'

She led the way upstairs, conscious of his heavy tread behind her. She realised she was nervous of him, though not in the way she was nervous of Len. His manner reminded her of her old headmaster, who had also liked to 'have a word'. She felt a lot more than nine years his junior, and wondered if he was going to tick her off about something.

'You want a coffee?' she asked, closing the bedsit door behind them.

'No, thanks.' Dave strolled over to the window, stared through it, and then swung round to regard her gravely. He occupied more space in the room than Billy had ever done.

'I went down to see Billy at lunchtime. I told him to get out of Len's place.'

'You did what?'

'I told him I thought Len had had enough and he was . . . um . . .' He hesitated, choosing his words, '. . . outstaying his welcome. That it was time he moved on.'

Barbara stared at him. She could just imagine the original. 'And what did Billy say?' she asked tightly.

Dave shrugged, and stuck his hands back in his pockets. 'Not much. Did his frightened rabbit bit. You know what he's like. I felt like kicking him.'

'Does Len know you went to see him?'

'Nope. But I know he ought to go. There's a big bust-up brewing. I've known Len a long time. Billy's pushing his luck.'

Barbara folded her arms, taking it slowly. 'And you think Len wants Billy out?'

'Sure,' said Dave, surprised. 'Who wouldn't? He's been there over a year, for Chrissake. Just sponging. I don't know how Len's put up with it so long.'

'So why have you come to see me?'

Dave stroked his nose, then laughed shortly. 'Why indeed. Well . . . I kind of got the impression . . . correct me if I'm wrong . . . that you might have some influence on him. Something Len said.' He smiled.

Barbara didn't know whether to trust him. For a wild moment she imagined a plot between him and Len, some sort of test for Billy.

'What makes you so sure Len wants Billy to leave, and it's Billy outstaying his welcome?'

Dave frowned. 'Well, it stands to reason, doesn't it? Billy's really bugging him.'

'Why doesn't he throw him out, then? If that's what he wants. He'd be entitled to. Billy doesn't pay any rent, he's got no rights. Why not just throw him out?'

Dave looked at her closely. 'What are you getting at?'

Barbara decided she'd have to trust him, that things couldn't get any worse. Abruptly she said, 'You're looking at it upside down. Billy wants to leave. Or at least he's thinking about it. Len must know. And he doesn't want him to. That's what's bugging him. You've got it all wrong.'

'You must be joking,' said Dave contemptuously. 'He despises Billy. Why the hell should he want him to stay?'

'You ought to ask him that. I'd like to know too. And I agree he despises him. But he still wants him to stay.'

Dave looked disbelieving.

'Listen,' Barbara felt herself start to grow angry. 'Why doesn't he throw him out, then? Don't tell me he's not capable of it, if that's what he wants. Or that he can't bring himself to tell Billy to go, because you know that's rubbish. He can do what he likes. And I don't know what he said about me and Billy but he won't have me round there any more, and shall I tell you why?'

'Why?' said Dave, still frowning, but listening.

Barbara caught herself, before the anger took over. A just-conceivable vision of Dave as ally – or non-combatant, more realistically – entered her mind. She steadied her tone.

'Because he decided I was getting too friendly with Billy and wanted to put a stop to it. He's jealous, I can feel it. The last time I was there I went to see Billy on his own, after Len made him stay in. The weekend he banged his head. Len came back from the pub early because he guessed I might be there, pulled a great lump of Billy's hair out, and virtually threw me out. Even Sonia was frightened.'

Dave's frown had deepened. He shook his head, looking faintly repelled. What's he going to make of it, thought Barbara, there's no way of dealing with it as if it's normal.

'But if Billy wants to go,' he said slowly. 'Why doesn't he just go? I mean, what the hell is he doing there? It doesn't make sense.'

Barbara sighed. 'Because he's got nowhere else to go. He can't afford a place of his own. Not on what he gets paid. That's another thing. Did you know Billy was offered a permanent job in the spring and Len put a stop to it?'

'No,' said Dave.

'He told Billy he'd make a mess of it and got him the playground job instead, through someone called Springfield.'

'Yes,' said Dave. 'I know Springfield.'

'He actually told Billy it'd be better if he worked on his own because then no one would know if he made a hash of it. He didn't want Billy meeting new people, I'm sure of it.

And he didn't like the idea of him getting a permanent job. He likes him as he is, completely insecure and dependent on him. Even if he could afford it, no one would rent Billy a place, knowing his job, and he doesn't have any friends he could share with. What d'you expect him to do? Walk the streets? Join the kids under the pier? I tell you he's done that, I'm sure he has. Before he met Len. He was really at rock bottom. He'd put up with anything, just about, rather than go back to that.'

Dave considered, scratching a sideboard. He shook his head. 'But Len doesn't behave as if he wants Billy around. I tell you, it was getting really heavy over the weekend.'

'What d'you mean, heavy?' asked Barbara worriedly. 'Christ, Billy's all right, isn't he?'

Dave shrugged. 'All in one piece at lunchtime . . . I suppose I only saw them Saturday night. Maybe they'd just had a row. But Len's very twitchy at work. Taking a lot of time out, and chewing everybody's heads off. Even worse than usual. I can't overlook it for ever.' He smiled briefly, seeing Barbara's incomprehension. 'I'm his boss,' he explained. 'Thought you knew.'

'No, I didn't.' Barbara was amazed. 'I mean I knew you worked together. I didn't realise. Are you really?'

'Yes,' said Dave, amused. 'Really.' He rubbed his jaw. 'Ah, Christ. What's he playing at. Are you sure you're right?'

'Positive,' said Barbara, beginning to think she had convinced him.

'Why doesn't Billy go back to his parents, then? Christ, they only live down the road, don't they?'

'He can't. It's the situation there that caused all this mess in the first place. He shouldn't be forced back there. He wouldn't go, anyway.'

'But he did go back,' Dave argued. 'They both went there, a couple of weeks back. Len said they had tea there and the little twerp puked all over the car on the way home. He had the inside virtually fumigated.'

'Did he tell you Billy didn't want to go? Did he tell you he picked Billy up straight from work and simply took him there? I saw him afterwards, and he wasn't sick because he'd had such a good time and stuffed himself with cream cakes, I can tell you. Len found something Billy really didn't want to do, and made him do it. I don't pretend to know what he wants with Billy but, whatever it is, it isn't very nice. I agree he ought to go, and the sooner the better. Christ, I've been telling him that myself. If it was you or me I daresay we'd just get the hell out and never mind where to. But Billy's not us. I don't suppose he's ever been very good at taking decisions and he doesn't think he could manage, and he may well be right. He's scared of Len but he's scared of lots of other things as well, and he knows that Len does at least care about him, even if it is the wrong sort of caring. It's sick, the whole thing's sick, but they both are, not just Billy. Len doesn't hurt him because he wants him to go, he hurts him because he likes hurting him. He frightens me, I can tell you.'

'Ah, Jeez,' sighed Dave, and stared down at the carpet. Barbara thought she was probably witnessing the closest he ever got to embarrassment.

'Well,' he said finally, 'something's got to give. You couldn't have him here, I suppose?'

'No,' said Barbara firmly. 'Not permanently, anyway. I don't want him, and my landlady wouldn't stand for it.' She studied him anxiously. 'D'you really think it's that bad?'

Dave lifted his shoulders. 'Christ, I don't know. Perhaps it'll blow over. If I've got it wrong about who wants what, maybe I've got it wrong about that as well. Shit, and I tore Billy off a strip too.'

'You're horrible to him,' said Barbara, distressed. 'Both you and Len.'

'Well . . .' He pulled a face. 'He's such a wimp, isn't he? Sorry, but he is. And he set himself up. It isn't all Len's fault. He didn't ask Billy to dump himself on him. Billy wormed his way in. Yes, Len, no, Len, three bags full, Len. You didn't see it. Enough to turn your stomach.'

'Billy was desperate,' Barbara said heavily. 'He thought he needed someone. You wouldn't understand.'

Dave studied her, then looked away. 'No, well, perhaps

you're right.' He sighed. 'So what next? You want to go round there and lift him?'

Barbara blinked, dazzled by the simplicity of the idea. She was almost tempted to say yes, until questions like 'Where to?' and 'Suppose he doesn't want it?' intervened. She shook her head.

'I think he's got to do it. It didn't help when I interfered, and he's scared of you. I think you ought to stay out of it.' She glanced at her watch. It was nearly half-past-six. 'I'm going to see if I can catch him. He usually swims after work. He won't know what on earth's going on.'

'Well, if you see him set him straight, will you? But get him to leave or sort things out with Len for Chrissake. Shit . . .' He moved towards the door and muttered in an undertone, '. . . it's like Len and Maggie all over again.'

Barbara heard him. Without thinking she said, 'Except Billy's hardly going to go running to you, is he?'

'What?' said Dave, halting and looking at her sharply. 'How the hell did you know that?'

Barbara flushed. 'I bumped into Maggie in town. She was very friendly. I've been to her place a couple of times.'

'Have you, now.' He didn't look tremendously pleased. 'You do get around, don't you?' He waved a sudden finger in the air. 'Which reminds me. My excuse for visiting, almost forgot.' He moved back into the room. 'Jane wanted to know if you'd like to come over Sunday. She'd have asked you herself if we'd seen you over the weekend. Don't suppose you will now, though. I've asked Len. Still, I'll leave the number.' He dug in his jacket for card and pen and scrawled a number down. 'Give her a ring if you fancy it.'

'Is Sonia invited?' Barbara asked.

'No,' said Dave, and smiled.

Barbara took the card and stuffed it into her handbag. 'I won't, but thanks. Look, I must go. I'll ring Jane and explain. You do understand, don't you?'

'Sure,' said Dave. 'Some other time, perhaps.'

*

The wind had been getting up all afternoon. Billy hadn't noticed it, since it seemed merely a reflection of his mood and might even have been a product of it, but it had driven the children from the beaches and into the diversions of the lower prom, and seemed to infect them with a wild and reckless excitement. Their shouts into the salt-whipped gusts grew louder, their movements faster and more impetuous, their deeds rasher. The mothers with little ones soon gave up even the lower prom and retreated into the shelter of town. Billy was left with the older, unaccompanied children, all boys, who, freed from junior obstructions and their adult guardians, bonded with fellow inheritors of the earth and became even more wild and adventurous. He found he was dealing with a tribe of small unpredictable aliens, bent on self-destruction.

Two boys dragged a plank of driftwood off the beach and attempted to manufacture a lethal weapon with it, by slotting it into the fast-spinning handrails of the roundabout. Twice it bounced off violently, narrowly missing nearby heads. Billy was compelled to intervene and take it off them. When he called them 'stupid fuckers' – language stronger than he normally used to junior miscreants – they reacted angrily, offended as well as thwarted, and drew up battlelines. Their tactics were undefeatable: they were the warriors of opposing armies and it was their lives put at risk, but Billy was the enemy and the first fatality would mean victory for them. One battalion sought to scale the slide from the slippery end, while another crowded on the steps and the platform at the top, shaking the rusty guard rail and shouting battle cries into the wind, before crashing down to meet the invaders, either sweeping them down in the descent, or log-jamming mid-slide in a teetering scrum of arms and legs. Even the see-saws, normally regarded as infantile by older children, came into their own as human catapults: one boy sat on the ground-resting end while another ran up the see-saw away from him, the trick being for the sitting child to gauge exactly the moment to leap off, so as to spill the running boy before he reached the other seat. In fact the sitting boy ran the most risk, as the wood snapped up with the sudden removal of his weight, catching elbows and knees, and whipping past the chins of spectators.

Billy halted the slide assaults by tipping a bucket of water down the chute and telling them that next time he wouldn't wait until they had cleared it, and the see-saw abuse by exhortations and threats. But the atmosphere of challenge and antagonism was only defused by a blood-letting incident, when a boy hurled an empty plastic swing seat quite deliberately into the head of a running compatriot. As Billy patched up the child with shaking hands – in the event the boy's knees had come off worst, his head must have been bullet-hard – the others crowded round openmouthed, transformed instantly from malevolent conspirators to trusting infants, astounded at this bolt from the blue that had left one of their number maimed and weeping. Billy, who was already feeling quite ill with frustration, trying to keep one eye on the children and another on the prom for a car that might be Len's, and trying not to think at all about Dave, whose threats meant he now stood to displease one of two powerful men whatever he did, found himself cast in the role of responsible and competent adult; the boys' trust in him to take over and deal with the carnage they had wilfully created was at least as oppressive as their earlier defiance.

At six o'clock he left the few remaining children to their own more subdued devices and scrunched down the beach in swimming trunks to the sea. He noticed the pebble-roaring breakers and white horses further out, but ignored them. He waited for a gap between foam breaks, dived into the murky swirl, and struck out strongly.

It was difficult to maintain a rhythm in such a turbulent sea. But he persevered, welcoming the chance to be properly tired before turning himself over to the care of the water. He gave up only when the muscle ache reached his shoulders and neck, and by then his legs were singing with exhaustion. As he stopped, an exquisite weakening sensation rushed into them. He rolled on to his back and spread his arms wide, revelling in it.

The first wave that bore down on him undulated his body violently and swirled foam over his face. For a moment he thought it exhilarating, to plunge feet-first into the trough and watch the next monster, its crest whitely crumbling, tower over him: like riding a glorious and living rollercoaster. But then the foam crest covered his face, forcing his head up, which made his legs drop. He had to make an effort with arms that were already tired to get them up again, and the tumble down the next slope broke his shape completely, tipping him face first into the next wall of water.

He struggled to get back into position, annoyed with the sea for conspiring, along with everyone else, to force action on him. For a few seconds he relaxed completely, refusing to play along, but knew almost immediately he would drown and, after inhaling an unpleasant lungful of water, that he couldn't deliberately choose to die.

He trod water, coughing the brine out, keeping the back of his head to the swell so that the foam parted round him, giving him space to breathe.

The sea no longer felt as if it wanted to look after him. It felt indifferent, enormous, engaged in its own powering pursuits. He no longer felt the security of its support: his body felt heavy, like something the murk would willingly swallow up. He wondered if he'd left it too late, and in a moment of panic couldn't work out where land was, until he glimpsed it, frighteningly distant, from the crest of the next wave.

He struck out frantically, and found the exertion calmed him. It wouldn't matter if he drowned now, he was tired enough for it and angry enough for it, and he was trying, so it wouldn't be his fault.

But the land seemed to race towards him. He was swimming with the seas: they picked him up and flung him forwards, as if they had no use for him and wanted to be rid of him. They punished him only at the end, by knocking him down as he struggled to be free of them, then sucking him back so they could do it again, taking their chance to reprimand him when they could do so without killing him.

As he wrenched himself free and staggered up the pebbles an old man walking his dog further up the empty beach shouted 'Stupid bugger!' at him. Billy grasped the meaning from the man's face and his gesture as he shouted, though the sound itself was lost in the crash of an incoming wave.

A few yards from the foam he had to sit down. He drew his knees to his chest and hugged his trembling calves. The sea, which had once been his friend, pounded and sucked in front of him. He gazed at it resentfully. He felt hustled: by Len, by Dave, by Barbara, by the sea, by the howling chaos within him, by everything.

Barbara almost turned round when she reached the front and saw the sea. There was no one on the beaches near the pier, from above even the lower prom looked empty. But then it seemed silly not to check now she was so close.

As she walked she peered at distant faces, using a hand to hold flying hair out of her eyes, in case he was on his way home. Halfway down the steps to the lower prom the sea disappeared from view, hidden below the slope of the beach. She crossed the road at the bottom and hurried past the deserted funfair.

The playground structures were visible first as she rounded the dodgem car stadium, and then the hut behind. The door was ajar. She rushed across the concrete, face averted to snatch air from the wind, and wrenched the door wide. On the floor was a towel and a pile of clothes.

'Jesus Christ!' she gasped, and half ran, half scrambled over the pebbles, scanning the sea as it came into view. She almost fell over Billy before she noticed him.

'You haven't been swimming in this!' she cried, though it was obvious he had. She slithered to a sitting position beside him. 'You might have been killed!'

'Go away,' muttered Billy. He turned his face away. The moment I touch land, his thoughts groaned, they're on to me again.

Barbara wasn't sure if she'd heard him correctly, above the

wind and sea. She repeated the sounds in her head and decided she had.

'Don't be like that,' she said, hurt. 'I came to see how you were. Dave's just been round. He's sorry about lunchtime. He didn't understand.'

'Doesn't matter,' said Billy, still not looking at her. 'I'm going anyway, you needn't bother.'

'What?' said Barbara loudly, wishing he would face her, so hearing wasn't such a strain. 'What d'you mean, I needn't bother?' She pulled at his arm, wrapped round his legs. 'Hey,' she said reproachfully.

Billy shrugged.

'Where're you going, then?'

Billy shrugged again. 'Anywhere. I don't know. It doesn't matter.'

'But of course it matters.' She tugged at his arm anxiously. 'Billy? Of course it matters.' She wondered if something had happened she should know about. His arm was shivering.

'You're cold,' she told him. 'You can't sit here in this wind. You ought to get your towel.'

Billy swung round. His face was savage. 'I ought to do a lot of things,' he shouted, at pointblank range. 'Everybody's telling me what I ought to do. Dave wants me to go, you want me to go. Len wants me to stay. It's fucking easy for you lot, isn't it? All you've got to do is say it, you don't have to fucking do it.' He stabbed at his chest with a thumb. 'It's me's got to go, me's got to stay, me that's got to do everything. Shit . . .' He transferred the thumb to his forehead and rubbed it despairingly.

'Don't cry,' Barbara said, hearing a tremble in her own voice. 'Please don't cry.'

'I'm not crying,' he sobbed. 'I just can't do it. It's too much. You don't know what it's like. Nobody knows what it's like. I don't feel well, I think I'm going to explode . . . everything's happening at once and I can't do it all, I can't . . .'

Barbara recognised emergency. 'Come back to the hut,' she said, trying to sound very calm. 'We can't talk here.

210

Come on.' She stood up. 'Billy, come on.' She started to walk slowly back.

Billy rubbed his eyes with the balls of his palms, gave the sea a last desolate stare, and lurched to his feet.

Back at the hut Barbara picked up the towel from the floor. She tossed it to him as he approached.

'Get inside,' she said. 'Out of the wind.'

She waited outside while he changed, trying to set herself limits on what she could offer, when the desire simply to take him home with her was so overwhelming.

'Sit down a minute,' she said, when he was dressed. She pulled another deckchair into the shelter of the hut and patted it. 'Sit down. I want to talk.'

Billy sat down. 'I gotta go,' he said, more in control now. 'I've got to. It's killing me. I just gotta go.'

Barbara leant towards him. 'But what's killing you? What are all these things that are happening? Can you explain?'

Billy shook his head desperately. 'It's Len. Everything's Len. I gotta go. It's him. I've got to.'

'All right,' she said. She looked at him. 'OK,' she nodded, accepting that whatever was going on, it centred on escape from Len. 'I'm glad you've decided. But don't treat it as if it's the end, and nothing matters afterwards. It should be the beginning. You've got to have some idea where you're going to.'

Billy shook his head again.

'It's not all going to stop because you want it to,' she insisted. 'There's tomorrow and the next day and next week. You've got to think about it.'

Billy groaned and shifted position in the chair. It's too much for him, she thought hopelessly, it would probably be too much for anyone. She was silent a moment, then placed a hand on his knee.

'Listen,' she said. 'It's your day off tomorrow, isn't it? Leave tomorrow. It's too late tonight. Tomorrow you'll have the whole day to get organised. And you could have a look round. I know you won't find anywhere in a day but you might get a few addresses, something to start from. Use my address and phone number if you need to. You can leave your stuff in my room. Come round after work with it. You know when I'm back.' She sighed, and because there was no way she couldn't say it, added, 'And you can stay with me tomorrow night. I can see how frightening it must seem to jump off into nowhere. You can't stay long because I'll get chucked out if Mrs Barnstaple finds out, and news gets round however careful you are. But a couple of nights will be all right, I'm sure it will.' She squeezed his knee. 'You mustn't think that just because you've decided you're leaving I'm not interested any more. I don't know how you can think that. But you had to decide. And you must promise to look. We'll do it properly and sensibly. You buy the local paper tomorrow and make a few phone calls. And don't worry about deposits. I'll lend you the money if it comes to it.' Her father would help, she thought urgently. She never asked for money, he'd realise it was important. 'People do manage to find places,' she promised. 'Honestly. I'll help.'

'You think I'll find somewhere?' Billy was blinking and hugging his chest. He was rocking himself, Barbara noticed: the material behind him was moving.

'Of course,' she assured him. 'Don't get in a panic. We'll do all the things we have to. There's a couple of agencies near my work. It'll mostly be expensive central stuff, but they might be able to suggest somewhere else. That's how you do it, just keep asking, you get there in the end. I'll pop in at lunchtime. You do this end. That's how we'll start.' She was aware of convincing herself, as she reassured him.

Billy nodded, staring fixedly at the ground. Barbara leant forward, willing him to show more enthusiasm.

'Barb?' he asked, and lifted his head to look at her steadily. 'Why're you doing this?'

She nearly shrugged it off with a smile, but then saw that he meant it, and that her answer was going to be important to him. She thought about it a moment, seriously.

'Because I'm involved . . .' she started, and then paused. She didn't want to say 'And I feel I haven't any choice,' though it was true. She tried to work out why. 'Because I'm worried about you, and I know I'm a bit responsible. For the situation, I mean.'

'Do you like me?' he asked. 'Len says no one could like me. He says . . . he says horrible things about you. About why you bother with me.'

'Of course he does,' she said quickly, not wanting to hear them. 'You mustn't listen to him.' She hesitated. Billy was still looking at her. 'Oh, Billy,' she sighed, hating Len, 'of course people could like you. I do care about you, I promise.' That was what she should have said, she realised suddenly, never mind why; that she cared.

'I want you to like yourself,' she said gently, urging him to understand that she was trying to be honest. 'The more you like yourself, the more I'll like you. But I'll care about you anyway. You know that. I can't bear to see you so unhappy. Don't listen to Len, he's only trying to hurt you. People say horrible things to each other when they're angry, believe me, I know. Don't let him upset you.'

Billy dropped his eyes to work it out. He grasped that she was saying that Len might be right about him being unlike-able, but that he shouldn't worry about it because it was irrelevant to her feelings for him. In the end he was relieved because he had known Len was right, and now could believe both of them. And she seemed to be suggesting that *why* Len was saying it might be more important than the truth of it, and that she knew something about this too.

'Did you say horrible things to . . . I don't know his name . . .'

'Peter. Yes. And he said horrible things to me. I thought horrible things about him too, until I wrote him off.' She decided not to say anything about maybe writing him in again; she didn't want Billy to think her full attention wasn't on him.

'How did you write him off?' Billy thought it sounded rather frightening, writing someone off, though oddly attrac-tive, too.

'Oh . . .' Barbara shrugged, smiling. 'Told myself he wasn't worth it. Concentrated on all the things I didn't like about him. I've always found it easier to lose things when I've convinced myself they're worthless. I suppose I prefer being angry to being sad. It works too . . . I feel quite good while I'm doing it.'

'Was he really worthless?'

'No. Of course not.'

'Len thinks I'm worthless,' Billy said bleakly. 'He's been telling me that a lot.'

'No he doesn't, or he wouldn't say it. He wants you to be worthless. It's not at all the same.'

'Why should he want to make me worthless?'

'I don't know. Perhaps because he knows he's losing you. He needs to make you nothing, like I tried to do with Peter. Or perhaps he resents caring about you at all.'

'I don't know what he wants from me.'

'I don't think he wants anything from you,' she said emphatically. 'He just thinks you're his. It's a power trip, that's all. You can't win. But it's not your problem, it's his. Don't worry about it. Poor Billy . . .' She touched his leg. 'Has he been giving you a rough time?'

Billy didn't reply. He was staring upwards, at the coast road. For an instant he thought he had seen Len, leaning over the railings, but it wasn't, just a passing likeness.

'What is it?' asked Barbara, following his gaze.

'Nothing.' Billy shook his head. 'Thought I saw Len. He's been watching me. He said he saw me Friday . . . he knew I'd been to see you. He said he'd give me a thumping if I went round again.'

'Jesus,' whispered Barbara, and felt her skin crawl. She got to her feet hastily. 'Why didn't you tell me? Christ, I don't want to get you into trouble. Will you be all right tonight? Jesus . . .' A wave of outrage broke over her, at what they were being forced to accept, when it was perverted and dangerous and shouldn't have been allowed. She was angry too, and a little at Billy, for being so helpless and letting her sit there.

Billy nodded mutely, and suddenly found her fear intolerable. He sank back in the deckchair, turning his face away, and comforted himself by stroking his cheek against the cloth.

Barbara stared down at him, appalled. There ought to be someone you could ring, her thoughts cried, someone who would drop everything and come, when things were desperate and you didn't know what to do. And was he going to be safe, even after he'd left Len, when he would still be here at the playground, and so easy to find? And should she warn him, and frighten him more?

She squatted beside him.

'Billy?' She grasped his shoulders and made him stop the movement. His eyes were half-closed, he looked sleepy. 'Billy? Answer me. Are you going to be all right tonight?'

His eyes opened properly. 'Yes.' He nodded jerkily. 'I'll be OK.'

'He hasn't been hitting you, has he? You must tell me if he has.'

'No. He just says things. I'll be all right.'

'And you are going to come tomorrow, aren't you?'

'Yeah.' He nodded again. 'I'll come.'

'We'll do it,' she said, deciding they had to press on, that there was no other choice. If anything happened out here it would be public, it would be a crime, officially. Other people might help, he would be entitled to it.

She forced a smile. 'You wait and see. People move all the time. They manage. You will too.'

'Yes,' said Billy.

She squeezed his hand, and left.

Billy watched her until she was out of sight, then turned back to the cloth, and closed his eyes.

Barbara had a terrible dream, too, that night, so real it went on being terrible for seconds after it woke her, until her mind sorted out what was memory and what imagination.

She saw Len coming out of the sea, like he had the night Billy hit his head. Everything was the same, the darkness, the oily texture of the water, the fairytale lights of the pier, Sonia beside her, except that Len was carrying Billy in his arms this time. Billy was unconscious and soaked, his head hanging back, arms trailing. Len walked towards her up the pebbles, carrying him easily, as if he weighed nothing, and then just as she thought he was about to pass, turned and said, 'Here, you have him, then,' and thrust him at her. She tried to take him, had to take him, the way he was pushed at her, but he was large, because he was a man, and a man's weight, and she dropped him. His head hit the stones and he slid down the pebbly slope towards the sea, his body twisting and turning, so hideously limp and doll-like she knew he was dead, and she'd killed him. Sonia came and stood by her shoulder to peer down at him, and then sighed, putting a consoling hand on her arm, and said, 'There you are, then.'

22

The next morning it took Billy less than five minutes to bundle his possessions into the cardboard box, and pile his sleeping bag on top. By nine-thirty he was ready to leave.

Though he hadn't decided what to do about the food. He really ought to take it because he was definitely going, whatever happened, but on the other hand it was bulky, and would mean another cardboard box and two trips. And one trip might be hard enough, if what he was planning came off, never mind two. It was like having to consider two people, with different destinies; and in fact the notion was helpful, since the preparations weren't incompatible, until the end.

He resolved for the present to stick to being the Billy who was going to do things sensibly, as Barbara had told him. It would give him activities to fill the day, and then if Len called his bluff and he had no chance to be the other Billy, he would have done all the right things and they wouldn't have been wasted, and no one could accuse him of not intending to go in the first place.

He cleared the cupboard in the kitchen and heaped the contents on the table so he wouldn't forget about them. Then wondered what to do next. It was too early to get a local paper.

He lay down on the sofa for a rest: he'd had a bad night and thought he needed it; but after a couple of minutes decided it wasn't rest he needed, but action, and that he might as well spend the time checking out the newsagents' and sweetshop boards. For this, he remembered, he might need Barbara's address and phone number. The address was easy, because her house had an enormous twelve over the door, but he had no memory of her giving him the phone number. Then he realised it would be the same as Sonia's, and went to the window sill to look in Len's phone book.

There it was, under S, in curvaceous green-ink scrawl. He felt pleased to have solved that by himself, wrote the number in ballpoint on his hand, and let himself out the back.

Walking to the shops he began to wonder if he might not perhaps be ill, after all. When he had had the trouble with his ear he had felt fuzzy and remote too, his heart had missed and skittered in much the same way, the same white noise had buzzed in his head. He pressed the back of his hand against his forehead. It felt all right – if anything, rather cool – and he wasn't aching, or coughing, or feeling sick. He wasn't even, strictly speaking, feeling unwell. Just peculiar.

There were several 'suit professional couple, no children' on the three noticeboards he studied, and one 'fourth girl'. No single bedsits at all. That took twenty minutes. He decided to stroll on another mile to the council offices, where he remembered they had a large public noticeboard at the entrance to the foyer, under a 'Transfers' sign.

The walk took another twenty minutes. There were quite a lot of cards here. Among them were two offering lodgings, but both specified over twenty-fives. He went inside and asked a man behind a glassed-in desk why this was. The man said it was complicated, but it was to do with the new regulations and the advertisers were just covering themselves. Billy told the man he didn't have anywhere to go and needed somewhere pretty urgently, and the man smiled as if he'd heard it all before and asked if he were pregnant or married with children. Billy was offended because he didn't like being made to feel stupid, but then the man sighed and said he was sorry, he had only been kidding and he'd like to help, but there was nothing he could do. He pointed to a poster advertising a housing surgery at the Citizens' Advice Bureau on Monday evenings and said he might try there.

Billy was quite into being sensible and organised by now and let himself be encouraged by this, since it meant other people must have trouble with housing and something could be done about it, else they wouldn't bother to hold surgeries for it.

By now it was eleven-thirty, and the midday edition of the local paper was out. He bought a copy, picked up a cardboard box from a supermarket plus two Mars bars for his lunch, and went home.

As soon as he got in he flicked through the paper to the classified pages. There were lots of housing adverts, under two headings: 'Accommodation to Let' and 'Houses and Flats to Let'. Looking at the long lines of print made him feel quite excited, despite himself. He left it for a moment, to stash the food from the kitchen table into the box and dump it next to the other one on the sitting room floor, then spread the paper open on the carpet beside the boxes, unwrapped one of the Mars bars, and settled on his stomach to study it.

He dismissed the 'Houses and Flats to Let' after a quick skim through; even the one-bed flats were far too expensive. He turned to the 'Accommodation to Let'. Before he started reading he counted the entries: there were thirty-two.

He decided to be methodical and got up to get the ballpoint from the window sill. Then he read all the entries through. Then again, striking out the nine that specifically asked for young women. He scanned the rest. Among them, a few read oddly: they didn't seem very clear about the details of the accommodation they were offering, nor the prices they were renting at. They said things like 'central location' and 'from £25'. They must be agencies, he realised; he knew about agencies and to take no notice of the cheap come-ons, which wouldn't exist. They'd probably want big deposits too. Still, he didn't scrub them out. He did however strike through the five 'Full Board, DHSS welcome' which were all over a hundred pounds a week.

He seemed by now to have struck out or written A beside a fair number, and whatever was buzzing even louder in his head made him get up and go into the kitchen. The clock said 12.45. For something to do he filled the kettle and retrieved the coffee and sugar from the cardboard box. Moving around brought back a sugary aftertaste of the Mars bar he had eaten; he was suddenly aware of it as an unpleasant obstruction in his upper chest, as if he had swallowed the bar whole and it had jammed halfway down. He went to the bathroom, vomited into the toilet, and immediately felt better.

His concentration had returned by the time the coffee was made. He carried it back and placed it beside the paper on the floor. He picked up the pen and this time struck out the doubles, which ranged from forty-five pounds to seventy. He counted and found he was left with fourteen entries. 'Professional men' figured in several, but he hesitated before scoring them through as he wasn't quite sure what they meant by 'professional'. He had only heard it applied to lawyers and doctors and the like, and couldn't believe there were enough of that type to go round all the landlords who apparently wanted them. None of the ads specified 'young men' as they did with young women. He felt vaguely resentful on behalf of his peer group, whom nobody wanted; and at that point crossed out the 'professional men' because, whoever they were aimed at, he was sure it wasn't him.

What he had left now ranged from twenty-five pounds to forty pounds, depending on whether they were *incl.* or *excl.* He wondered how much you had to add to *excl.* to make comparisons with *incl.* Whatever it was, it looked as if he was going to have to be prepared to spend more than half his income on rent, and stay organised for a long time.

And then he remembered – it had been rather slipping away from him – that it wasn't going to happen until more important things had happened first, which made it less of a worry. He crossed out the three at forty pounds a week, circled the remaining six telephone numbers, and stared at them. He tried to imagine making the calls and what they might ask him, and had a horrible suspicion that he wouldn't be able to do it, that it was impossible.

He looked at his watch. It was two o'clock. Then he rolled on to his side on the carpet and closed his eyes, because he was feeling very odd.

A while later he thought he would like to hear a record

because, although he'd got the cassette player, he wouldn't have a proper stereo after today. He knelt in front of the alcove and started to leaf through Len's LPs, trying to make up his mind what he wanted to hear. But before he could decide the oddness attacked him again and he had to withdraw his hands and rest them on his knees.

He wondered if it was fear that made him feel like this and, if so, why he should be afraid when he couldn't lose, whatever happened. He wondered if your body made you feel like this when it knew it was going to get hurt, however much you told yourself it didn't matter and that there were more important things to protect. And that perhaps it was natural and didn't mean you were afraid in yourself, and might even be necessary to gear you up for what you had to expect.

He reminded himself that he didn't have to win, which was unlikely, anyway, as long as he got the chance to express what he wanted to express, and tried not to lose.

But he still wished Len would come home, so the waiting would be over and he wouldn't have to think about it, and imagine losing.

Barbara half-expected to see Billy waiting outside the house when she got back from work, and was relieved to find the street deserted: she had Sonia with her and hadn't told her about inviting him to stay. It would be obvious tomorrow morning, but she hoped to pass it off as a fait accompli: pretend Len had thrown him out, and she'd had no choice about it. She wanted to warn Billy to say this too; Sonia's mouth wasn't intentionally big, but her mother was friends with Mrs Barnstaple. She thought it would sound better all round if it came across as a crisis arrangement, agreed to in a moment of weakness and sympathy, rather than a pre-planned strategy.

This had seemed particularly important after visiting the two agencies at lunchtime. She hadn't been expecting much but it was still depressing to be proved right. Their best advice was that Billy get together with other youngsters and hunt for a house or flat as a ready-made group; in their opinion that was certainly the cheapest, and these days probably the only, way to do it. It meant finding a group first, then the accommodation. Both might be advertised, but a two-stage operation like that was never going to be completed in a couple of days, she could see.

Upstairs she changed into jeans and sweatshirt and lay on the bed to re-read the letter she had received from Peter that morning. The first love letter, indeed, she had ever received from anyone, since people who lived together didn't need to write, and the only serious boyfriend she'd had before Peter had lived within shouting distance, and so hadn't needed to either.

It read as if authorship was a new experience for Peter too, but somehow that made it seem more genuine, and it was gloriously long and gave the impression of something he had simply sat down and written, without worrying about style or structure, and gone on writing until he'd said what he wanted to say. Because it was written like that she could hear him saying it, and could feel her face pulling the tenderest expressions in response to it. She had even kissed one of the pages at work. It was the page where he wrote 'You put laughter in my heart'; the letter was crammed with clichés like that, but they were so innocently written, and so patently original for him, that they melted into sincerity in the mind.

The same words touched her again now. An image of herself was conjured up, as she had been: an implanter of laughter, a soft, giving, shining image, lovable and cherishable, because she had been loved and cherished. It's a loaded game, she sighed – though with the secret joy of the advantaged – to be more likeable when you're liked, more lovable when you're loved.

There was no mention of future footings in the letter, for which she was grateful. It was all about feelings and friendship, without any attempt to organise her into anything. Only at the end, as an afterthought, almost, was tacked on *Can I come and see you Saturday? Eleven o'clock your place. Ring if I can't.*

And somehow the thought that Billy might still be here – almost certainly would be, bar a miracle – did not diminish her delight. From the first, Peter would see her new self; in her new life, on her own ground, and beside her own new friends.

'I'm going, Len,' said Billy, rising from the sofa as Len entered the room. 'Thanks a lot, but I'm going.'

Len stared at the boxes. Billy stood beside them and waited.

'Creeping off, were you?' asked Len, expressionless.

'No. I was waiting for you. To tell you.'

Len lifted his gaze from the boxes to Billy.

'Where the fuck you going, just like that?'

'I'm going to get a room somewhere.'

'You've got a room here, shithead.'

'I want a place of my own.' Billy was keeping his voice low and soft, it was the only way he trusted it.

'You're setting up with that bitch, aren't you?' Len said nastily. 'Told you she'd get her claws into you.'

'No, I'm not. On my own. Not with her.'

'How the hell d'you think you're going to manage on your own? You can't wipe your arse without being told what to do. Where the hell's this place, anyway?'

'I've got a couple of numbers to ring,' Billy said evasively. 'I'll see you around, 'spect.'

'Like hell you will, pillock. What a thing to announce.' Len put on a whiny falsetto, 'I'm going, thanks a lot but I'm going. You can't just go.'

'I can,' nodded Billy. 'I'm going now.'

'Like hell you are.' Len snatched up the clothes box and shook the contents over the floor. 'Fucking little shit. Where're you going?'

Billy said nothing. He stared at his possessions tumbled on the floor, and squatted down to start piling them back inside. It was very difficult to do with Len standing over him.

'Answer me,' hissed Len, and made to cuff him. Billy flinched at the feinted blow. Len gave it to him the second time, with the side of his hand against his ear. The force knocked him off balance, on to his knees.

'I'm going,' he repeated, getting back into position. 'I'll still see you round.'

He piled the things back into the box. He stuffed his towel round the personal stereo, just in case. He felt his ear grow hot.

As he rose to his feet Len caught him again, across the cheek. Billy staggered but kept his footing.

'I don't want to fight about it,' he lied. He felt a brief impulse to fly at Len there and then, but nothing happened. He prayed it would come instinctively, when the moment was right.

'I don't care what you want,' sneered Len. 'She put you up to this, didn't she? You're not telling me it was your idea. You're going round there now, aren't you? You've nowhere else to go.'

'It's me who wants to go,' said Billy. 'She's just helping out. She's a friend.'

'Friend like shit,' snapped Len. 'She wants to take you over. Like the rest. Bloodsuckers the lot of them. You don't want to fall for that one.'

'I want to go.' Billy indicated himself with a thumb. 'I want it.'

Len lunged at him, but Billy was ready and sidestepped the blow. He was aware of making Len look silly.

'It's not such a big deal,' he murmured, wishing things wouldn't happen so fast, making him react the wrong way. 'I should have told you before. Barbara said I should. It was me who didn't want to. Barbara said it wasn't right just to go. That's why I stayed, to do it properly.' He knew that every time he said 'Barbara' he was inflaming the atmosphere. He was tempted to shout 'Barbara, Barbara!' to bring it to a head quickly.

Len was removing his suit jacket. He tossed it on to the back of the sofa. Then undid the top button of his shirt and yanked off his tie.

'You should have just hopped it, kiddo.' He laughed

unpleasantly, rolling up his sleeves. 'Never mind what that bitch said. Now you've screwed it both ways, haven't you? Left it too late, but not late enough.' He beckoned. 'C'm here, Billy, c'm here.'

Billy frowned and shook his head. However it started, it wasn't going to be by obeying orders.

Len gestured at him impatiently. 'Come here, Billy. What're you afraid of?' He stood back to regard Billy, and smiled. 'You're shaking again. You only have to think about leaving and you're shaking. What're you going to be like in a place of your own, eh?'

'I'll be OK,' breathed Billy, trying to appear more in control. 'I'm just nervous.'

'Scared of me, are you? So you should be. You can't do anything right, can you? Can't arrive properly, can't live properly, can't go properly. You're a mess, aren't you?'

'If you say so.'

'And you can't even fucking stand up for yourself!' shouted Len, infuriated. 'You're such a prick I don't know why I ever bothered with you. You're nothing, you hear, nothing.'

'I'm going, aren't I?' retorted Billy. 'I'm not nothing. I'm doing something now. I can't win with you. If I don't do anything I'm nothing, and if I do, it drives you mad.'

'That's it.' Len nodded triumphantly. 'You can't do anything right. That's it exactly. The way you are. Born loser. Hope Barbara realises that, lucky girl.' He had been moving forward as he spoke and was now close enough to reach Billy, who could have retreated, but didn't.

He put his hands on Billy's upper arms.

'You want to leave,' he said smoothly. 'Go on, then, you leave. Go on, go now.'

Billy looked at Len's hands. Now the moment was near he was scared. He was still going to do it, but it didn't stop him being scared.

'You like me doing this?' asked Len, wrapping his fingers more tightly round Billy's arms. He shook him lightly. 'Come on, Billy, don't be a girl. Have some pride. Show me how much you want to leave.'

'I'm going now,' said Billy, fear making him give Len one last chance, and tried to turn.

'Not yet you aren't,' hissed Len.

Billy could see all sorts of things in Len's eyes, some of them not Len at all.

'I hate you,' he whispered, fury rising at last; and knew this was the moment, now.

Barbara was patrolling her bedsit. She was trying to decide if she was going to let Billy share the bed with her, or make him use the sleeping bag on the floor. All in all, to be in keeping with the arrangement and bearing in mind what had happened last time, it should really be the bag. The foam cushions of the armchair put end to end would make about five feet of mattress, and he must have slept on more uncomfortable floors.

She looked at her watch. She wished he would hurry up, so she could get things organised. She'd gone down to check the hall earlier, in case he had dumped his stuff during the day and she had somehow missed it on her way in, but found nothing. She was doing her best to imagine him wandering around town, oblivious of the time, though the mental picture did strike her as slightly odd, when he must have a large cardboard box in tow. Surely that at least would remind him. Typical of him to be late, she thought impatiently, he can't do anything right.

Len's right eye was streaming where Billy's fist had landed a direct hit.

'You're trying hard,' he said breathlessly, wrestling Billy across the upstairs landing. 'It won't do you no good.'

Billy didn't reply, because he was trying so hard, but he didn't agree. He had lost the offensive early on, but he had had it for a time, until Len recovered from the onslaught. Long enough to appreciate his achievement, and glory in it. He had seen no reason to conserve his strength – there was nothing to save it for – and his anger had waited so long its release astounded both of them, for a short while. Even now he was losing he didn't need to push himself into resistance. His body was doing it all for him, without being told, even when it was most pointless and wasteful.

In the doorway to Len's bedroom his legs buckled.

'Uh uh,' said Len, hoiking him up by the front of his t-shirt. 'This way.' He twisted the material tight into his fist and dragged Billy across the room.

'Hurting now?' he asked savagely, crashing his hand across Billy's face.

Billy sprawled back on to Len's bed, his nose pouring blood. His strength had gone. Len could hold him down onehanded and hit or strip him with the other, as he chose.

'I don't agree to this,' he gasped a few minutes later, as Len yanked at the waistband of his jeans.

'All the better,' hissed Len, rolling him on to his stomach and punching him in the kidneys.

'You're doing this,' mumbled Billy, too exhausted even to arch with pain. 'I'm not to blame.'

'Too right,' rasped Len's voice, from above him. 'Too fucking right.'

By seven o'clock Barbara's vision of Billy trailing round town with a cardboard box which had escaped his notice was no longer sustainable. Either he had changed his mind about coming, or something was preventing him. She worked at convincing herself that the former was more likely, since he had had the whole day to escape; even if Len had been taking time off work to check up on him he would hardly do it on Billy's day off, when his location would be unpredictable.

However, the alternative was still a possibility, which made her very anxious. And, indeed, even if Billy had decided not to leave, it seemed the height of thoughtlessness not to have let her know – a note through the door would have been enough – when he should surely have realised how much it would worry her.

At seven-fifteen she suddenly couldn't bear it any longer. She grabbed her handbag, slammed out of the bedsit, and set off for the house. As long as she was tactful when she got there, she told herself – in case he had genuinely changed his mind – the only person likely to receive abuse was herself, and she was willing to put up with that.

Len's Montego was outside the house. From the doorstep she tried to get a view into the sitting room through the bay window. But the room was unlit and the net curtains prevented her from distinguishing anything except a general sense that the room was unoccupied. There was no movement in the greyness and she heard no voices. She rang the bell.

The figure of Len opened the door to her, turned his back immediately, and walked down the corridor towards the kitchen. Barbara could only assume from this that he had been expecting her. She followed, stepping over a pile of jackets that had fallen from the coat rack at the bottom of the stairs.

In the kitchen she found him washing his face in the sink, bent low over the bowl. She glanced through the archway into the sitting room and saw two cardboard boxes on the carpet, one overturned and its contents scattered about. The house seemed very quiet.

'You want him,' Len said thickly, still hunched over the sink. 'You fucking have him.'

Barbara thought he sounded upset, and that perhaps that was why he wouldn't face her.

'I don't want him,' she said calmly. Since the boxes made it obvious, she went on, 'He's only leaving. You must have known it would happen some time.'

'Right,' said Len, dabbing at his eyes with a tea towel. 'See how you like him dumping on you instead.'

'He's not going to be staying with me,' repeated Barbara. 'He's going to find his own place.'

'You really think that?' sneered Len. 'Pull the other one.'

'He is,' said Barbara, irritated. 'And he might have done it sooner if it hadn't been for you, knocking him down every time he tried to do something for himself.'

Len swung round, furious. Barbara stared at his face. There was a livid bruise along the line of his jawbone and one of his eyes was hugely swollen.

'So it's all me, is it?' he shouted. 'What d'you know about anything? Interfering cow. D'you know what that kid was when he came here?' He pushed his face close to Barbara's; the distortions made it look inhuman. 'Dead on his feet, that's what he was. No home, no money, no friends, except junkies and worse. Out of his head half the time. He shook. You seen a kid that shakes? Like an old man. Don't you tell me it's my fucking fault. I took a risk having him here. He could have stabbed me while I was asleep, ripped the place off, you name it. I took all the risks, he did nothing, not a thing. He lives off my back, ungrateful little sod.'

'So why'd you do it?' Barbara shouted back, fear making her angrier. 'Why pick him up to treat him like dirt? He's got to go.' She lowered her voice. 'Where is he? Please tell me.'

Len's mouth tightened. For a terrible moment Barbara thought he was going to hit her. She froze, suddenly sensing that if she retreated or showed her fear, he would. He stood motionless, until the tension left his body, then brushed past into the sitting room and snatched up his jacket from the sofa.

'Little shit,' he snapped, putting it on jerkily. 'You're welcome to him. I don't want to find him here when I get back, you understand? You want him, you fucking have him, and good luck to you. And if I find he's taken anything of mine I'll come over and finish him off, you tell him.'

'Oh, Jesus,' whispered Barbara. There was only the bathroom and Len's bedroom; she didn't like to think of Billy, silent, in either.

Len lurched out of the sitting room. She heard the front door open, and slam behind him.

Billy wasn't in the bathroom. She mounted the stairs, feeling she was entering forbidden and dangerous territory.

Halfway up, she noticed that two of the banister struts were broken, and the stair carpet rucked.

229

23

Billy couldn't believe that he could be this tired, and still be awake. He had managed to roll on to his back, then discovered that it wasn't such a good idea, but couldn't seem to do anything about it. His arms turned out to be above his head and didn't respond to any of the normal messages, although he hadn't completely given up on them. He wasn't sure if it was the messages or the arms themselves that were at fault, but hoped the connection might come soon, when he stopped being so tired. The worst thing was the blood flowing from his nose, which, now he was on his back, he was being forced to swallow. It had run into his eyes as well, and not being able to see properly was bothering him. But he wasn't feeling that bad otherwise, because although the swallowing was an effort it seemed to happen more or less automatically, and nothing else hurt too much, and he knew he'd done everything right.

He had heard the door bell ring, and movement in the corridor, and then angry voices in the kitchen, Len's and Barbara's, and although they were angry he thought they were probably sorting something out, and someone would come up soon and tell him what was going to happen. He hoped it would be Barbara, as he had had enough of Len, and while he knew Len couldn't hurt him any more, and probably didn't even want to, he would prefer never to have to see him again. The front door slamming worried him a little, since it meant someone had left, but then he heard footsteps on the stairs and knew they weren't Len's.

Barbara couldn't make sense of Len's bedroom. It was huge and full of machinery. There was shiny metal and red plastic and all sorts of unfamiliar shapes and angles. Then over by the window she saw a kingsize bed and, lying on the bed, a brown body, smeared with red.

'Oh, Billy!' she cried, running over. 'Oh, God!'

'It wasn't my fault,' Billy whispered, seeing her through a red haze. 'I didn't let it happen.'

'No,' Barbara gasped, using the edge of the sheet to wipe the blood from his eyes. 'I've seen Len. Oh, Jesus, what has he done?'

'I'm OK,' Billy murmured when he could see her expression properly. 'I'm OK.' He tried to smile and disturbed a swallow. It made him cough, a horrible strain.

'Oh, God,' Barbara moaned, seeing him spitting up blood and not knowing where it was coming from. 'I've got to call an ambulance.'

'No,' Billy spluttered. The coughing seemed to have released something. The feeling in his arms was returning. 'I don't want to go to hospital. Please.' He would get lost in hospital, he knew he would, he couldn't start again. 'Barb!' he called, suddenly convinced she had gone.

'I'm here,' she said, very close to him. She wiped the side of his face with the sheet.

'I want to stay with you tonight. Just tonight. I won't be any trouble.'

'Oh, shut up,' Barbara choked. She stared at him, anguished. The thought of sending him away seemed awful to her too: strangers in uniform touching him. 'Is anything broken?' she asked, giving him a tiny chance.

Billy thought back to arms and legs and couldn't remember anything like that. He shook his head, showing her a bit of movement. 'I've packed,' he whispered.

'But Billy, I can't carry you.' She wasn't even sure she could dress him.

'I'll manage,' said Billy. 'Give me a minute. I'm just tired.'

'But there's blood in your mouth. I don't like it.' It was an effort to speak, through the crush of indecision.

'It's only my nose.' Billy braced himself on his arms and managed to sit up. 'I'm OK, Barb,' he said. 'Please.'

She picked up his jeans, in a bundle at the end of the bed.

'Dress yourself, then,' she said.

'OK,' said Billy.

She passed him his clothes. She only had to help with his jeans and trainers.

She stood back. 'All right,' she sighed. 'You wait there. I'll ring for a taxi.'

She raced downstairs and called a taxi. They askèd where to, and sounded reluctant when she told them, pointing out that it was only round the corner, a couple of hundred yards or so.

'It's for a disabled person,' she gabbled. 'And he's got luggage. I'll pay anything you like. Please.'

The man mulled it over and then said, 'Ten minutes,' grudgingly, as if he wanted her to know he thought she'd pulled a fast one.

When she emerged from the sitting room she saw Billy at the top of the stairs, hanging on to the banister.

'Where's Len?' he asked.

She ran up to him. 'He's gone out,' she said, grasping his elbow. 'I don't think he'll be back for some time. Just take it slowly.' This is crazy, she thought, if he falls I'll never catch him.

'I waited for him,' Billy said, halfway down. 'I told him I was leaving.'

'*Why* did you?' Barbara groaned. 'You didn't have to do that.'

'I wanted to,' said Billy. He couldn't think of a better way of putting it. He nodded. 'I wanted to.'

'Sit down,' she said, when they reached the bottom. She pushed him on to the third step. 'I'll get the boxes.'

She flew round the sitting room repacking the spilled box. Someone had trodden on the headphones of Billy's personal stereo and broken them. She sobbed 'Oh, no,' inexplicably – they were only stupid headphones – and then inside a towel found the player, which looked undamaged. She placed it carefully in the box.

When everything was packed she dragged the box into the hall. She looked at Billy, his head sagging, and wondered if the taxi driver would take them. If he passed out she would definitely call an ambulance. Once he couldn't object, she would have to.

She went back for the food box and then opened the front door.

Billy raised his head. There were fresh red splashes on his t-shirt, from his nose.

'Oh, Christ,' she moaned. She rummaged through the heap of outdoor clothes on the floor and tossed his jacket towards him. 'Hang on,' she said, to save him struggling to get it on yet. 'I'll just get a cloth.'

He looked less gruesome after she'd cleaned him up again, and at least the jacket was black, so new spots wouldn't be as conspicuous. She zipped it up to his neck. A white minicab pulled up outside.

'Get straight in the back,' she urged. 'Don't look at him. I'll do the talking.' She had to help him get up. 'Can you make it?' She was reluctant to let go of him in case he fell. 'If you can't, I'll have to call an ambulance.'

Billy nodded, strengthened by the threat. The problem was in his thighs: they felt horribly stiff and trembly.

'Quick,' Barbara hissed, ducking down to view the driver. All she could see was a weasly face, and glasses. 'Now,' she said, tugging him on. 'Before he gets out of the car.'

They made it to the back door of the taxi. As she was bundling him inside, the driver got out.

'What's up with him?' he frowned, walking round the front of the car. He had a disgruntled expression on his face, as if they had drawn lots for this useless trip in the office, and he had lost.

'He's an epileptic,' she said desperately. 'He's had a fit and he hit his nose but he's all right now, just tired. I'm taking him home.'

'Oh,' said the driver, looking faintly disgusted.

'There's a couple of boxes too,' Barbara added. 'I won't be a minute.' Please take him, she pleaded silently, we're almost there.

She stored the boxes in the boot and climbed into the front

of the car. The driver got in beside her and adjusted the interior mirror. She wished Billy would sit up properly, instead of sagging sideways on the seat. The upholstery was fawn, and would show anything.

'It's just round the corner,' she said, willing the man to turn the key.

'I realise that,' he said. He glanced round. 'Are you sure he shouldn't go to hospital?'

'No,' said Billy loudly, sitting up and taking notice.

Barbara leant towards the man. 'They don't like to be taken to hospital for a fit,' she confided, with silent apologies to Billy and the epileptics of the world. 'He'll be fine after a rest.'

The driver sighed and switched on the ignition. Barbara expelled a vast quantity of air, as quietly as she could.

The journey took less than twenty seconds. The driver unloaded the boxes but left Billy to her. She propped him against the wall in the hall and hustled the driver outside to pay him.

Billy murmured, 'Oh, shit,' as she returned, and slid down the wall to the floor. She couldn't get him up.

'I'll get Sonia,' she panted, more to herself than him, and dashed for the stairs. Please God, she prayed, let no one else appear.

She banged her knee on one of the treads of the upper flight. She wouldn't have believed it possible, if it weren't for the painful evidence she had done it. Her eyes were watering as she pummelled on Sonia's door.

'You've got to help me,' she burst out, as the door opened. 'Len's beaten up Billy and I can't get him up the stairs.'

Sonia stood before her, immaculate in white jersey silk over tight yellow jeans, looking quite unfitted for carrying injured men up stairs. Barbara felt an awful distance between them, sensing she was part of a world Sonia had left and had no desire to be dragged back into. She grabbed her arm and hauled her through the door. 'Please,' she begged, realising momentum was her best asset. 'Just come.'

She got her as far as the half-landing on the first flight.

Billy was in sight below, huddled against the wall, knees drawn to his chest, looking unconscious.

'What are you doing!' cried Sonia. 'For God's sake, call an ambulance!'

'No,' said Billy instantly, raising his head. He pulled his legs in tighter and groaned.

'What's wrong with him?' Sonia was creeping down the stairs, despite herself. 'Why's he sitting like that?'

'He must be OK,' Barbara insisted. 'He walked to the taxi. He must be all right. It's just the stairs. Please help. I'll take responsibility.'

Sonia approached gingerly, pushing up her sleeves.

'He's bleeding,' she said accusingly. Sonia was squeamish about blood, even her own.

Barbara thought that, like the stairs, if she started getting him up, Sonia would help without being forced to make a decision about it.

'Come on, Billy,' she said, and slid her hand under his armpit. Len had picked him up easily on the beach, she remembered; she wished she knew how.

Sonia helped, but in tight-lipped silence. Barbara felt more and more criminal. As they approached her door and she began to think further than just getting him there, she thought again how much simpler it would be if he fainted, and she could send for an ambulance.

Sonia released him at the door, as if determined to do only the minimum asked. 'I'm not going to help any more,' she hissed. Her voice had a tremble of anger in it, or it could have been fear. 'I'm going out in ten minutes. This is stupid. You can't keep him here. You know he ought to go to hospital.'

Barbara was too busy supporting Billy's weight while she struggled with the door to reply. By the time it was open Sonia's feet were clattering reproachfully upstairs.

She got him two steps into the room before she had to let him go. Billy, safely home, and with no reason to try any longer, slid slowly to the floor and curled up on the carpet.

She closed the door, stifled the wail that wanted to tell her that this was all too much for her, and gave up the idea of trying to get him on to the bed. I'm out of my depth, she moaned to herself, no one could expect me to cope on my own.

Suddenly she knew who she wanted to help her cope. But there was no way of contacting her, or getting her here. She leant back against the door and squeezed her eyes shut. Then snapped them open, pushed herself abruptly away, and fumbled with the clasp of her handbag. There was one way, and it was ridiculous and quite unreasonable, but since it was the only way, she was going to do it. She rifled through the handbag, dimly aware of saying 'Oh, God, oh, God,' to herself as she scrabbled, and, on the second search, found it, the little card with Dave and Jane's number on it.

'I'm going downstairs to make a phone call,' she said to the air around Billy, and ran downstairs.

As she dialled the number she prayed it would be Dave. Please let it be Dave, her lips said, as the number rang.

It was Jane, cool and business-like. For a moment Barbara thought she was an answering machine.

'This is Barbara,' she said uncertainly. 'Jane?'

'Oh, hello.' It was a real person; the voice had a tinge of interest in it now.

'I'm sorry to bother you,' Barbara found herself saying, dredging up a telephone manner. 'But can I speak to Dave? It's . . . it's rather important.'

'He's in the bath,' Jane said, shifting into neutral. 'Can I take a message?'

'Oh, God.' Barbara felt it all slipping away. There didn't seem to be any way of putting it in a message. 'It's terribly important,' she begged. 'I'm sorry. I must speak to him. Please.'

The conversation was briefly deadlocked.

Then Jane said, flatly but miraculously, 'Right, hang on, I'll get him.'

There was a clattering noise in her ear, followed by a distant, 'Phone, Dave,' a gap, and then a slightly exasperated, 'Well, you'll just have to, it's important.' A longer gap was followed by a quieter, 'Barbara. Christ knows.'

'Hello?' said Dave's voice. Barbara had to steady herself against the wall. She was crying, she realised, the mouth-piece was wet.

'Dave,' she gasped. 'I need Maggie. Len's beaten Billy up and he's lying on my floor and I can't move him. I want Maggie.'

'Barbara?' asked the voice sharply. 'Are you all right?'

'Yes yes . . . no no, I'm not. I want Maggie. I need her. She's not on the phone. I'm sorry. I couldn't think of anyone else to ring.'

There was a short pause, then Dave said in a low voice, almost to himself, 'I'd better come over.'

'I want Maggie,' sobbed Barbara. 'I want you to bring her. Please.'

'Barbara,' said Dave sternly. 'Calm down. You say Billy's at your place?'

'Yes, I found him at Len's.' She took a shuddering breath and tried to sound rational. 'I got him here in a taxi and he nearly didn't take us but he's here now and I can't manage on my own. I don't know what to do. I must go back to him. Please get Maggie. She lives . . . oh, God . . .' She rubbed her face frantically. She couldn't think how to explain it. She didn't even know the number of the house.

'I know where she lives,' said Dave. The words hovered, wondrously, over the silence that followed. 'OK,' he said at last. 'If she's there and agrees to come I'll bring her. See you in twenty minutes.' He rang off.

Barbara put the phone down, astounded that something so enormous could be achieved simply by demanding it. Even with Jane. Jane had believed her and made Dave listen, just because she'd begged her to.

She wiped her face properly and picked up one of the boxes. Dave had said twenty minutes. They must live near Maggie, she thought, that's how he knows her address.

Upstairs she had to elbow the door open; it hit Billy's legs as it swung wide.

She put the box down and knelt beside him to stroke his head. There was no point attempting to move him now, with the others coming. She had no doubt it would be both of them: that Dave would find Maggie in, and prepared to drop everything for her sake. It was a crisis; other people had acknowledged it.

'Are you all right?' she murmured, thinking he didn't look too uncomfortable. 'Can I do anything?'

She had interrupted Billy in the middle of a fantasy. He breathed, 'OK, I'm OK,' hearing her words from a long way away. In his fantasy his mother's face had just dissolved into surprised and tender delight. He'd borrowed the story line from an Interflora advertisement on the television. In it a small child walked up the path to a suburban house, rang the bell, and stood by patiently. The door was opened by a woman with an expression of polite inquiry, transformed instantly into delight as she recognised the child, and had the flowers he was carrying thrust into her hands. In the advertisement the woman was meant to be the child's grand-mother, but in Billy's fantasy she was his mother, and it wasn't flowers he pressed into her arms, but himself. He dragged himself reluctantly away from the image; Barbara was still speaking.

'Dave's coming round,' she was saying. 'Billy, can you hear me? Dave's coming round. I can't manage on my own. He's coming to help. You don't mind, do you?'

Billy sorted it out. He didn't mind what she did, as long as she didn't send him away. 'I want to stay here,' he whispered.

'That's why he's coming,' Barbara said, hoping it was true. 'So you can. He's going to bring Maggie. You remember Maggie, Len's wife. She's nice, you'll like her. If you're going to stay I'll need some help. You do understand?'

'Yes,' said Billy. The image of his mother's face was fading. He thought how awful it would be to tell her, especially when he had just delighted her. He wondered if he was brave enough, and whether she would ever forgive him; or herself. Then, whether he would ever be able to forgive her, for wearing the mask, and not knowing.

'Are you cold?' asked Barbara, noticing his legs were trembling.

'No,' said Billy. 'I'm fine. I just got cramp.' Saying it made it happen again. 'Oh, Jeez,' he moaned weakly, as his legs jerked.

Barbara didn't know what to do about cramp. People took salt for it, she thought hazily, but didn't feel she could ask him to eat salt. She rubbed his thighs, because she couldn't think of anything else to do, and watched the dial on the back of her wrist.

After eighteen minutes the doorbell rang. Two short rings; Maggie, Barbara thought with a rush of gratitude. She got to her feet.

She couldn't escape the feeling, as she let them in, that the grown-ups had arrived. For a moment she saw them as a couple, as parents almost, coming to deal with everything.

She hid her relief by picking up the other cardboard box, which Dave immediately took off her. Maggie grasped her arm. 'Oh, Barbara,' she said, with such concern Barbara wanted to give up and howl. She battened it down, but let Maggie keep her arm around her as they mounted the stairs.

'Careful with the door,' she managed waveringly, as Dave prepared to push it open. 'Billy's behind it.'

'Oh, my dear,' Maggie breathed as she entered, and released her to kneel down beside Billy.

'How the hell did you get him here?' Dave's voice was grim. He put the box on the floor against the wall.

'He walked,' Barbara said. 'And I got a taxi. Sonia helped me get him upstairs, but I think she's gone out now. She thought I ought to call an ambulance.'

'No,' mumbled Billy.

'He just keeps saying that,' she said, crying. 'He keeps saying he's OK and he doesn't want to go to hospital. I don't know what to do.'

'Billy?' asked Dave, squatting down opposite Maggie. 'If you're so fine, why won't you get up? What's wrong?'

'He's got cramp,' said Barbara. 'And he's tired. He says that's all it is.'

Maggie reached for one of Billy's wrists and felt for his pulse. They all waited.

She nodded. 'It feels OK.' She passed the wrist over to Dave. 'You feel it. It's quite strong and slow. He's not in shock.'

'He did walk,' repeated Barbara. 'Honestly.' She was beginning to feel that she had been terribly stupid, that she probably shouldn't have moved him at all. She'd never thought of things like pulse.

'Have you been unconscious, Billy?' Dave asked. 'Can you remember?' He peered into Billy's ears, and then opened his eyes, one by one; like the policeman, thought Barbara, it must show all sorts of things I don't know about.

'I'm OK,' said Billy tetchily, averting his face. 'I remember everything. I don't want to go to hospital.'

Dave exchanged looks with Maggie. She shrugged minutely. He rose.

'Are you prepared to have him overnight if he doesn't go? Like this?'

'Yes,' said Barbara. She cleared her throat. 'Yes,' she repeated, less squeakily. 'He was coming here, anyway. Those are his things. Just for a couple of days, till he found somewhere. That's why Len . . .' Her voice choked. She gestured at the floor.

Dave rubbed his jaw, staring at Billy. Then turned to Maggie. 'What d'you think, then?'

'He ought to see a doctor.'

Dave nodded, as if she'd confirmed his own thoughts. He swung round to Barbara. 'You're definite he's moved under his own steam since this happened?'

'Yes.' She swallowed hard. 'It was only the stairs he couldn't manage.'

'OK,' he said. 'One thing at a time. Let's get him on the bed before someone falls over him.'

240

Billy's legs jerked, very noticeably. He made an urgent gasping noise.

'Shit,' said Dave, and knelt down again quickly. He grasped one of Billy's legs and straightened it, kneading the underside of the thigh, then replaced it and repeated the procedure with the other. Billy's gasps eased.

'Just relax,' Dave said, waving Maggie into position the other side. 'We're going to get you on the bed. You don't have to do anything. Don't think about it.' He slipped his hands under Billy's shoulders and the backs of his knees. Maggie did likewise.

'Christ, Billy,' he muttered, when he was upright and Maggie had pulled away. 'You're heavier than you look.' He carried him to the bed and laid him on the quilt.

Maggie started to unlace Billy's trainers. Dave flexed his shoulders and took out his wallet.

'Don't suppose you've got a doctor, have you, Billy?' Billy didn't reply, but Dave didn't seem to expect it. He leafed through a wad of cards. 'I'll ring mine. He's a lazy sod but he'll come for money.' He shot a glance at Maggie, who nodded, and then at Barbara. 'You happy with that?'

'Yes,' said Barbara. She was conscious, suddenly, of their dependence on his power: his car, his strength, his money; and experienced a stab of anger, alongside the gratitude. Then she recalled who had summoned up that power, and that he had just – this minute in fact – sought her approval to use it. The anger withdrew.

Dave was bending over Billy. 'We're going to call a doctor. Hey, you listening? If you're as all right as you claim you can stay. OK?'

Billy said, 'OK,' automatically. He was only vaguely listening. Ever since being placed on the bed he had been wrestling with the bizarre conviction that this room, and its occupants, were his mother. Barbara was a bit of her, definitely, and the woman with the gentle voice who was sitting beside him, holding his hand. But Dave seemed to be as well, which was odd. He wondered if he'd got the word wrong, and 'mother' wasn't exactly what he meant. He thought it comforting, though, to realise that whatever it was, it could be found here, that he might not have to pin everything on his real mother, in case it was too late for her.

The kind woman at his side smiled at him. He smiled back but he must have done it wrong, because it made the corner of her eyes crinkle and her chin bob, as if he had hurt her instead. She squeezed his hand tightly and looked away.

Dave disappeared downstairs to the phone. Barbara wanted to say something very important to Maggie, but not in front of Billy.

'What have you done with Jacey?' she substituted. 'I'm sorry, I couldn't think of anyone else.'

Maggie looked up. 'It's all right. The couple next door have got her. She was ready for bed. I told you they were a godsend. She'll spend the night.'

'Dave lives near you, does he? You got here so quickly.'

'Not really.' Maggie gave her a flickering smile. 'He drives fast.' She paused, replaced Billy's hand on the bedcover, and walked over.

'Did you see Len?' she asked quietly.

'Yes. He told me to take Billy away.'

'Were you frightened? You must have been.'

'Not really. Well, yes . . . I don't know.' Barbara glanced over to the bed. 'Maggie . . .'

What she was going to say was cut off by the sound of feet pounding up the stairs.

'Right,' Dave announced, bursting into the room. 'Ten minutes.' He regarded Barbara. 'Take her out for a drink,' he told Maggie. 'I'll have to wait. He won't want us all crowded round. Go to the Eagle, on the corner. Nobody goes there. I'll join you afterwards and give you the score.'

Maggie nodded. She nudged Barbara. 'Tell Billy you're going. Tell him you'll be back soon.'

'OK,' said Billy, when she'd told him. 'Can I stay here?'

'If the doctor says so. Dave'll stay with you. We won't be long.'

'I'll get these things off him,' said Dave, and started to

unzip Billy's jacket. 'Ah, shit,' he muttered. He reached for tissue to mop blood spots off the pillow.

Barbara watched him hopelessly. She felt she ought to be stopping him, or at least warning him, before the doctor examined Billy, but she couldn't think how to say it.

'Come on,' said Maggie, catching her arm. 'Dave'll deal with it.'

Barbara followed her out of the room but halted halfway down the first flight of stairs. Maggie hesitated a few steps further down and glanced back up at her.

'He didn't have any clothes on,' Barbara said.

'What?' Maggie frowned.

'Billy. When I found him. He was on Len's bed. There was blood . . . I think they're going to know. Oh, God.'

Maggie stared at her, and then at the closed door above them. She shook her head, and snatched at Barbara's hand. 'C'mon,' she said, her voice hollow.

'That's why I didn't call an ambulance,' sobbed Barbara as they walked towards the pub. Passers-by were staring at her but she didn't care, because it was terrible, and she had every reason to cry. 'I thought he had the right . . . I can't explain . . . I couldn't make him, not when he didn't want to. And, Christ, I felt so responsible. I had to do the right thing, only I didn't know what it was. I should have known . . . I did know, really . . . Billy knew . . . I didn't take it seriously enough. If Billy had been a girl and I'd been a bloke we'd never have behaved like this, we'd have known how danger-ous it was. And I kept telling him to be reasonable, I'm sure I did, as if it wasn't happening. I even told him to explain to Len, to see if he would help, Christ, I remember saying it. He told me all these terrible things and I knew they were making him ill, I should have kept him with me. He was so frightened yesterday, and I left him, because I was frightened too. He kept saying he'd got to get away from Len, and I just told him how to do it sensibly, and walked away. I should have taken him home with me, I wanted to, I knew he was ill and it wasn't safe. He actually waited for Len, as if it was some great showdown. And now he's got hurt and it's all my fault.'

Maggie listened to her, grim faced, all the way to the pub.

'Come on,' she said, tugging Barbara through the swing doors. 'Let's get you a drink.'

Dave's 'nobody goes there' turned out to be almost literally true; fortunately the barn-like interior of the pub and piped music ensured some privacy.

'You don't know what's happened to him,' wailed Barbara, slightly more quietly now, when Maggie returned from the deserted bar with two brandies. 'It's all so awful. His step-father was so wicked, he's ruined his life. He's always thought nobody cared about him. He doesn't think anybody *could* care. He's sick, he's never going to get better. And he keeps saying he's OK, I can't bear it. Oh, God, what have I done?'

'Barbara,' said Maggie firmly, sitting down opposite her. 'Stop this. I mean it. You're going to frighten Billy if you don't. Try to take your cue from him, whatever you feel inside. If he says he's OK, don't tell him he's not. He may be right or he may be wrong, but it's up to him. You're not going to improve anything by being so tragic.'

Barbara nodded repeatedly, closed her eyes, and exhaled deeply.

Maggie leant forward and spoke slowly. 'Even if he is sick, he can get better. You mustn't write people off because awful things have happened to them. Awful things do happen to people, all the time. People can survive. And you're not responsible. All right you may have pushed him to leave, but it was the right thing to do, even now you know it was. It's not your fault. You did what any friend would do, probably more. And you couldn't possibly know what Len would do, or Billy, for that matter.'

'Sonia told me not to get involved. She said it would only cause trouble. She knew when to pull out, she kept telling me. But I couldn't. He wanted to see me, what could I do?'

'Nothing,' Maggie said emphatically. 'You haven't done anything wrong. There's nothing wrong with caring about people and wanting to help them. Calm down and have a drink.'

Barbara downed her brandy. After a couple of minutes she said, much more composedly, 'What's going to happen to him? I mean if he doesn't go to hospital. We were going to try to find him a place. Oh, dear . . . I don't know what we're going to do . . .'

Maggie was frowning over the glass in her hand. She raised her eyes.

'What sort of place was this?'

Barbara shrugged. 'I don't know . . . a bedsit . . . maybe a flat share . . . anything.'

'I thought you said he couldn't afford a bedsit. And that his job was temporary, and no one would rent to him, anyway?'

'Well, I know . . .' Barbara was taken aback, 'but we were going to try. We had to try.'

'I'm not denying that,' said Maggie. 'I'm just wondering what, realistically, you expected to happen?'

Barbara thought about this.

'I wasn't thinking realistically,' she said at last. 'I just knew he had to go.'

Maggie leant an elbow on the table and cupped her chin in her hand. She covered her mouth with her fingers and appeared to be exhaling slowly through them.

'But he did have to . . .' Barbara repeated, finding her gaze uncomfortable.

Maggie nodded.

'Why're you looking like that?' said Barbara plaintively. 'Are you angry with me?'

Maggie took her hand away and her face cleared. 'Of course not,' she said. 'Not with you. You're right. He had to move.' She blew out through her teeth. 'Jesus Christ, that man. Jesus Christ.' She snatched up her drink. Barbara sensed her anger was largely private, and that any contribution would be out of place.

Maggie put the glass down, stared at it, and sighed heavily.

'He can have the room.' She lifted her gaze. 'If that'll help.'

'What?' said Barbara.

Maggie's expression became belligerent. 'Well, he can't stay with you. At least not for any length of time. And he certainly can't stay with Dave. And he's not going to find a bedsit, is he?'

Barbara blinked. 'But . . . what you said about Len . . .'

Maggie shrugged. 'Billy's solved that, hasn't he? He's hardly going to want to see Len again. And I have a feeling that Len is going to want to stay well away from Billy. Poor kid, honestly . . .' She put fingers to her mouth, then shook her head rapidly. 'I don't know what I'm making such a fuss about. It's all right. I'll have him. For a bit, anyway.'

'But all those regulations . . .' Barbara reminded her. 'I thought . . .'

Maggie waved a hand at her. 'Just leave it, please. If it doesn't work it doesn't work. He's got a job at the moment, so that's all right. He might not want to stay, anyway. We're only talking about now.'

After a second or so Barbara said, 'I'm sorry. That isn't why I rang you. I don't want you to feel forced into it.'

Maggie gave her a short smile.

'I believe you. I wouldn't blame you if you had. We all push things when we're desperate. Christ, I should know that. Nothing happens until you do. You called the right people.' She hesitated, then reached across to touch Barbara's arm. 'Actually, I think you've done everything right. Billy too, maybe. I want to help. I just need time to get used to it.'

Barbara accepted it and wanted, suddenly, to tell her that most people wouldn't have let themselves be forced into it, and that the only reason she had was because she was the kindest, most generous, most magnificent person in the world, but the desire to say it swamped the words.

'You're so good,' she sighed, managing only the essence.

'I'm not,' said Maggie. 'I'm doing it because I'm bloody angry and I'm in a position to help. But listen . . .' she tugged at Barbara's wrist, 'I'll do it, but I've got other responsibilities. You will still see him, won't you?'

'Oh, yes,' said Barbara fervently. 'I'd want to see him. I even like him. It's not just that I feel sorry for him. Well . . .' she paused, remembering with pain her inability to tell Billy this. 'I did like him. I slept with him once. It didn't really mean anything, but I wouldn't do that unless I liked someone.' She stopped, aware Maggie was trying not to smile at her. 'I think I'm a bit drunk,' she admitted. 'I haven't eaten since lunchtime.'

'It's the stress,' said Maggie, releasing the smile. 'Don't worry.'

When Dave arrived, ten minutes later, he went to the bar first and bought himself a whisky. Walking over to them, his expression was inscrutable. He placed the glass on the table.

'He hasn't gone, has he?' Maggie asked, looking at him anxiously.

'Nope.' He pulled up a chair next to her, his eyes on Barbara. She switched her gaze to the triangular ashtray on the table and waited.

'Christ,' he sighed, after a moment. 'You might have warned me. You knew what Len did to him, didn't you?'

'I should have told you. Sorry,' Barbara murmured, although she realised she wasn't, particularly. A light-filled shaft had opened up at the top of her skull; she felt in danger of drifting right through it.

He flicked his eyes at Maggie. 'She's told you, has she?'

Maggie nodded.

He sighed again. 'If that bloke didn't think I was some sort of hoodlum before, he does now. Made me wait outside half the time.' The muscles of his jaw hardened, as if the mortification of this had particularly rankled. 'Then he wanted to call the police. Would have done, if Billy hadn't surfaced long enough to tell him not to. Jesus, he's like a stuck record. "I'm OK, I'm OK". Little twerp.'

'Perhaps he is OK,' said Maggie mildly. 'I mean, he should know.'

'I wish people wouldn't keep calling him little,' complained

247

Barbara fussily, emerging briefly through the top of her head. 'He's at least as tall as Len.'

Maggie put a restraining hand on her arm. 'So what did the doctor say? Should someone go back?'

Dave shook his head. 'No hurry. He's asleep. He might have a broken nose, but he can breathe OK, and he might have cracked some ribs but ditto, and he's exhausted, but otherwise . . .' he pulled a sour face, 'he's all right.' He took a scrap of paper out of his jacket pocket and held it out to Barbara. 'That's his number. Ring him or an ambulance if you're worried about anything. He's given him some valium, and there's a couple by the sink for the morning. It's a muscle relaxant, he's going to be very stiff. And if he has to get up for a slash you go with him, right?' He looked at her closely. 'You're going to be able to manage this, are you?'

'Of course,' said Barbara loftily. She took the note, frowned over it, and tucked it in her handbag.

'Right,' said Dave, leaning back and picking up his whisky. 'So what's next?'

'I've said he can stay with me,' Maggie said, without looking at him. 'For a while, anyway. We've just been discussing it.'

Dave lowered his whisky. 'You're joking.'

'I'm not.'

Dave looked at Barbara swiftly, who couldn't see what possible business of his it was, but crammed herself back inside her head, anyway, in case she was needed.

He turned back to Maggie. 'Jeez,' he said urgently. 'You don't know what that kid's like. He'll drive you mad.'

'Got a better suggestion, have you?' Maggie's tone was aggressive. 'How about you having him?'

'No way.'

'Well, Barbara can't have him. It's going to be no help to anyone if they're both walking the streets. I can't see an alternative. Christ, Dave . . .' She became fierce. 'Nobody else is going to do anything. What the hell choice is there?'

Dave stared at her, then said, 'Are you sure about this?'

'Yes. Quite sure.' She regarded him evenly. Barbara wanted to kiss her.

Dave pursed his lips, then shrugged and said, 'It's your house.' He looked away.

Maggie smiled to herself. Barbara glanced between them. Other messages were flying about; she felt outside them, and confused.

'I know,' she said loudly, suddenly working it out. 'You're Jacey's dad, aren't you?'

Without looking back, Dave said, 'Jeez,' in an exasperated voice.

'He is, isn't he?' Barbara checked with Maggie. She dipped her smile and nodded.

Dave picked up his glass of whisky, and gave Maggie an annoyed glare. Maggie's smile broadened.

Irritably he said, 'So when's Billy moving in, then?'

'Tomorrow night?' Maggie said.

'Oh, God.' A thought struck Barbara. 'Billy's meant to be working tomorrow. He mustn't lose his job. Who do I ring?'

'Springfield,' Dave said. 'Leisure and Tourism.'

'You do it,' said Maggie. 'It sounds suspicious if it's a girl. He's a mate, isn't he?'

Dave said, 'Christ,' but then caught Maggie's eye and gave a weary sigh. 'OK,' he said, 'I'll do it.'

He threw the remains of his whisky back and placed the glass on the table. He rotated it slowly, frowning. Maggie sipped at the remains of her drink. Barbara watched them, feeling outside them again, but no longer confused by it.

Dave looked up at Maggie. Guardedly he said, 'Len wasn't always this bad, was he?'

'Yes,' said Maggie. 'It just didn't look so bad with me.'

'Shit.' Dave frowned down at the glass again. 'And I've said some crass things to Billy. Look . . .' He dug out his wallet. 'I've got to find Len. Will you get a taxi home? Here . . .' He held out a fiver.

Maggie hesitated, smiled at the impatient flap, and took it.

'What on earth are you going to say to him?' asked Barbara, amazed.

249

'Won't know till I see him.' He stood up and patted his pockets. 'Tell him Billy's gone . . . Christ, I don't know. Depends how he's feeling. We'll probably get paralytic.'

He rested his hand on Maggie's shoulder. 'See you soon, OK?'

'OK,' said Maggie, twisting to smile up at him. 'Any time.'

She watched him leave, then turned to Barbara.

'Those two,' she shook her head. 'They'll probably end up fighting, if they're not too drunk. I'm not sure it'll clear the air this time, though.'

'I hope it doesn't,' said Barbara.

They left the pub. It was dark outside now. Barbara's mind no longer felt in danger of escape. It felt more as it did coming out of a cinema at night: glutted, and slightly stunned.

As they turned the corner she asked, 'Does Jane know about Jacey?'

'Yes,' nodded Maggie. 'Dave had to tell her. He sees Jacey . . . he couldn't have it coming as a terrible shock later.'

'Didn't she mind?' It suddenly occurred to Barbara that she didn't know Jane at all. All these surprises. She only knew what Sonia and Maggie thought about her.

Maggie smiled; almost a grin. 'I believe she did, at first, More about me than Jacey, I think, though I'm not sure why. It can't have been the first time. Perhaps she didn't like having to hear about it. I understand that's one of their rules.' She gave a reminiscent sigh. 'I don't know why I did it. I've just always trusted him and I suppose I was lonely, stuck out in that bedsit, and perhaps I wanted to see if I could still do it. And of course he's not one to turn down an opportunity. She's OK about it now. There's nothing between me and Dave any more, except Jacey and what there's always been. I gather Jane doesn't want children, because they'd mess up her life, so maybe she even feels a bit let off the hook. I can imagine her rationalising it like that. Anyway, she knows he sees Jacey every week and she's never tried to stop him, which must say something.'

'Yes.' Barbara thought it said rather a lot.

Maggie walked on a few paces, then moved closer, till they were brushing shoulders. 'You mustn't take any notice of what I say about Jane,' she said quietly. 'Or perhaps you've realised that. You'd probably like her. She's actually very like Dave, which is why they get on so well. The difference is that he's always been fond of me, because we've known each other since we were kids. She only knew me when I was married to Len and thought me pathetic, which I expect I was. Rather like Dave and Billy now. Maybe that's why she did mind so much. But in any case . . .' She moved away and became brisk, 'I've given up feeling bad about it, because I reckon it's a selfish arrangement all round. We've all got more or less what we want.'

'I hope Billy gets what he wants,' sighed Barbara, staring up into the orange-tinted night. 'He's been so brave, really he has. I would like him to be happy.'

'Well, he's made a start,' said Maggie. 'He's left Len, and he's got somewhere to go, and he says he's OK . . . it doesn't look quite so bad now, does it?'

'No,' admitted Barbara. 'I suppose it doesn't.'

At the house they waited in the hall by the phone for Maggie's taxi, so they could make arrangements for the following night without disturbing Billy. After she had left Barbara walked slowly upstairs to her room, thinking how fantastically lucky it was that good people existed, alongside the bad, and how important they were; and how embarrassingly mushy and emotional, when mixed with alcohol, they could make you feel.

Dave had left her bedside light on but lowered it to the floor, so that the curled shape in the bed was in shadow. She picked up the clothes he had left in a heap under the window and put them in her washing bag, then shifted Billy's foodbox into the corner. Doing it reminded her she was hungry, so she made herself a sandwich using the remains of a sliced loaf from the top of the box, and the peanut butter she found beneath. The texture was like dental cement, but the taste a lot better. It took a long time to eat and while she chewed she scribbled a note for Sonia to give to Mr Fiddick tomorrow,

251

since she knew she wasn't going in to work in the morning. It was to have claimed some trivial illness, but in the end she couldn't see what was wrong with the truth and wrote, *A friend has been hurt and I am looking after him today. Please count it as holiday. Sorry.*

Eventually she went and looked at Billy, but from a distance, so she wouldn't be tempted to touch him and perhaps wake him. Someone had washed his face properly and turned the pillow over; from where she was standing the view was peaceful, and could almost have been ordinary: just any young man, fast asleep.

She wondered how much she would tell Peter about all this, and thought that she would probably tell him most of it, in time. She had missed talking to him and, anyway, she'd be seeing Billy and she'd want to be able to explain why.

Then the temptation became too much and she couldn't resist moving forward and kissing Billy goodnight, very lightly, which made his eyelashes flicker but not much else.

She went out immediately to the bathroom to brush her teeth and become practical again, and when she was back in the room she made up the bed on the floor and wriggled into the sleeping bag, which smelt of Billy and salt, and was quite gritty in places.

In deference to Billy, she left the light on.